DEADFALL

DEADFALL

A NOVEL BY
JANE MACLEAN

TC
Thomas Congdon Books E.P. DUTTON NEW YORK

For information contact:
E.P. Dutton, 2 Park Avenue, New York, N.Y. 10016

Library of Congress Cataloging in Publication Data

MacLean, Jane. Deadfall.

"Thomas Congdon books." I. Title
PZ4.M16333De [PS3563.A317983] 813'.5'4 78-13770
ISBN: 0-525-10585-9

Published simultaneously in Canada by
Clarke, Irwin & Company Limited, Toronto and Vancouver

Designed by Barbara Huntley

10 9 8 7 6 5 4 3 2 1

First Edition

FOR HAL

O rose, thou art sick!
The invisible worm
That flies in the night,
In the howling storm

Has found out thy bed
Of crimson joy,
And his dark secret love
Does thy life destroy

—WILLIAM BLAKE

deadfall.   A trap constructed so that . . . a weight falls
upon the animal and kills or disables it.

—*Webster's New International Dictionary*

DEADFALL

1 ZIHAUTENEJO

I forgot my straw hat, Stephanie thought.

She hesitated under the shadow of a palm on the fringe of the beach, shrugged her shoulders, and then stepped out onto the lighted sand. Stephanie McMillan. Stephanie Borders McMillan, a fair and attractively fragile woman from San Francisco, on vacation, alone. Age thirty-four.

The sand was loose. She walked on it placing one sandaled foot in front of the other, precisely, the way her mother had taught her to do on holidays the Borders family had taken years ago in Florida. ("You're going to have a nice figure," her mother had told her, "and you must learn to carry yourself properly, one foot in front of the other.") It was difficult maintaining her balance walking that way in soft sand, but she held her shoulders back stiffly and continued. The beach was deserted. There was no one to see her in her first bikini, no one to appreciate the new blond streaks in her hair. It didn't really matter.

Back home in San Francisco she had often taken her children down to the small harbor beach near the Marina

Green. It was wholesome on that beach, in spite of an occasional stray hot-dog wrapper or a piece of broken glass. Dogs galloped, naked two-year-olds bared their tanned bottoms to the breeze, and she and the other mothers sat and read, or exchanged recipes. The sun in San Francisco was never too hot, the water never too deep, the tide never too strong.

But it was different in Mexico. Here the beach was a stretched out and barren hot curve, empty of children and everyone except her. Of course it was empty; at three o'clock in the afternoon all the sensible people in Zihautenejo were taking siestas under whirring wooden fans or on straw mats inside their grass huts. Everyone except Stephanie. She sighed, spread her white towel on the sand halfway to the water, removed her white sandals, and lay down on her stomach. After a while she closed her eyes.

A man appeared in the distance, on the far northern end of the beach, and started walking in her direction.

From somewhere far off, the ruffled sound of a derelict engine sputtered on the water, hummed, sputtered again, and then died. Stephanie raised her head and glanced out over the calm blue Pacific. There was nothing out there to see, nothing at all to mar the flat, blue blankness, and that was good. Because she must not think about Jonathan.

The horizon was an empty space where hollow sky faded into blank water. The horizon was an illusion.

There aren't even any birds here, she realized, and wondered why not. She must remember to look for birds later, in the evening, when it wasn't so hot. Later she would have to shower and change and force herself to go to the terrace and drink with the other hotel guests and eat with them, and act normal. There weren't even any sandpipers on the beach, nothing. . . .

She lowered her face again to the rough terry cloth

of the beach towel. *Casa del Sol* was embroidered in uneven green letters where she rested her cheek. Through the sand she could feel the surf pound the shore, the waves rolling in and out, over and over, attacking and retreating, attacking and retreating. Like Fitz. But she knew she mustn't think about Fitz, either. . . .

She lifted her head again, and a blast of vacant heat slapped her face. Some small object had landed on her back; she reached over her shoulder to brush it away, and the palm trees behind her that fringed the beach like lowered lashes jumped into view. She shivered in the heat and shut her eyes, trying to forget the endless questioning in San Francisco a month earlier. But it didn't work.

A police car might as well be parked under those palms, she thought. Or that insurance inspector Mr. Sommers, crouching behind the shrubs, peering at her. God, what a nightmare. . . .

Were the children safe, back home? Of course they were; Angie and Kent were in good hands with Mrs. Hayes. She had to stop worrying about them; she knew her fears were exaggerated.

If only Fitz had never returned from Europe.

Stephanie sat up. She looked to her left, searching for something else, something more immediate to concentrate on. A bleached, dessicated crab shell lay in the sun about twenty feet away from her; she squinted at it. What had happened to its innards? How long had it lain there, gradually disintegrating into white dust? But Jonathan was disintegrating too, and she was the one who was empty.

The man who had been walking along the beach was nearer now; if she had looked more closely she would have seen yellow swim trunks and a large straw hat.

She picked up a handful of sand and began examining each grain of it. She picked at it with her fingernails, separating each small grain from the other. Separating herself from Jonathan. Fitz from Jonathan. The children from Fitz, herself from the children, until she could bear the separations no longer and started pouring the sand from one hand to the other, back and forth. Back and forth from the past into the present, the present into the future, the future into the past. . . .

She flung the sand into the flat air and fell exhausted onto her back, squeezed her eyes shut, and felt the heat creeping over her skin. The sun blazed on her eyelids, trying to penetrate behind them. But there was only darkness inside her head, only a black, amorphous tumor of doubt that kept creeping forward inside her brain. . . .

Jonathan was going to be dead.

Jonathan was dead.

She sat bolt upright. The man in the yellow swimsuit was only fifty feet away from her, standing very still and staring at her. She couldn't see his face; the wide-brimmed hat was pulled too low over his eyes. But she thought he was smiling, and his body was beautiful. She rolled over on her stomach again, dismissing his stare.

Jonathan was dead! Oh God, she knew he was dead. But she was trying to forget it, trying to bury his black death in the white sand. She wanted to obliterate the memories of that last dinner with her husband and her best friend, of too much good wine (Was that the reason? Was it really as uncomplicated as that?), of some stupid quarrel between Fitz and Jonathan out on the McMillans' deck, high above the city, after dinner. . . .

She had turned away from them, hadn't she? For one of those moments when a thin-lipped God pulls the wrong string to distract you, and then the moment is gone. And part of your reason for being there is gone with it, and part of your life. . . .

Jonathan's gaping mouth, a horrible black hole

below his staring rounded eyes falling away from her—down, down. The dark pinwheel of his arms and legs spinning into space, and his long white scream fading into the night. . . .

The police had come almost immediately, a phantom force swarming around her in a blue blur—dim, swimming faces and moving mouths, jaws opening and closing, asking her questions she couldn't answer. Who had called them? It had to be Fitz, of course. Someone had given her a sedative, and the next morning the house was full of people. Full of her parents and Jonathan's parents, and his brother, and the police, and friends, and the doctor. Full of everyone except Jonathan.

On the second day they had let her see her big-eyed, silent children, but she couldn't tell them about their father. She had broken down, and her mother had told them instead. Then came Lieutenant Brinton, so young and sympathetic, and Mr. Sommers from the insurance company. They returned every day, asking more and more questions, but at least the lieutenant was polite. "Mrs. McMillan, I hate to keep bothering you," he always said, "but there are just a few more details. . . ." Mr. Sommers just grumbled to himself and fixed her with eyes of stainless steel. She thought he must have been angry about all the insurance Jonathan had left her; she had no idea there would be so much. But she should have known; Jonathan had always taken such good care of her.

The days had passed by somehow, full of fewer and fewer people. The days and then the weeks, until Dr. Pedersen told her that she had to get away from the house, that she needed a change. So she had called Mrs. Hayes to look after Angie and Kent.

Part of her had wanted Fitz to come with her to Zihautenejo. But the other half, the part of her that doubted . . .

Mr. Sommers had continued to bother her every few

days until she left, even though Lieutenant Brinton said he was satisfied that Jonathan's death was an accident.

Fitz was satisfied, too.

But Stephanie was weakened by suspicions. . . . No, by more than that—by a cold nagging fear that the Mexican heat wasn't dissolving. By the fear that she knew something she couldn't remember, didn't want to remember, couldn't bear to know. . . .

Because Fitz was her only true friend.

○●

She lifted her head and looked around. The man in the yellow swimsuit was gone.

2

The Casa del Sol put up its guests in a dozen bungalows called *casitas* nestled among tall coconut palms on the edge of the beach. There was a picturesque main building in the center, a low-lying, white adobe structure, with a large, tiled dining terrace stretching toward the ocean. Fifteen circular tables dotted the terrace, set with pink linen tablecloths and hurricane lamps containing pink candles. Lush, looming mountains abutted the sea, dwarfing the small hotel; there was a remote and somewhat wild quality about the resort.

Stephanie sat at a table near the low stone wall that bordered the terrace, and wondered what her children had eaten for dinner in San Francisco, and what the other guests thought about her eating by herself in such a romantic place. She wondered if they had noticed how tentatively she tipped the headwaiter to seat her alone, facing the ocean with her back to the other guests. Jonathan would have tipped the waiter with more aplomb; he might have picked at the skin on his left thumb, as he sometimes did when he felt unsure of himself, but at least he wouldn't have tried to conceal the money as she had done. Had the people behind her guessed how foolish she felt? Had they sensed her feelings when she had arrived on the terrace an hour earlier, and looked into their contentment? The rush of mournful hatred brought on by their gaiety, the shy reluctance to impose herself on them?

Stephanie hadn't noticed the other lone diner on the terrace, a tall man who had taken the table behind hers and to the right, shortly after she was seated. He was dressed in white slacks and a madras shirt. He watched her throughout dinner.

In March, Mexican nights are fat with stars. Solitude is a northern star, locked in black ice, Stephanie was thinking. She'd never reached for a star, had she? Never dreamed of solitude, never done much of anything—except love her family.

"Excuse me," the man behind her said.

Stephanie smoothed her white skirt over her knees, not hearing him. Some people craved solitude, friends of theirs—of *hers,* now: she would have to get used to that—who moaned into their martinis about the need for true solitude because it hadn't been handed to them on a cold marble platter, on an engraved tombstone platter. They were lucky to have marital fighting and infidelity served to them on warm china plates. She would settle for that again, with gratitude. Even for infidelity . . .

"I beg your pardon : . ." The man in the madras shirt tipped his head to the right, as though trying to see around her.

Stephanie heard his voice vaguely but didn't turn. They should have come there on their honeymoon, she

and Jonathan. All the things they should have done. . . .
He would have loved the hotel, the view, the terrace, the
paths that wound in and out among the palms, paths
made of flat, rounded stones which seemed to float on the
sand. It would have been a childlike adventure to skip
from stone to stone on the way to their honeymoon *casita*. . . .

Jonathan had smelled so warm, in the morning. A
"natural man" smell, she had called it—

"Please forgive the intrusion."

The man had pushed back his chair and was now
moving around her table. She didn't want to talk to him,
she dreaded strangers, she dreaded everything. She
wanted to think about Jonathan.

"My name is Nicholas Hanson."

Stephanie looked up.

"I'm sorry to break into your privacy this way, but I
couldn't help noticing that you're alone, and I thought we
might share an after-dinner drink."

She saw his plaid shirt, a tanned face above it. Jonathan had a shirt almost like it; she would have to force
herself to go through his closet one of these days. "I'm
sorry," she answered. Her hands played with her napkin.
"I don't think so."

Nicholas Hanson lowered his face to the level of hers
so that she could see him clearly across the candlelight, so
that she could see his eyes. He knew they were his best
feature: light green, heavy-lidded, electrical. They took
her by surprise. The rest of his face fell into focus around
them, a long face, handsome with imperfections: the nose
almost too small for the length of the face, the chin round
and not quite firm enough. But his mouth was strong and
broad. His hair was dark blond and beginning to thin.

"It's a crime to be alone on a night like this," he
declared. "May I sit down?"

Stephanie wanted to say that it wasn't a crime; it was a necessity. And she wanted to tell him not to sit down.

He was still smiling.

"Yes," she heard herself say, "please do." Politeness versus intuition, the old training coming to the fore. Or was it more than politeness? There was no time to sort out conflicting instincts.

"Would you like a brandy?"

"Yes, thank you." She fingered the collar of her orange silk shirt.

"What kind?"

"It doesn't matter."

He stretched his long legs, crossed his ankles, and signaled the waiter with an upward flick of the chin. How self-assured he was, Stephanie thought. And somewhat arrogant. Jonathan would have raised his arm and smiled at the waiter.

Nicholas ordered two Martells and then turned to her; his eyes narrowed slightly. "Are you enjoying your vacation?"

She nodded and touched the thin gold chain around her neck. His smile was charming, but the thought that there was something slightly hostile in it crossed her mind, in the way his lips lifted in the center and dropped down at the corners. Something almost antagonistic, yet sensual and appealing . . .

"Aren't you going to tell me your name?"

"Oh," she said, and let go of her necklace. "I'm sorry. My name is Stephanie. Stephanie McMillan."

"Delighted!" He smiled and lifted an imaginary hat to her. "My pleasure."

Their brandies arrived, and Nicholas touched his snifter to hers. "Here's to Zihautenejo. *Salud y pesetas y tiempo para gastaralos—*"

Stephanie lowered her eyes, feeling embarrassed at

●○ 9

the intimacy of a toast she didn't understand. Why was he going after *her*? Because she was the only single woman there, that was why. Not because she had freckles that bridged her nose and an ordinary nice face and an ordinary nice figure—except for her legs, which were particularly good. If it were Fitz sitting there, that would have been different. Of course he would have gone for her; men always did.

Nicholas Hanson was looking at her, unsmiling.

Maybe he liked her eyes. Jonathan had loved them, had called them "as wide and spacy as the blue sky. Innocent, and naive—"

"I'm glad you're here," he said.

"What?"

"I hoped you would be here." His eyes were a contradiction: beneath lazy bedroom lids the green was alert and probing.

"I . . . I don't understand," Stephanie said.

"I mean," he said, smiling, "that it's a shame to be by oneself in a place like this, isn't it?"

"I . . . I wouldn't know." She looked away from him, flustered. He was too attractive, too certain of his appeal. Wasn't he exactly the sort of womanizer her mother had always warned her away from? She didn't trust his mouth; it would demand too much. And his eyes; they would find weaknesses. Or his self-confidence; it could destroy what little she had left since Jonathan—

"Sorry," she heard him say. "I didn't mean to come on too strong. Where are you from, anyway?"

"San Francisco." She twisted the stem of her brandy snifter between her thumb and index finger.

Nicholas threw back his head and laughed, a long, relaxed roll of laughter that caught her off guard. "So am I!" he exclaimed. "What a marvelous coincidence."

She smiled weakly. He continued to look at her. She

took a sip of brandy; he said nothing. The intensity of his look was flattering and embarrassing.

Take me back home, she thought. She wanted to go back to her brown shingled house, back to her children. She wanted another night sitting by the fire with Jonathan, the comfortable feeling, the sharing, the love that was as consoling and delicate as a lace handkerchief. And now that handkerchief had been torn to shreds, while they were both so young—

"Is anything the matter?" Nicholas Hanson asked. "You're trembling. Would you like some hot coffee?"

She looked at him, wondering what she was doing there with this stranger who made her feel flustered and nervous. She should excuse herself and go to bed.

"I don't know," she murmured. "I guess so."

"I'll get some," he said, and again flicked his chin at a waiter.

That was a mistake, she thought. She should have said no. She never should have spoken to him in the first place. His eyes frightened her. . . . But he was so attractive.

"Would you like a cigarette?" He offered her a Marlboro; she shook her head.

Jonathan hadn't spoken to her at all, at first. Jonathan had opened a door and stood there looking at her without moving, a photograph framed in a frozen moment—

She started in her chair as the loud arpeggio of a guitar scalloped the silence; a mariachi band had begun to play at a nearby table. Nicholas lit a cigarette and turned to watch the musicians, six happy men with big teeth and big-brimmed hats. Their music faded into Stephanie's background.

Jonathan was a photograph that would never fade; she wouldn't *let* him fade. She would keep his image—his wavy hair and gentle face always before her eyes, the memory of his kindness, his strength, his reliability. Jonathan was a solid man who knew what commitment was, and how to increase it each year by binding the practical to the emotional. . . . He had become so good about helping her around the house, especially those last few months. He'd done some cooking, washed the dinner dishes, cleaned the refrigerator, shopped for the children's clothes on Saturdays—

"Your coffee will get cold," Nicholas said gently. He was watching her out of the corners of his eyes.

"Oh," she said, and took a sip of it. Nicholas smiled at her and looked back at the mariachis.

The coffee was lukewarm and bitter; she put it down. She had begun to take Jonathan's consideration for granted, hadn't she? She had begun to accept his help as her due, as automatically as she would accept change from the grocer or a letter from the postman. She had gathered the convenience of him, like coins, into the pockets of her daily life to be dipped into, extracted, used. Had she thanked him often enough? Had he gone from her without understanding her gratitude? No, no. Of course he knew. . . .

Nicholas turned back to her. "Isn't that a beautiful song they're playing? It's called 'Quando Caliente el Sol.' Do you speak Spanish?"

Why was he so interested in her?

"Stephanie?"

"What?"

"I asked if you speak Spanish."

"No," she answered faintly. "I'm afraid not. I did study French in college, though. I used to speak a little French. . . ." Her voice trailed away inadequately, and she turned to look out over the black ocean. The cold stars were just as near as they had been earlier, and just as far.

12 ◐

For a moment she saw Jonathan's warm eyes smiling reassuringly down at her.

Then Jonathan's face fell away from her again, into the darkness. His wide, startled eyes. His mouth a black hole, screaming! And Fritz's wild shout, just before he fell. . . .

If only she could remember what had happened!

"I'll teach you some Spanish," Nicholas said, and pulled his chair closer to hers.

3 SAN FRANCISCO

It was the dark of the moon, and love-ritual time.

The tall, solitary figure of Fitz hovered like a dark angel, high on her balcony above the midnight quiet of the city lights. Far below, pale small lights like asterisks sprinkled the darkness. Beyond them swelled San Francisco Bay, its black waters stretching into space and silence.

Above the waters there was more vast blackness, the sky, the night. A satin night that lounged above the city, waiting; a night that gazed glossy and unwrinkled into her eager eyes. A night that was perfection: black, smooth, and brooding.

A night that waited to love her.

No one could see Fitz; she stood alone on the fourteenth-floor balcony of an old apartment building at the crest of Russian Hill. Her privacy was guaranteed, her communion with the dark. She wore jeans and a suede jacket; her black hair stirred faintly in the breeze. She leaned forward, propping her elbows on the redwood rail of her deck, and settled her chin into her hands. Her long hair fell around her face, and she ran her fingers through it slowly, thinking that it would have to be trimmed soon, that it had grown much too long. . . .

But it was love-ritual time, sacred time. Not a time for thoughts of hair or anything else. Nothing but the ebony night and the pleasure it would give. She lowered her hand to the belt of her jacket and loosened it.

The whole beautiful panorama belonged to her, she was thinking. The profound waters, the ruminating sky, the tongue of mist that curled above the water, the blinking eyes of city lights. They were all hers to play with, and to love. She could make of them what she wanted with the trick of an eye, could change them into any form she chose, could fly out to meet them or make them come to her in any shape she desired. . . .

She leaned farther out over the railing, narrowed her eyes, and stared hard into the darkness. Through nearly closed eyelids the distant lights began to blur, to merge, to mingle with their own reflections in the water, forming new patterns. The black sky lowered, compressed, began to beat against the pulsing surface of the water. The mist over the bay was fighting against the sky, pushing up against it, against the black roof of the mouth closing down on it. . . .

Fitz opened her eyes wide. The bay was a giant mouth, expanding to fill her vision. The bay was a mouth, and the lights along the water's edge were uneven rows of gleaming teeth inlaid with yellow-gold fillings. The tongue of mist was rising and twisting as the sky yawned sleepily. . . .

She pulled off her jacket. *Listen!* she murmured to herself. *Listen* to the sound of that yawn, to the thick, slow inhalation of air, to the soft suction of the atmosphere receding into an infinity of darkness. *Feel* the hushed pause, the breathless pause at the center of the yawn, and now hear the sky exhaling in a long, husky sigh. . . .

A colossal mouth, eternal instrument of love.

She unzipped her jeans, kicked off her shoes, removed her yellow T-shirt and dropped it to the deck. Now she stood naked, her face lifted to the smooth moist, sky. She was listening to its heavy breathing, waiting for it to pant to the rhythm of love, waiting for the huge mouth to press against her flesh, letting the cool night air caress her bare and shivering skin.

Because Fitz had decided, a long time ago, to demand as much love from everything in life as she gave to it.

She lay down on the deck, arched her back, extended her arms, and spread her legs wide. Her eyes were fixed on the ebony sky, on the roof of the giant mouth that descended on her slowly, slowly, forming into a quivering black nimbus, a great black cloud that was breaking up, dispersing into a whole galaxy of soft smoky spheres that hovered over her. Innumerable cool cosmic orbs danced around her, floating, swirling, changing form, refracting shadows, palpitating. . . .

They fell upon her, skimmed across her skin, her lips, her hair, the tips of her fingers. The tongue of mist curled its way through the swirling galaxy and flickered lightly over her body, licking her belly, her breasts, lazily probing her open mouth. . . . The glimmering lights, rows of gleaming teeth, tugged lovingly at the lobe of her ear, nibbled gently at her dusk-pink nipples. . . . The cold, dark waters of the bay rolled over her belly, surged voluptuously between her thighs, and then rushed into her, pounding, pounding. . . .

In time, the waters would subside and flow smoothly

away from her, back into the waiting throat of the bay. The gleaming teeth would root themselves again in the soft gums of the shore, the gray tongue of mist would curl up and sleep once more over the peaceful waters, and the infinities of floating, dancing specks of night air would coalesce into the black mass of the sky, satiated.

But meanwhile Fitz exulted in all of them; she lay twisting and groaning, ecstatically entwined in nature's loving embraces, trembling under its moist lips.

○●

Thirty minutes later she sat up, stiff with cold, and began gathering her clothes from the deck. The next morning she would begin her painting of the giant mouth. Like most of her other works it would be a large, abstract canvas, and her gallery in New York would sell it for at least $15,000. They would obtain an agreement from the buyer that it would be available for her next big show. The critics always praised Fitz's unusual technique, and her universality.

When her clothes were all picked up, Fitz looked out over the bay again, and smiled. The mist had developed into a massive gray fog that shouldered its way past the Golden Gate Bridge, nudged against the breasts of Marin County, shoved its weight into the sides of the city, and jostled the yellow lights. The sudden wail of a foghorn heralded its entrance into the bay. Thank God for the everchanging cycle, she thought. If only things could change even more often, giving her and everyone else new perspectives, new colors. Even one new color.

She turned abruptly and walked across the balcony to the glass doors of her studio. A new color, a whole new color. What a marvelous idea! Could it be done? Not just a different tone or shade to add to the spectrum, but a color unlike any other. Why not? Something added to nature, rather than stolen from it. Something dark and brilliant . . .

Her large studio was dark. She walked through it, tossed her clothes on a chair, and went into the galley kitchen at the far end of the room. There was a bottle of Courvoisier somewhere on the counter; she groped for it.

The new color would be a question of chemistry, not her *forté*. But Raoul could help her, back in Paris; he knew all the right people, that scientist from London, what's-his-name—

And think of all the fun she could have giving it a name! Peridoria, Talahaye. Burnt Addendum! Fitz laughed, turned on the main light switch by the kitchen door, and poured herself a brandy. It was probably a nutty idea, but worth trying nonetheless. She would work on it, when she could leave again.

When Stephanie came back from Mexico.

The snifter of brandy warmed in her palm. She walked naked back into the lighted studio and looked around it with satisfaction. What a find! So high on Russian Hill that she could see forever, but no one could see her.

The room was large, over thirty feet long and half as wide, and filled with the organized clutter of her life. All her treasures: at least twenty of her own paintings hanging at random on the redwood walls, three of them upside down and one on its side, for the sake of change. Her painted version of Michelangelo's sleeping statue *Night* hung to the right of the brick fireplace, and opposite it, to the left of the chimney, the huge and hideous *Cronus* by Goya. Crazed, fearful Cronus, devouring one of his sons.

Fitz looked at it, remembering the days it had taken her, in Madrid, to copy it from an enlarged photograph. Days of running back and forth to the Prado, days of painstaking care as she watched in appalled fascination while Cronus's Lear-like form emerged again under her brush. Wild, silly Cronus, who knew not what he did, holding the bloodied stump of a headless child before his frightened eyes. Stupid Cronus, symbol of all the bestiality and ignorance in the universe. Symbol of what exists, and what to avoid. Fitz considered it the most powerful masterpiece ever painted.

She shuddered and turned away from him, remembering another painting and another night. The night of Jonathan's death. It could have been avoided. . . .

She looked across the room, at the bright print pillows scattered over the leather furniture, the piles of books and records stacked on tables, on hi-fi speakers, on the floor. A Mexican shower tree stood potted in blue and gold ceramic near the sliding glass doors, and next to it was her large easel, waiting to be used at any hour. Fitz often painted at night—"making love," as she called it, to her canvas with soft brushes.

An old Steinway grand, stoic under the weight of mountains of sheet music, stood against the far wall. And beyond it in the corner, an open spiral staircase led to her bedroom loft and bathroom. Near the foot of the staircase stood *Colo-Cocka-Mumba,* her favorite sculpture, one of the few she had accumulated in her travels. Fitz smiled at him, feeling the usual technical thrill. What a challenge! He was over seven feet tall and sculpted entirely of wood but for his erect iron penis, and someday she'd figure out why the weight of it didn't topple him.

She took a sip of brandy and tilted her chin up to look at another technical achievement, her own self-portrait, which hung from the ceiling in the center of the room. She had painted it on a canvas ten feet long by four feet across and tied it to three redwood beams in the middle of the high ceiling. Fitz had hung the portrait from several different ceilings since she'd painted it five years earlier, but the effect in San Francisco was certainly one of the best. Maybe she had been more powerful against the stark white plaster of her rented villa on Mykonos, during the year she'd spent there. Or more mysterious in Paris; but here against three rustic beams she was elegant. . . .

She floated in the air, looking down on her room with smoky eyes. Eyes the color of old cognac, one of her favorite lovers called them. Eyes that glowed as liquid and golden as ambrosia. Her long, bare arms stretched gracefully above her head, palms outward, and the silken strokes of her dark hair spilled downward into space in a fine display of trompe l'oeil. The curves of her body and her full breasts pouring down were tantalizingly visible through the diaphanous, lemon-yellow folds of a Greek hetaera's toga.

The background was solid black.

Fitz yawned, took a final sip of brandy, and flicked off the lights before climbing the stairs to her bedroom. She had painted its four walls a warm deep red, a sensual red that was the color of cardinals, the color of whores. A Titian red, stolen from Venice; a dark scarlet, stolen from Hawthorne. And an Ingmar Bergman red, stolen from the membrane of the soul.

She didn't bother to remove her make-up; she was too sleepy. She brushed her teeth quickly and fell into bed.

○●

At one o'clock in the morning the telephone rang.

Fitz rolled over twice in the darkness and reached for the receiver.

"Fitz, lover! Hey, Kitty Cat!" said a distant, blurred voice.

Kitty Cat. Only one man called her that, Mike Higby.

Wonderful, crazy "Midnight Mike" Higby whom she'd met in Paris years earlier, when his Jaguar convertible had hit her Citröen broadside, late at night. He'd been going around the Etoile in the wrong direction, just for the hell of it—

"Mike," Fitz muttered. "What time is it, anyway? Where in the world are you?"

"New York, kitten. Gonna watch the sunrise. Feeling Fitzgeraldish and I want you. I want to dance with you in the dawn and then make love to you until you're black and blue. Let's go to Saint Cloud."

It crossed her mind that he was drunk, but then she remembered that Mike was never drunk. She could see the twinkle in his eyes, behind his thick glasses.

"That's a double-entendre," he said. "Fitzgeraldish."

"Saint Cloud," she murmured.

"Saint Cloud," he repeated.

There was a long pause, while they both remembered. The eighth fairway of the golf course at Saint Cloud, high on a northeastern rise of Paris. His convertible parked on the grass with the top down, the radio playing music at top volume while they danced barefoot on the green, while they tangoed, and waltzed, and cha-chaed, and boogy-woogied, and belly danced, and then stripped under the stars.

"You're the best goddamned dancer in the world," Mike finally said.

"You taught me how to hula-hoop," Fitz answered. "To Harry Belafonte." She knew it was a nonsequitur. That had been a different night.

"I'm the best goddamned hula-hooper in the world," Mike remarked.

"I can't come now."

"Didn't think so."

"Are you all right?"

"*En pleine forme*," he said. "Just wanted you."

"Me too . . ."

"Good. How about Saint Cloud this summer? Are you coming back?"

"For sure."

"Then I'll just have to wait," he said. "Guess I'll dance alone and then go play with five-fingered Mary. Bye, Kitty Cat."

"Goodbye, Mike darling—"

Dance alone, Fitz thought, and rolled over on her back in the dark bedroom. Dance alone, as she used to do for hours in her room when she was young. "You're the best goddamned dancer in the world," Mike had said. Because she'd learned to dance alone. She would love to see Mike again. How many men had she seduced with her dancing, she wondered. Her world—just she and the music. It was the only way to learn. . . .

No, that wasn't right, she thought as she rolled over on her side, feeling sleepy again. She hadn't learned; it came naturally. She didn't need to go to dancing school, like all her friends. Like Stephanie. Miss Adam's Dancing School. Good old proper Miss Adam and her proper dancing school for proper young people . . .

One! Two. Three. Four. . . . One! Two, three, four. . . .

One side! Two side, Three back, Four side!

One, side. . . . Two, side. . . . Three, back. . . .

Four side. . . .

○●

"No one's going to ask me," Stephie said. "I'm too tall."

"I'm as tall as you are," Fitz pouted. "We're all too tall, all the girls."

"I wish Pete Arnold would ask me," Stephanie remarked hopefully.

●○ 21

"This is for the birds," Fitz answered. "Who needs it?"

They were sitting against the wall, on a long line of straight-backed chairs. They wore white gloves and Capezios; their full-skirted dresses came to below their knees. Stephie's blond hair had a pink ribbon in it.

"Mother says it's a social necessity," Stephie said. Johnny Van Kemple and Irvin Jenkins were swaggering toward them with sneering grins on their faces, elbowing one another. Johnny bowed his head to his knees in front of Stephanie, and then kicked Irvin in the shin with his heel.

"Oww!" Irvin grimaced, and ducked his head at Fitz, as a form of invitation.

"One, side!" Miss Adam yelled over the microphone. "Two, *side!* Three *back!* Four, *side!* . . ."

The music on the record player was a scratchy rendition of Lawrence Welk's "Cheek to Cheek." Johnny clasped Stephanie around her fanny with one hand, and with the other he held her arm out stiffly. He pressed his cheek against her bosom, which was level with his head, then sighted along their arms as if they were a rifle and started walking sideways, with his knees lifted as though he were stalking deer.

"Two *side!* Three *back!*" Miss Adam barked.

"The happiness I seek," the music played, "When we're all alone and dancing cheek to cheek. . . ."

"Toot! Toot!" Johnny shouted, and switched his maneuvers. "Toot! Toot!" He was walking straight ahead across the dance floor, staring maliciously at Stephie's breasts as he shoved her backward. "Toot! Toot! . . . Toot! Toot! . . ." Stephie made quick little movements backward with her Capezios, trying to escape being stepped on. "Toot! Toot!" Johnny shouted, blinking at her breasts. Everyone was laughing.

"Leave her alone!" Fitz yelled over Irvin's head. "Johnny Van Kemple, you leave Stephanie *alone!*"

"Heaven," the music played, "I'm in heaven. . . ."

"Three *back!*" Miss Adam yelled. "Sour *side!* . . ."

"*Toot! Toot!*" Johnny shouted. . . .

And then Fitz did what Stephie wished she could do but lacked the nerve. Fitz ran at Johnny, kicked at him, pulled at his hair, clawed at his face, hit him hard. Fitz gave Johnny Van Kemple a bloody nose and was told that she should have controlled her hot temper and behaved like a young lady, and that she was not welcome back at Miss Adam's Dancing School.

Fitz would have preferred to walk out on Miss Adam first.

She begged Stephie to quit dancing school. She told her that she didn't need that kind of humiliation, that they could have more fun swimming together after school, or writing plays, or even dancing by themselves. But Stephanie had stuck it out. It was a social necessity, her mother said.

So Fitz had taught herself to dance, hour after hour in her own room, alone.

And she still had a hot temper.

Stephanie couldn't seem to move.

She had been sitting alone on the darkened terrace for over an hour, looking at the sky, listening to the ocean, and watching the long strands of waves heaving on the dark chest of the beach. She wasn't sure how long it had been since Nicholas Hanson had finally gone back to his room, and since the last waiter had retired, smiling uncertainly about leaving her there alone.

Nicholas Hanson had been too familiar and persistent for her taste, and he had declared that he was going to take her scuba diving tomorrow. She didn't want to go with him. She didn't want to be sitting on the terrace, she didn't want to move. Until a month earlier, motion had been her many-chambered cage: up and down the stairs, in and out of the house, in and out of rooms in the house, in and out of the car, back and forth to the market, the laundry, the pantry, the kitchen. Perhaps that was why she couldn't move, now. . . .

She shivered and rubbed her arms, thinking that she should force herself to return to her *casita.* But she didn't want to go to bed alone again, without Jonathan.

Jonathan. Think about Jonathan, she told herself. His safe eyes, the thin rim of vulnerability around them that only she could detect. His wavy hair, his boyish grin. His eyes warm over the rim of a red-wine glass, that last night at dinner, before Fitz got angry with him. His boyish grin turning inside out into a horrified death hole, out on the balcony . . . his round eyes receding from her into space—

No, no! She couldn't think about him that way, she wouldn't. She would think about him as he was, the very first thrills, the beginning, the happiness. . . .

Telegraph Hill, on a cold night in November. She had been wearing a plum-colored skirt and matching sweater the night she met Jonathan. She had raced down the steep Filbert steps near Julius's Castle and turned left into Darrell Place, a walkway bordered by small apartment buildings and enclosed in thick greenery. It was the most romantic area of San Francisco. Her footsteps were short, quick, excited, impatient. Two bachelors, her friend Joanie had said. Two bachelors.

She rang the doorbell and tried to smooth down her hair. Two bachelors and a girl named Samantha. Would Samantha be pretty?

Jonathan opened the door and just looked at her. He was around six feet tall and strong jawed, and his hair scooped across his forehead. She liked his dark eyes. Beyond him was a scene of perfect domesticity: a fireplace filled with orange flames, a table set for six, Joanie Barchfield bending over a sofa and offering hors d'oeuvres to Bob, her husband of two years. A man to care for.

Some moments stay locked in memory; others escape quickly through a keyhole in the mind. But some moments hang suspended on the wall of the psyche even before they are a memory. Jonathan was part of such a moment. She was home safe, and didn't know it yet.

"Hello," he finally said.

"Hi . . . I'm late, aren't I?"

"And I'm Jonathan McMillan." There were crow's feet at the corners of his eyes. "And you must be Stephanie. I've just been hearing about you—"

He stood back, holding onto the doorknob, and let her pass. Oh God, hearing what? That she worked as a secretary with Joanie and they both hated their jobs? That she was nice-enough looking and a nice-enough nice-girl, not a sexy divorcee? That she worried too much about what people said about her when she wasn't there? That she hated entering a room and feeling circles of eyes around her and on her, judging? (What will it be, folks? A red, white, or blue ribbon for this canned pickle?) That she copied what poise was supposed to be, and concentrated on where to hold her elbows, at what degree to set her smile for the judges?

"Greetings!" Joanie called, and came over and gave her a kiss on the cheek. That takes care of one elbow, Stephanie thought, as Joanie led her by the arm. She was aware of Jonathan standing behind her; she directed a seventy-degree smile at the other guests, which was the best she could manage.

"Stephie, this is Samantha Peters, and Ron Meadows." Joanie wrinkled her nose; she was a plump bubble of a hostess. "Stephanie Borders, my companion at the keys."

"Oh?" asked Ron Meadows, arching an eyebrow. "Do you both play the piano?"

"Jesus, Ron. Don't be such a smart-ass," Samantha said.

Stephanie looked at Samantha. Of course she was beautiful and probably smart; with a name like that you had to be. Her hair was long and auburn; she was familiar with Ron and friendly to Stephanie, which meant to Stephie that she might be interested in Jonathan.

"Sorry." Ron smiled weakly. He was sandy-haired and all angles. "Just asking."

Stephanie returned his smile in kind. As a matter of fact I do play the piano, she thought. As a matter of fact I play the piano quite well, which is why I can type so fast. So why don't I just say so?

"Would you like a drink?" It was Jonathan's voice, strong and safe at her side. She followed him into the kitchen.

Ordinary, ordinary.

Compared to Samantha.

"—blowing the damned bagpipes full blast at three o'clock in the morning," Samantha was saying. She sat next to Jonathan at the dinner table. "Can you imagine? Stoned to the skies, weaving along the Marina Green, convinced we were marching like the Highland Pipers, and waking up half the city. George can really blow those things! He likes to dance on tabletops too. He's a nut."

"So are you," Joanie remarked, amused.

"So I gather," Jonathan said pleasantly.

Ah, yes, Stephanie thought. Samantha was a free spirit, like Fitz. A wild, free creature sending out electrical challenges: Tame me, if you can, laddies! Grab me by my auburn hair and just try to subdue me! Just *try* to make me cook and clean for you—

"Samantha's a classic," Bob Barchfield stated. "A genu-wine thoroughbred-filly nut. More wine, anyone?"

"Nonsense," Samantha said, smiling. "I'm just a sweet young thing."

Jonathan looked at Stephanie, and she knew from his look that everything was going all right.

○●

He was a stockbroker, he told her after dinner. From Connecticut originally. He worked for Dean Witter, was twenty-six years old, had graduated from Lawrenceville and Princeton, loved to play tennis and loved San Francisco. He wore a tweedy ivy-league sport coat and a gold signet ring with the family crest on his left hand. He was perfect.

She had tried to keep the eagerness out of her eyes, as they sat on the floor by the fire. The insecure hope. At one point it occurred to her that Fitz might not approve of him, that she would think he was too stuffy, being a stockbroker. . . .

"You're rather cool and self-contained, aren't you?" Jonathan had said.

She smiled and shook her head.

"Well," he said, "you'll have to prove it. How about a game of tennis next Saturday?"

And she hadn't cared what Fitz would think of him. . . .

His first kiss, after he had taken her to Sally Stanford's Valhalla restaurant in Sausalito, on their first date the Saturday after tennis. ("Where the hell did you learn to play tennis so badly?" he had asked, laughing, and she didn't mind because he'd said that he'd have to do something about *that!* . . .

His first kiss, sitting in his brown Buick. An uncertain kiss, and she had wanted more. But he walked her to her front door and thanked her like a gentleman and didn't offer her another kiss. And she had wanted it. ("I knew what I was doing," he confessed to her later, "I planned my tactics . . .")

The romantic restaurants he took her to, always outside the city. The soft contentment in candlelight, the talk of his family in Connecticut and hers in Missouri. . . . The first time he held her hand in public, at the Danville Inn in the East Bay. His love for Mabel Mercer, a singer, whom she'd never heard of; his desire to take up skiing over the Christmas holidays. . . .

His delight at the way she played the piano that night at Bev Martin's party, when he stood by her at the piano for hours. "I can't do anything," he said. "I have absolutely no talent whatsoever . . ."

The kisses that lasted longer and longer, after each date. But he was always a gentleman, he never pushed. . . .

The big night, sitting on the sofa in her Greenwich Street apartment. "You don't have to make up your mind right away," he had said. "I mean, I don't want you to feel rushed, or anything—"

She had interrupted him, had taken hold of his hand and replied before he'd actually asked the question. "Yes, Jonathan," she had said, "Oh yes, the answer is definitely *yes!*"

Because he was perfect. . . .

Stephanie blinked, realizing that she had been staring at the same spot on the ocean's shallow edge, a dark and seemingly immovable area under white, crisscrossing waves. But of course the dark spot of water was moving; everything shifted in nature. The palm leaves stirred, the breeze drifted, the ocean lapped the salt of its shores, over and over. And maybe it was the unseen that moved the most.

Hang on to Jonathan, she thought, and closed her eyes. *Keep moving with your memories. . . .*

"He's a little nervous, isn't he?" she remembered her mother saying when they flew back to her home at Christmas. "I mean, under all that Eastern sophistication. But I guess that's natural, given the circumstances. I never knew anyone who could pack his clothes the way he did, without a single wrinkle. Amazing."

"Good-looking," her father had remarked. "Sure you know what you're doing?"

She knew what she was doing. She remembered sitting in that pale living room with the heavy English furniture, and thinking that it was more important to defend Jonathan—the almost-stranger changing into a dinner jacket upstairs while they discussed him behind his back— than to agree with her mother and father, no matter what they thought. Jonathan had become her first loyalty. She remembered the way she smiled at her father.

"He . . . he seems just fine," Stephen Borders muttered.

"If you're happy," her mother murmured. "He seems more than respectable. Frankly, I was beginning to worry about you."

"I know it's old fashioned these days," Jonathan said from the doorway, "but Stephanie's sort of an old-fashioned girl. I wonder if I might talk to you, Mr. Borders?" He ran his fingers through the freshly combed lock of hair that fell forward over his left eye, and smiled at her.

He looked beautiful dressed in his dinner jacket for the Kansas City Country Club; she had never seen him look so handsome and refined. She could picture him in church. And at that moment she didn't care if he told her father that he had no ambition and no money, or if he told him he was queer. Except that she didn't really know what it meant, then. She thought queer men walked funny and liked to decorate; she didn't understand that it was physical. She had been overprotected. At that moment she didn't care if Jonathan told her father to jump into the Prudential Sea of his regional, Prudential, vice-presidency—

"Of course, young man!" her father boomed.

"I guess these talks are necessary." Jonathan said, grinning, at her. "Like death and taxes. Ouch! I didn't mean it that way . . ."

"We're going to pop a few champagne corks tonight!" her father said when they came out of his study. "You've got a fine young man, honey. We're going to celebrate in style!"

"I don't want to wait till June to get married," Jonathan whispered in her ear while they were dancing at the country club. "I don't want to wait at all. I just want to live with you . . ."

It was difficult for him to remain a gentleman, he told her later. But he never pushed too far; he respected her. . . .

○●

"You're kidding!" Jonathan laughed. "You've got to be kidding me! I don't believe it. . . ."

They had been married two weeks. They were sitting at the dining table in their first apartment on Green Street and had just finished a bottle of Beaulieu Cabernet, which, Jonathan informed her, was one of the best California wines. It complimented her broiled lamb chops beautifully, he told her. . . .

"I don't understand," she remembered saying.

"The joke. How could you *not* understand that joke?"

It wasn't very funny in the first place, she thought, and it was rather crude. It was the first vulgar joke he had told her, something about an elephant defecating on the ground and saying, "That remains to be seen." It wasn't typical of Jonathan, but maybe it was the wine.

"I don't understand how it could remain," she had said. "It evaporates."

"You're kidding! You've got to be kidding me, I don't believe it. . . ."

And then he told her why it wouldn't evaporate, and explained what the famous four-letter word that began with *s* was. She blushed; all she knew was that it was a dirty word that she had first heard when she was about twelve and had heard many times, but she had always thought it was pee-pee! She had never wanted, or never bothered to ask anyone. She remembered blushing because she was so naive. . . .

"You're incredible," Jonathan said. "I love you. . . ."

○●

Something moved in the near darkness, in the coconut palms to the right of the terrace. Stephanie turned her head quickly toward the sound and into the present, but she could see nothing. The Casa del Sol slept; only a dim nimbus of light from one distant bungalow shone through the palms.

Fitz would go wild over Nicholas Hanson, she thought. He was really her type, so unlike Jonathan. . . .

She stood up abruptly, left the table, walked over to the low stone wall of the terrace, and sat down with her back to the ocean. The breeze seemed to increase, and she hugged herself, imagining the conversation she would have with Fitz about Nicholas.

"What an attractive man!" Fitz would say. "Those eyes—"

"You would think so. He's the kind you like: charming, and superficial. A real lady-killer."

"Now, Stephie," Fitz would sigh, "you know that no one is superficial. No one and nothing is just a surface. Not skin, or water, or words or wood. Not even Formica, for that matter—"

"That sounds like a pretty good description of Nicholas Hanson to me."

"My, my—" she would say, smiling. "Aren't you getting saucy in your widowhood! I think you're lucky. I mean, imagine how awful it could have been down here, nothing but couples and bridge-playing old biddies. The blue-rinse brigade. It seems to me that you're really lucky!"

"Please try to show a little sensitivity, could you Fitz?"

Fitz would lean toward her at that point. "I show more sensitivity to your needs than you do, dear heart. I always have, even if you don't want to admit it. Now is now, and you're a lovely widow with half of your life ahead of you—"

"Sometimes I think you're glad I'm a widow."

"Shhh . . . shhh . . . shhh . . . ," the waves behind Stephanie remonstrated. "Be silent, shush up . . ."

But that was it; that was the source of her fear. Fitz had never really liked Jonathan, not from the beginning. She had never wanted Stephanie to marry him; she didn't think he was exciting enough for her. She wouldn't even stay for the wedding. "Diamonds and diapers are not my thing," she had announced, and that was all. She had left town, was gone for seven long years, and then a month after her return from Europe Jonathan had died that hideous death. . . .

Stephanie shivered again. All she could hear was the steady, certain unfurling of the waves behind her and the sound of the long-jawed palm fronds whistling through their fringed and tattered teeth. All she could hear was the waves, the palms, and Fitz's whispers.

"It seems to me," Fitz had said about a week after her return, "that you and Jonathan are letting the days sift too uniformly through your years, Steph. Like sand in an hourglass . . ."

And: "Maybe you should get out by yourself more, just to see if you can stand alone? I think you and Jonathan depend on each other too much . . ."

And, "You're in a bit of a rut, don't you think? . . ."

Damn her anyway, Stephanie thought, and kicked off her sandals. She swung around on the stone wall and buried her toes in the cold sand. Fitz had gotten her way, all right. She usually did—eventually. Stephanie *was* standing alone now, because she had to. She was all alone and still listening to Fitz. . . .

Fitz was a moth, Stephanie reflected—a moth drawn to Stephanie's own dim light. It circled around her, fluttering dissatisfactions in her ear, provoking envy of the glamorous, exciting, creative life that Fitz led. Fitz had always known what she wanted, and now she had achieved it. Hell, Stephanie thought—compared to Fitz she was only a clock ticking away the years, doing the right thing, tick! Doing the expected thing, tock! Doing the safe thing, tick! But Fitz was an alarm clock, clang clang clanging in the face of conformity. So Stephanie was jealous and wanted to suspect Fitz of something terrible. Maybe that was it, she realized; maybe she was just jealous. . . .

She picked up her sandals and started walking across the sand toward the path which led to her *casita*. The breeze seemed to grow stronger each time she moved.

No, she realized, there was more to it than jealousy. There was anger at herself, for letting Fitz's influence filter slowly through her tight web of domesticity, for letting the moth into her lighted den. And there was something sinister about the accident itself, about the fact that Fitz was there and had had her way, now that Jonathan was gone. . . .

But she hadn't even put up a fight, years ago, when Stephanie told her about marrying him. It was the first time in years that Fitz hadn't tried to dissuade Stephanie from doing something she didn't really want her to do, since childhood. And that seemed strange, now. At the time Stephanie thought Fitz was probably happy to be rid of her, tired of trying to change her into someone more like Fitz herself. Maybe I was dumb, Stephanie told herself. *Maybe I should have realized that Fitz seldom gives up.* . . .

Stephanie stubbed her toe slightly on a stone, the first rounded stone of the path that wound toward her cabin under the palms. The tall trees were clacking in the wind. *Maybe I was really dumb,* she repeated to herself. The stones were cold under her feet. Maybe she should have known that Fitz wouldn't leave her permanently alone to discover her own, chosen world. Stephanie had been so happy, so content at the prospect of her new life with Jonathan that she never actually gave Fitz much thought.

She'd been home free.

The palm trees overhead thrashed louder and Stephanie moved faster, suddenly remembering Snow White in the forest, where leaves had faces and long-armed trees reached out to grab her. She looked over her shoulder, feeling foolish, knowing it was a childish fear. . . .

And it was foolish treason to suspect Fitz, wasn't it? No one had loved her more, except Jonathan. Or loved life more, or crusaded more for its joys than Fitz. She would be hurt, if she was aware of these thoughts; Fitz would never do anything to harm her best friend. . . .

But something violent had happened between Fitz and Jonathan that night on the balcony. Something passionate, and Stephanie had been left out of it; she had missed what was going on between them. *Don't be absurd,* she told herself as she hurried toward her *casita. Neither one of them was ever unfaithful to me.* . . .

It was something else, something that went back farther than that night, something that originated years earlier. Stephanie felt it, sensed it, and she had to figure it out—

Her cabin sat among the palms, dark and waiting. It was the farthest one from the main building, the closest to the ocean, the most secluded. She saw its low outline and heard the rusty wind chime tinkling by the screened-in front door.

I have to figure it out, she thought, *or I'll go crazy living with this fear of Fitz, not knowing whether to blame her or not, whether to love her or hate her. And I need her, now. Except for Angie and Kent I'll be so alone. I'll be so horribly lonely.* . . .

She stepped inside the dark casita, and the full terror of solitude wrapped her in blackness, like a serape.

5

It was dawn, and Stephanie's wedding day.

Fitz was letting Stephanie drive her along in a white Buick convertible with a red leather interior, and they were somewhere on the outskirts of their childhood city. The bright pink backdrop of the early-morning sky was smudged with clouds of dull gray. The air was muggy.

Stephanie drove slowly, because the road was narrow, rutted, and dusty. It was bordered on either side by small shacks, dirt-covered and shabby. Fitz felt uncomfortable; she couldn't understand what they were doing in such a bad neighborhood.

The whole gray and pink sky was suddenly moving, driven by some unseen force, moving faster than they were. Their open car seemed to stand still. Fitz felt a sudden pause in time—a breathless premonition—which huddled about them like motionless, hot air. Then it was gone.

They drove on and passed an ink-green pine tree on the side of the road. Fitz looked closely at the tree, and suddenly she saw Jonathan standing in its shadow, watching them silently. She shouted at Stephanie to stop, that it was Jonathan! Stephanie slammed on the brakes, her blue eyes wide with delight, and before the car was fully halted Fitz jumped over the convertible door and ran across the loose brown powder of the road toward his shadowy form.

"Jonathan!" she cried. "What on earth are you doing here? Of all the places to find you—"

His face was dark and unfriendly, and his teeth were set like small pieces of porcelain in a ghastly, smug smile. He held a gun; a short stubby black gun in front of his stomach.

And then Jonathan shot Fitz, twice.

She felt the explosion in her abdomen. She felt its fire and saw its flames. She *knew* what it felt like to be shot. If she heard the word *gun* today she could feel that explosion and could see the bits of clotted red, black, and orange flesh and fire shooting upward under her eyes.

She could feel her body falling into space and her eyelids closing, overpowered by a fuzzy black, foamy haze. She knew what it felt like to be dying.

Stephanie was screaming, screaming! She jumped out of the car and started running to Fitz, who could still see her through the black foam. "No!" Fitz yelled to her. "No!"

And then she heard the third shot.

Stephanie was a tawny ragdoll, a pretty scarecrow full of straw, dancing in the dawn. Stephanie was a hazy vision bending, twisting, spilling, crumbling into the fluffy brown dust. . . .

The last thing that Fitz saw before the thick black foam filled her eyes completely was Jonathan's awful, complacent smile hanging over her head.

○●

"Diamonds and diapers are not my thing," Fitz had said to Stephanie the next morning, and then turned away to hide her emotions. *What a dream,* she thought, *God what a horrible dream! It was the worst of all.* . . . She walked over to the closet and reached up on the shelf for her suitcase.

"What are you doing?" Stephanie said.

Fitz lifted the heavy red suitcase off the shelf and dropped it onto the bed, opened it, and walked back to the closet. She still saw the appalling smile on Jonathan's face, that sick smug smile. . . .

"Fitz, answer me!" Stephanie was standing in her pink nightgown in the center of their bedroom on Greenwich Street.

Fitz was already dressed. "I guess I'm going to leave," she said calmly. She was shaking inside, wondering if she knew what she was doing. "I'm tired of San Francisco anyway. I want to start painting in Paris, I've always wanted to paint in Paris. I'm sorry, Stephie."

"But you can't leave now!" Stephanie said, incredulous. "You have to be my maid of honor!"

Fitz opened the chest of drawers, took out a pile of underwear, and placed it carefully in the bag. She couldn't look at Stephanie. Why was she letting that dream do this to her? Why was she giving Jonathan this power? . . .

Because that dream means something, she said to herself.

Because I really do want to paint in Paris: I've been itchy-footed for months. Maybe that bad dream is doing me a favor. Yes, that's it, a big favor. I believe in the power of dreams. . . .

She dropped another armful of blouses and sweaters into the suitcase and opened another drawer.

"Fitz, please!"

Dreams always meant something, Fitz knew; they told you what you were missing, what you really wanted, what you should do. She emptied the bottom drawer. Dreams were actually more organized than your daily life, when you thought about it. They provided the missing links—

But damn that smug smile on Jonathan's face.

"You just can't leave now," Stephanie said.

"I'm really sorry," Fitz repeated, and went to the closet. She started pulling her dresses off the hangers, folding them carelessly, placing them in the other half of the red suitcase. Damn Jonathan for wanting to be rid of her, even in a dream.

"You can't walk out on me at the most important time of my life—"

Oh yes I can, Fitz thought, and walked into the bathroom to pack her cosmetics. Now's exactly the right time. Jonathan wants me to go, and you don't need me, you've got him. Even if he's all wrong for you; I can't change that. But I'll be back, one day. I'll come back and get even with him for that smile. I'll wipe that smile right off his face. . . .

How?

She took her toothbrush out of the rack, her eye liner and mascara and eye shadow, her shampoo and cleansing cream and conditioner off the counter, her aspirin and vitamins out of the medicine cabinet. She closed the door and looked at herself in the mirror.

By seducing him, she thought. That was how. She would make him beg for her, when the time was ripe. She would make him ache for her—

That would get rid of his smugness.

If she could do it without Stephanie's knowing. . . . She didn't ever want to hurt Stephanie. . . .

But someday she would seduce Jonathan.

"Fitz?" Stephanie said again. "Please stay long enough to be my maid of honor . . ."

Everything was dead at three o'clock in the morning.

Stephanie lay on her back in the black bedroom of her *casita.* Her eyes were open. There was no shape to her room, no form to the night, no substance to the air. Everything was flat, black, formless, dead. Dead like Jonathan. She could feel the deadness touching her hands and feet and heart, where only Jonathan used to touch. . . .

Only the mechanical clicking of her clock, only its two luminescent hands glowing and floating in the darkness like two disembodied creatures in hell . . . only the clicking told her she was alive. Tick. Click. Tick. Click . . .

She should take a Seconal.

Tick. Click. Tick . . .

She wished she could hear the ocean. Any sound of real life, of something that breathed naturally and not mechanically.

If only she could fall asleep naturally, and wake to the warmth of Jonathan's arms around her. . . .

○●

"Shush," he mumbled sleepily. "Here." Had she been dreaming again? He curled around her so conveniently. He wrapped her up in waking warmth, his cheek on her hair, his chest pressed to her back, his left arm looped around her. His knees nudged the backs of her knees, their lower legs overlapping. They fit perfectly.

"Mmmm," she murmured. A private package; a reciprocal gift each dark cozy morning. The somnolent minutes slipped by. . . .

She wiggled; they turned together, rolled together in ritual until he lay on his back and her head snuggled against his chest. Warm and safe, pressed against each other the length of their bodies. This ritual was the best part; it was more real than anything else.

The curly hairs on his chest tickled her cheek. She rubbed against him; he pulled her tighter and closer in their silence and sense of commitment, the best security in the world.

It was enough; it was all she needed.

"Darling." He was above her now. He nibbled her ear, and she lifted her face. His lips were soft, his hands gentle. She felt his weight, and smiled into his eyes, watching them glaze over slowly, watching his round glazed eyes gradually closing, sliding shut into a faster deeper different kind of sleep that filled her too, that poured his dreams inside her. She was a cup containing his love, and that was enough for her. It was all she would ever need.

But sometimes, she wondered if it was all Jonathan needed. . . .

○●

Tick. Click.
Tick. Click.
She should throw that clock out the window. Into the sand. She should have done with him the things other women do in bed, wild things. She should have let herself go a little.

That picnic, after they'd been married only a month. That picnic up in the Napa Valley, after they'd visited some wineries. Maybe that was when she made her first mistake. . . .

○●

"Hey, Stephie!" Jonathan yelled. "Up here! This is the perfect place!"

He stood in shorts, on top of a hill under an old oak that spread its shadow over the dappled brown grass behind him. He stood gleaming and healthy in the sunlight, her athletic, all-American hero, grinning down at her. Her young God on Olympus. She loved the strong muscles in his legs. . . .

His shorts were khaki-colored, and he was wearing a navy-blue Lacoste shirt with an alligator on it. He slipped the knapsack off his shoulders while she walked up the hill toward him, and then she began spreading the plaid blanket on the grass.

"Wait a second," he said, as she started to unpack a barbecued chicken and her first potato salad, some Rouge et Noir Camembert, French bread, and a bunch of green grapes. "Let's not eat yet. I have a surprise for you."

"A surprise?"

"Of course." He smiled and pulled a thermos out of the knapsack. "Thought we might have a couple of martinis, to celebrate our first picnic. And then maybe a little open-air exercise, before lunch . . ."

The gold and green of California hills was all around them, and no one was in sight. Tall blades of tan grass swayed in the breeze. The red Corvette that Jonathan had rented for the day, just to see what it was like, was parked far below them on the road—a shining, curved road that wound toward them, and not away. Like their dreams. The dark green oak leaves trembled overhead and the heat of the sun beat on her bare legs.

"Someone might come along," she whispered as he unzipped her yellow shorts. "What if—"

"Hush," he said, and swallowed her sentence.

○●

He grinned all through lunch, and Stephanie didn't notice what kind of grin it was. She thought it was just happiness, the satisfaction of the scene, the fact of being satisfied. They drank two bottles of BV Pinot Chardonnay with their food, and Jonathan finally started to giggle.

"What's so funny?" she asked, smiling too.

"Nothing!" He laughed.

"Come on, Jonathan! What is it?"

"Don't you have to go behind the tree pretty soon?" His eyes were devilish and expectant, ten years old.

"Not really, why? What's so funny?"

"I think you should go do pee-pee," he said. "You're in for a surprise!" He *was* ten years old again, hiding behind a door and ready to jump out at her, planting a frog between her sheets, springing a trap behind the oak tree. . . .

She stood up, dutiful and curious, half laughing because he was laughing, and walked warily around the oak tree. There was nothing there. She undid her shorts and spread her feet. . . .

It was a cork.

He had put a cork inside her, planted a cork in her private parts! It fell out because it wasn't in very far; she straightened up and stared at it.

"Hey honey?" Jonathan called. He was waiting for her laughter; now it was his voice that was expectant.

He had put a cork inside her! It had been there for over an hour and she hadn't known it, hadn't felt it. He had invaded her with a foreign object—

"Stephie?"

He had no business doing that, it was perverted, it was not a funny trick.

"Are you all right, honey?" There was anxiety in his voice, now. She heard him getting up, she couldn't imagine when he had done it or how he had done it, she didn't want to know. . . .

His hands were on her shoulders, turning her toward him. She couldn't look at his face.

"I'm sorry, honey. I thought it was funny! We were having so much fun, you were so dreamy. I don't know what came over me, really. Stephie? It was just a joke, honey. . . ."

○●

Tick! the clock in the dark *casita* said.

Click!

Stephanie closed her eyes. Maybe if she had laughed that first time, maybe if she had let him touch her and kiss her everywhere later. . . . Then maybe she would know what Fitz was talking about, she would understand her thunder-and-lightning, buttock-bouncing, hip-swiveling, soul-screaming descriptions. But they always seemed gross to Stephanie; they conjured up pictures of a prolonged and exhausting exorcism. Fitz made it sound like the expulsion of evil tensions, as if the lover were her partner in crime, an accomplice in the disposal of incriminating evidence, in the burning away of an excess of passion. . . .

She wondered if Nicholas Hanson was what they call a good lover.

Stop it! she told herself. *Stop thinking that way. Sleep. . . . Try to go to sleep. You have to get through life, somehow.* . . .

Tick.

Click.

Tick.

Jonathan is dead.

Tick.

Click tick click tick click tick click . . .

She opened her eyes again.

There was a crack—a thin, jagged crack—that hung over her head in the adobe ceiling. She could see it vaguely in the stillborn light before dawn; it was better defined than the other shadows waiting to be delivered by dawn's stretching fingers. Another day . . .

Tick.

Click.

Stephanie sat up. Why couldn't that clock make some other noise, say something else? Why couldn't it do something different, talk sense to her instead of seconds? The sense that Fate makes out of disaster. . . .

She should have been better for Jonathan. But he had never complained, and everything else between them was perfect, as good as a marriage could be, with a minimum of fights. . . .

"You take such good care of us," he used to say. "It's marvelous, the way the house is always spotless, my drawers in impeccable order, my socks rolled and matched up like granny used to do. The bills paid on time, the checkbook balanced. . . . I never see toys scattered around or handprints on the walls. . . . I know it takes most of your time but it's worth it, honey. You really are a superb wife and mother. . . ."

Mother.

Angie and Kent, their soft smooth cheeks . . .

Stephanie smiled wistfully in the half-light of dawn. It was always worth it, being a mother. Worth anything and everything to feel their smooth cheeks, to bend down to them, to smile into their innocence and see yourself reflected, long ago. To be an idol, a queen: dear little Angie following her around the house, her chubby hands clutching at her toy broom handle, sweeping up after Stephanie. And Kent all curled up in her lap, his six-year-old energy still for a while as he listened to another fairy tale told by his queen. Strong-willed and freckled, with dark eyes. The image of Jonathan, the essence of little boy . . .

Why did she fear for them so?

What was this cold premonition that followed her whenever she thought of Angie and Kent? They had to be fine; Mrs. Hayes was totally reliable, and they probably didn't even miss her. At three and six they were off in their own world. . . .

I should be home, she thought, and lay back down again. *I shouldn't be here at all.*

I wonder which cabin Nicholas Hanson is in.

7

Casita Numero Uno was the oldest and most decrepit of the bungalows at the Casa del Sol, and the last to be rented, when nothing else was available, as had been the case with Nicholas. The screened-in front door was rusty and creaked, and the small Maytag in the kitchenette coughed and quit at least once a week, dripping water and providing no ice. The shower leaked and had left a dark stain on the bedroom wall; only in Mexico could the shower faucets have been installed outside the shower above the cedar chest of drawers in the bedroom. But that was Mexico, and Nicholas didn't mind.

He rolled over in the bed that was too short for him, opened his eyes, and glanced at his watch. Six o'clock. Another hour before they would start serving breakfast. He yawned, he stretched; his feet stuck out from under the sheets at the foot of the bed.

He got up and walked over to the cedar chest, whose top was cluttered with a wallet, a large key ring, a hair brush and black comb, a paperback edition of *Shōgun*, a tube of Bain de Soleil, a stick of Brut deodorant, a bottle of Cardin aftershave, two cartons of Marlboro, two pairs of sunglasses in leather cases, and a box with two decks of playing cards in it. On one deck was the elegant, superior portrait *Blue Boy*, by Gainsborough, and on the other a sweet and innocent young girl called *Pinkie*, by Sir Thomas Lawrence. Nicholas loved those two portraits, so much that he drove all the way to the Huntington Museum in San Marino to see the original paintings each time he was in Los Angeles.

He reached now for the cards on the right, and took out the deck with pretty young Pinkie standing on a hill and looking out over the English countryside. He sat down on the rumpled bed, and began playing solitaire on the sheets while planning his general line of approach toward the widowed Stephanie McMillan.

There was something fragile and pathetic in Pinkie's face that reminded him of her.

It was eight o'clock in the morning.

Stephanie had dressed in a sleeveless pink cotton dress and white sandals, intending to go straight to breakfast. But instead she found herself on the beach far to the north of the hotel, walking aimlessly, listening to the waves slap the shore, hearing them spank the sand and then applaud their own punishing force with little clapping ripples. . . .

The beach usually reminded her of her children, of Angie and Kent smudged with wet sand, burying each other up to their necks and building moats, on balmy breezy days at the Marina Green or Stinson Beach. It reminded her of Jonathan teaching Kent how to throw a Frisbee, of Angie being knocked over by the waves and laughing. . . .

There was a small crowd gathering on the beach ahead of her, almost to the village of Zihautenejo. She soon learned that it was a disaster crowd, a flock of would-be vultures. Three boys had been playing a dangerous game in the surf. The youngest boy hadn't really liked the game; it frightened him. But he wanted to show that he was as strong and brave as the others. He wanted to be like the older, who had been superb when the younger two had held him under the water and pressed him down with their hands and feet against the grating, rolling sand until the count of 85. He hadn't even kicked! The youngest boy had been determined to do as well when his turn came.

His small body now lay breathless on the white sand, face up, eyes closed. Stephanie saw him and started running. Less than a dozen Mexicans stood in a circle around him, staring silently. He had been out of the water only a short while.

She ran to his body, knelt, and rolled him quickly onto his stomach. A little water drooled out of his mouth. The villagers did nothing.

"Get help!" Stephanie shouted. "For God's sake get help!"

They looked at her, uncomprehending. She rolled the boy onto his back again and clamped her fingers over his nose. "Get a doctor!" she pleaded.

They muttered to each other, but no one was moving.

She pressed her mouth to the boy's mouth and exhaled. Something about the chest; she knew she was supposed to push against the chest at the same time she breathed, to get a rhythm going. Oh God, if only she knew exactly how to do it! The head back. His head should be back more. . . .

She placed her arm under his neck, tilting his face to the sky, and breathed in and out, in and out, in and out while holding his nose shut with one hand and pressing her palm to his chest with the other, hoping she was doing it right, not knowing if she was doing it right.

"Doctore!" She implored the natives. "Oh please, someone go get a *doctore!* Help! *Au secours!"* Her eyes started to fill up. If only she could speak Spanish! If only these stupid people would do something—

Suddenly she saw Nicholas Hanson among them, speaking rapid Spanish in a quiet voice, pointing one man toward the hotel and a woman toward the village. She heard the words *madre* and *padre* as if in a dream. She wondered what he was doing there, thanked heaven he was there. . . .

Nicholas knelt down next to her, took the boy gently from her arms, and began breathing into his mouth exactly as she had done, pressing his chest with the palm of his hand exactly as she had pressed it. *Please let it be the right way,* Stephanie thought. *It has to be the right way, I can't stand any more death near me, I won't be able to bear it. . . .*

Nicholas stayed bent over the boy, breathing in and out, in and out for a long time, and still there was no breath in the little body. Finally he handed the child back to her and stood up, and while she continued the breathing in and out, in and out, she heard Nicholas haranguing the villagers angrily. This was almost worse than Jonathan, she thought, because there was still hope. When Jonathan had fallen into the night there was never any hope, none. Why didn't they have a respirator? She didn't love or need this boy the way she did Jonathan but she prayed to God to let him live . . . Each breath she gave to him was a kiss; each time she pressed her lips to his it was a kiss of life, willing him to live. She would make him live! She would give him so many kisses he would come to life again with her love. What if he were Kent? Oh Lord, what if this little boy were her son! . . .

She was blowing breath into him desperately now, too fast; she had to make him live. . . .

She heard the crowd murmuring. She heard loud

voices and then she felt the boy's chest move faintly under her hand. Nicholas Hanson took hold of her gently and pulled her face away from the boy's face. The small chest moved again. Nicholas bent over him and breathed with him five or six more times until he was on his own. The boy's eyelids fluttered and then fell back from soft brown eyes.

Jonathan's eyes.

Only alive.

Tears flooded the *"unfair!"* cry in Stephanie's throat.

○●

She kept her eyes lowered on the walk back to the hotel with Nicholas Hanson. She watched her white sandals moving across the sand heel-toe, heel-toe, and saw Jonathan's eyes alive again. The ocean murmured to her right; the ocean was a suffocator. The mountains on her left pressed down like heavy hairy pillows. Why was the boy alive, and not her husband?

"You'll have breakfast with me, of course," Nicholas said.

She was aware of his white pants, now sand and water-spotted, moving along next to her, aware of his blue espadrilles stepping along with her white sandals. It was lucky that he had happened to come along when he did.

"Stephanie? I know you must be hungry."

The casual, persistent familiarity, again. She looked up at him. Maybe it *wasn't* luck that he had come along; maybe he had followed her. He was the man on the beach yesterday; abruptly she was sure of that. And then he had sat next to her at dinner, last night. He seemed to be wherever she was, most of the time.

"That was a wonderful thing, saving that boy's life," Nicholas said. "We should celebrate." His eyes were a lively green.

There was something about him that troubled her, and she didn't know what it was. "I'm not hungry," she told him.

"Of course you are. How long has it been since you've had champagne for breakfast?"

The terrace was crowded at nine o'clock, and it seemed to Stephanie that all the people were watching her and Nicholas as they walked up the beach toward the tables and sat down in a corner. She didn't like people looking at them as if they were a couple. "You don't understand," she wanted to say. "This is not my man. Jonathan was my man—"

Nicholas ordered their breakfast without asking her if *huevos rancheros* and champagne were what she wanted. It wasn't the best of manners; Jonathan would never have done that. But maybe Nicholas thought she needed someone to take care of her. The waiter's name was Gabriel, she learned, and Gabriel returned almost immediately with an ice bucket and the champagne.

"Here's to the little boy," Nicholas said as soon as Gabriel had moved to another table. "Long life to him." His glass clinked against hers. She took a sip and glanced around, worrying about what these people would think of them drinking champagne in the morning. They probably didn't know about the boy.

"I'm not cheering you up," Nicholas said. "I guess that was a traumatic experience." His look was quizzical and probing. Stephanie tried to smile.

"I'm failing miserably," he said. "Should I sing a song for you, or wiggle my ears? I used to practice for hours, learning how to wiggle my ears—"

Why did she feel uneasy? He was charming, well dressed, and obviously experienced. Too experienced. That was it; his suavity worked against him. She shouldn't have been drinking champagne with a man like him, when Jonathan was barely cold. But it was silly of her to mistrust him; he had been wonderful with the boy.

Stephanie turned in her chair and looked out at the calm ocean. Why had death come so close to her recently? She'd always led such a sheltered life, a comfortable life—

She turned back to Nicholas and caught him looking at her wedding ring. The diamond was dirty; she knew she should remember to wash it more often. Nicholas looked up at her slowly, unsmiling. The clock in her bedroom. The clock that had ticked all night long in her bedroom was ticking and clicking with cold precision in his eyes.

Of course not, she thought. It's my nerves, and that little boy, and no sleep. . . .

If only she knew what to expect from people! If only the first steps leading into the knowledge of someone were not so difficult. She looked directly back at Nicholas. He sat before her like a picture she had seen, a magazine photo of a pyramid at Uxmal: suddenly mysterious, lofty, and constructed of steps so narrow and steep that you had to hold on to a chain to reach the cool temple at the top. She would need a chain with Nicholas Hanson, she thought. . . .

"More champagne?" he asked, his eyes on hers.

Stephanie nodded. It had been different with Jonathan. The steps leading to him had been broad and inviting—

"Tell me," Nicholas said, "are you a native Californian?"

Why did all his questions seem artificial? Jonathan had leaned on his tennis racquet and grinned, asking her where the hell she had learned to play tennis so badly.

"No," she answered, "I'm from Missouri. Kansas City." She twisted the stem of her glass nervously and waited for the smile that often came at the mention of her home town. But Jonathan hadn't smiled, and neither did

Nicholas Hanson. He already knew, she thought. He knew or had guessed that she was from the Midwest. She thought she'd lost her accent.

"The Bible Belt."

Gabriel served the *huevos rancheros,* and Nicholas took a large bite of eggs.

"Hardly! It's a very sophisticated city now, very swinging." Jonathan had nodded and said that he'd been to Kansas City on business, that there were beautiful houses and country clubs there, beautiful trees. . . .

Stephanie picked up her fork and pushed at her eggs; she really wasn't hungry. The early morning sun felt warm on her face; someone at a neighboring table laughed. And suddenly she saw Fitz. . . .

Fitz, sitting barefoot at the breakfast table of the apartment they had shared in San Francisco, years ago. Fitz munching on toast and muttering about Kansas City, about midwestern mentality and suburban bourgeois attitudes everywhere. Something about the destruction of the Zorba myth, and the everlasting search for the American Dream. Fitz had jumped up on her chair and done a carnival act, waving her fork in the air, pointing it at an imaginary screen, calling out in a hawker's voice:

"That's right, folks! Now we're gonna sing it all together now, gonna sing this glorious Hymn of the Hopeful Bourgeois, loud and clear! Just follow the bouncing red ball, sing along with old Mitch, and you'll get the meter! Here we go now, folksies: 'Drink to security wi-ith thine eyes, and I—I shall drink to thine . . .' "

Stephanie hadn't laughed much, at the time. Didn't everyone want security?

Nicholas had recalled the waiter and was chatting with Gabriel in Spanish. They were both laughing. "He forgot the toast," Nicholas said to her, "because it was burnt."

"Oh? I hadn't noticed."

"So I see." The humor was fading from his face. "You really should eat something."

She cut a bit out of the tomato-splashed eggs, remembering how Fitz had jabbed her fork at the air and continued her spiel in a strident, nasal voice: "Puritan paganism, little girl, yessirreee! That's how you were raised. A nice moral and material wall built around you, a censorious, middle-west nest! Step right up folks, and see the nest. See the bent twigs of bigotry? See the hard-earned, hard-baked bricks? All white, for right! No black bricks, and never any gray . . .

"This nest, ladies and gents, is in a big spooky jungle, called the Judgmental Jungle, but those who live in it are very safe, yessirreee. They're safe 'cuz they're insulated! Here's how it works. Just repeat after me, and you'll learn the secret to livin' in that jungle: 'Thou shalt worship thy neighbor's opinion above all else.' Good! 'Thou shalt be servile unto society's standards. Thou shalt covet the country club!' Excellent, folks, excellent! . . ."

Fitz had grinned at Stephanie and sat back down in her chair. And Stephanie had told her in a surly voice that she really should go on the stage, that she was a born actress—

"Such a scowl!" Nicholas said. "Is anything the matter?"

Stephanie looked up, startled. "No," she said.

"Are you sure?"

"Well . . ." She pushed her eggs around some more. "I . . . I'm drinking champagne with you in the morning, and I don't know anything about you. . . ."

Nicholas looked amused. "Let's see now," he said, and his mouth turned down in that mocking, slightly sinister smile. "Let's see. I'm a drug pusher." He arched an eyebrow. "A rich one. I own three nightclubs, one in Vegas, one at Tahoe, and one in North Beach. Carol

Doda is one of my favorite sweeties. That's my night work; in the afternoon I'm a banker on Montgomery Street, where all the secretaries are madly in love with me. In the morning I teach karate to young boys and seduce them too. On weekends I fly to Mexico and frighten pretty young ladies—"

Stephanie avoided his eyes. "Please don't make fun of me."

"Are you always this serious?"

She looked away and bit her lower lip. Was she always this serious? Was her husband always dead; did she always think about walking into the ocean in the middle of the night and decide not to do it because of her children? Was she always afraid; could she trust her best friend?

"I'm sorry," Nicholas said.

She didn't reply.

"I've done a lot of things, actually. Your eggs are getting cold. I've dabbled in archeology and geology, been a consultant for some American firms abroad, and done professional photography." He looked away from her, out at the ocean. "I'm down here now to take pictures for a travel article. For *New West.*"

"Oh," she said, and smiled weakly, thinking that that was hardly anything to be frightened of. What had she thought? She picked up her champagne glass and smiled at him again, trying to relax.

"Now that you know all about me," he said, returning her smile, "we can look forward to our scuba diving. Did I ask you if you've ever done it? Do you know how?"

Stephanie shook her head. "No, Mr. Hanson," she wanted to say, "I don't dive. I don't speak Spanish and I don't dabble in things. I'm not your type, really; I'm a dull Jane. I don't even travel, normally. Jonathan and I talked about it, though. We were waiting until the children were older—"

"I'm afraid of the water," she said. "Especially after what happened this morning."

Nicholas emptied the rest of the champagne into their glasses. "You have to go right back in, or else you'll be afraid of it the rest of you life. And I'll teach you how to dive; it's a fantastic experience!" There were flashes of excitement in his eyes. *Watch out,* she told herself. *Watch out for those eyes and that sexy smile.* . . .

"I'm not sure I like things that live in the ocean."

"That's because they're hidden," Nicholas smiled. "But—"

"Squishy things, things that go bump in the slime." She wrinkled her nose and her eyebrows.

Nicholas laughed. "You'll change your mind when you see them. It's a promise. I'll go into the village and get the equipment and a boat while you change into your suit. They know me here; I can take a boat out by myself. We can have lunch on the beach—conch, if I can find it—and then retire to the shade of a palm and drink white wine—"

The Girl Beneath the Lion. Hot sun, sandy beaches, sunlight spinning on the water, semen mixed with sand. *The Girl Beneath the Lion*—a book she had read years ago—that took place in Sardinia or Sicily, some place on the Mediterranean; it didn't matter. All she could remember was the hot sunlight on the water and the semen mixed with sand. Jonathan hadn't liked the book, but she had found it strangely exciting. And she could be that girl today; she could try to forget everything and become that girl. . . .

No, of course not. How could she think that way? Jonathan wouldn't understand those thoughts. . . .

It had to be the champagne.

9

The boat pulled away from the pier and accelerated across the bay, leaving a stream of foam in its wake. Stephanie could feel the throb of the engine under the faded blue pillows where she sat in the stern, staring at Nicholas Hanson's tanned back, skimming farther away from reality across the ocean, toward an unknown and frightening underwater world . . . with a man who still made her feel nervous.

Nicholas looked over his shoulder at her and smiled.

The boat was a battered twenty-three-foot fishing craft that felt sturdy despite its shabby appearance. The scuba tanks and gear were secured in its bow, next to a styrofoam cooler that contained their lunch, wine, and beer. Stephanie sat stiffly, her feet planted on the rough floorboards. Nicholas was standing at the wheel in the center of the boat, under its white roof. She guessed it was called a roof, on a boat. He was dressed only in red-and-white striped latex swimming trunks. None of it seemed real to her, and she didn't want to go under the ocean.

She continued to watch him, wondering what she was doing there. His back was broad, and the hair on his legs was golden and curly. Jonathan wore boxer swim trunks, not that tight European kind. She should have been alone with her memories of Jonathan, and Fitz.

They had crossed the bay and were nearing the southern point, where the scruffy mountains merged and twisted downward into the water. She wasn't even sure why he had wanted her to come. . . . Oh yes she was sure, and she shouldn't have agreed. It made her indebted to him, in a way.

"There's a reef in the next bay!" Nicholas shouted over the noise of the engine. "Around the point!" He gestured with his left hand and turned the boat slightly to the left. Was that port, or starboard? She never could get it straight. The sun had settled into her skin; she felt its warmth intensify as the boat throttled down. If only the boat would circle at that speed for hours and never stop, until she could step out on land.

She had worn her old brown one-piece suit, to feel safer. Nicholas had looked disappointed when he met her on the beach, but she didn't want to wear her bikini with him. She hoped he had gotten the message.

He throttled down even more, cut the motor, and threw an anchor over the side. The silence—cut by the sound of the sliding rope—the hot sky, and the smooth, blue green water . . . were unreal. Even the distant mountains seemed to hang above them through thin waves of heat, and now Nicholas was standing over her, his tanned legs spread wide to steady himself, handing her a can of beer. His dust-blond hair shone in the sunlight. She didn't like the way he was looking at her.

"Are you married?" she heard herself say.

"I never really found it necessary."

"Lucky you."

His eyes hung onto hers; small waves slapped the side of the boat. He hadn't missed the sarcasm in her voice, so why didn't he say more, defend himself? Now it was his turn to ask about her, to ask if she was married, or divorced, or separated, or a widow. She wanted him to know that she was a recent widow. . . .

"Drink your beer," he commanded, still looking down at her, a male peacock displayed before a dull hen.

He didn't care if she was married or not, she realized. His interest in her was only temporary. And now she was really afraid of the command in his voice, of being out there alone with him. Maybe he already knew about Jonathan. No, that was impossible. . . .

"Don't you *like* beer?" he said.

Stephanie took a sip of it; the taste was shockingly cold and bitter.

"Thanks," she said. "It's delicious."

"Do you always try so hard to please?" he said, grinning. "I'm glad. Now come on, let's go get our gear." He offered her his hand, and the boat rocked as she stood up.

"Watch out," the water seemed to whisper; "I'm in control now, you're in my power. . . ."

"Steady," Nicholas said, leading her by the hand to the bow of the boat. "Try these on for size." He gave her a pair of blue rubber flippers.

She was not a fish, she thought. She hated fish. She didn't want to commune with the fish, to have fins like the ones fish had. . . .

"Do they fit?" Nicholas asked. "They should be fairly tight."

She nodded. None of this was real. The rocking boat, the heat, Nicholas's tight swimming suit, the shiny bullet-shaped tanks, the waiting blue green water. This was not her life, and the body that kept responding to his orders was not her body. She didn't want to do this. . . .

"Now," he said, "let me give you a short course. The equipment here in Mexico is hardly the latest thing, but it'll work fine." He rolled a tank on its edge across the floor of the boat toward Stephanie and took hold of a long black rubber tube that was attached to the tank, near the top. "This is called a regulator, and it's what you breathe through. The mouthpiece fits like this—"

She tried to concentrate on what he was saying, to hear his voice and instructions through the barrier that was building in her mind. She couldn't do it, she was dizzy with fright and the heat, she was a total coward.

"—no air gauge on these tanks," she heard him say, "but that doesn't matter—"

"No air gauge?" She snapped to attention; here was her escape. "But we can't go under the water if we don't know how much air we have!"

He smiled patiently. "I *know* how much we have. We have three thousand pounds per square inch of air; that's what these aluminum tanks hold. Enough air to stay down for an hour, and I have a watch to keep track of the time. See?" He pointed to his left wrist. "Waterproof, made for diving. It's not the most intelligent way to dive, without an air gauge, but we're in Mexico. And we won't go deep anyway, since it's your first dive. If you go deep you have much less time. But there's nothing to worry about today."

"How do you know there's air in that tank?"

"Because I watched them fill it with the compressor, at the shop in the village."

"What's that on your other wrist?"

"A depth gauge, so we'll know how deep we are."

"I . . . I'm afraid."

"Stephanie." He said it softly, sympathetically. "Look, let me explain exactly how it works. This is the O-Ring, where the regulator is attached to the tank. And this is the K-Valve, where they fill the tank with air and let the air out. It's really a very simple principle. All you have to do is swim and breath naturally—"

"Which is the air valve?"

"This one, the K-Valve. I'll show you there's air." He turned it quickly, and a sharp, hissing sound whistled out of it. He closed it again. "There. Okay?"

"I don't like my life in the hands of mechanical things. I always think about that, in cars and planes—"

"It's not," he interrupted her solemnly. "It's in my hands. And I promise you we won't go deep; if you shake your head at me and point your finger to the surface we'll come right back up. Okay?"

"I . . . I suppose I should try it—"

"Of course you should. You'll love it. There's only one rule to be careful about. When you start for the surface, no matter how shallow or deep we are, always keep breathing and never swim up faster than your bubbles. Follow your bubbles up."

"Why?"

Nicholas was bending over, picking up a wide black belt. "Because you might get an embolism. If we were really deep, you could also get the bends. But we're not going down deep. It's just a rule to remember."

"I've heard about the bends, but what's an embolism?"

He looked at her, and his green eyes darted, the way people's eyes look when they're trying to make up their minds quickly. "We won't have to worry about that," he smiled, "If you follow your bubbles up. I'll explain it later, after you're hooked on the sport. Now this is a weight belt to counteract the buoyancy of the tank. . . ." He slipped it around her waist and fastened it. His body seemed very big standing so close to hers; some of his assurance was beginning to rub off on her.

"How deep is it here?" she asked.

"It's a giant reef that goes down over two hundred feet. But the top of it is only forty feet down. We'll just take a look at it."

"Can I practice on the surface?"

"Of course. Two feet under." He picked up a black mask with a snorkel stuck through the straps, slipped it over her head, and smoothed her hair. "Hold it right there, I want to take your picture."

"No! I—"

"Your eyes are even bigger and bluer through the glass."

Stephanie looked at him, knowing it was a line, knowing she shouldn't let it affect her, telling herself that the excitement she felt was only fear of the water, fear of the unknown. "The mask is too tight," she said. Nicholas took hold of her shoulders and turned her around to adjust the strap. His hands lingered on her bare shoulders.

○●

They were ready to enter a new world. Nicholas had taken three photos of Stephanie, the last one after slipping the tanks straps over her shoulders and buckling the strap around her waist. Then he lowered her into the water and they treaded water together for a while, which she found tiring. He laughed when she wrinkled her nose at the idea of spitting into her mask and rubbing the spittle around to keep the glass from steaming up; he laughed and said he liked the little freckles on her nose. He showed her how to clear the mask of bubbles when she first went under water, and he told her how to clear her ears as they descended, by holding her nose and blowing out and swallowing. He promised, with a glint in his eye, to hold her hand while they swam—

And then he told her that in the unlikely event that they saw a shark, they should swing the tanks over their heads and hold them out at arm's length, because sharks usually bumped first, to test before they bit. Their skin was a set of thousands of small teeth, and if you held the tank out and circled with the shark he was so stupid he would probably bump the tank, not like the taste, and swim away. . . .

Stephanie balked. She wouldn't go down, she said. She was terrified of sharks, she wanted to get back in the boat, she hated fish. She couldn't stand the thought that her bare legs were dangling below her right then, just waiting for a shark. She had read *Jaws;* she wasn't crazy—

"But I want you to overcome your fear," Nicholas had said. "You'll see a whole new world, something you'll never forget, and you'll be mad at yourself if you never try. You know you will. And besides, there aren't any sharks in these waters; I promise you, no sharks. It was just a precaution." He had put the regulator in her mouth then and told her to watch him go down a little first while she floated near the surface and got used to breathing through the regulator. He had swum down until he was directly below her and she felt as though they were both flying; the water was as clear and waveless as the sky. Stephanie floated above and he floated below, weightless, and she wanted to try to talk to him through the thin blue space. It wasn't so terrifying; it was calm and the water was warm. And she could breathe easily through that rubber tube, hearing the sound of her own breath echoing.

Then Nicholas swam back up to the surface. His wet hair had parted down the middle and looked thin; his ears seemed small and his green eyes very large through the mask. He removed the regulator from his mouth.

"Are you ready to brave it?"

She nodded. He replaced his regulator and took her hand, and they started down together.

But Stephanie wasn't ready for it. It was eternal blankness, an endless space of no boundaries and great power, an unnatural pale oblivion where she didn't belong. . . .

The fins made them swim too fast; they were going down too fast. The sound of her breathing was much too loud; she could hear herself trapped in an airless void, fighting it, not ready to be lost in the void, to end up breathless and suffocated like the boy on the beach. Nicholas was pulling her down. She stopped moving the fins, stopped breathing. She *couldn't* stop breathing; the noise of her breath was too loud, ringing in her ears. Her ears hurt, her head was pounding. She breathed too fast, descended too fast, breathed much too fast, panicked. Nicholas kept pulling her down, down. He wanted to kill her! He wanted her to fall downward into space, like Jonathan had fallen, and never return! The noise of her breathing stopped. Her head and ears and chest were all bursting at the same time; she would explode. . . .

She thrashed and kicked and tried to pull away from his hand; he held on firmly. She jerked his arm. He stopped swimming and smiled at her with his deadly green eyes. Then he reached out toward her mouth. He was going to pull the regulator out of her mouth!

She felt his hand on her mask, his fingers closing over her nose, pinching it shut. So this was it, she thought; this was the terror of dying, the terror Jonathan had known . . .

And then she remembered to blow out, and to swallow. She felt a popping inside her head and knew she was all right, knew she would be all right. Nicholas took his hand away from her face and smiled again with his eyes. They weren't deadly, after all, and her ears weren't splitting. She heard her own breath echoing through the rubber regulator and expanding in waves through the endless water, and then bounding back at her. She knew she would be all right now. The pressure was gone.

But Nicholas was still holding on to her hand, and she was still trapped. He pointed to a school of tiny silver fish that were gliding past them, miniscule red-streaked silver fish shimmering in the green water. Stephanie saw thousands of streaking bullets, an army of wriggling sperm, millions of bloodshot teardrops surrounding them. He pointed to the left, to where two black-striped angelfish swam along, trailing wings of gossamer, ethereal fins. But she saw two crazy faces running away, with straggling gray hairs rushing behind them. The warm water curled around her; she felt icy. It should have been beautiful, an extension of her dreams instead of a descent into nightmares—

Nicholas pointed to the right. A round blowfish, bright yellow with a purple circle in the center of its side, drifted calmly in space. She saw a solitary, staring eye floating in formaldehyde. He squeezed her hand and pointed down; an arch of bright coral reef stretched across deeper, dun-colored and spongy rocks below, where a five-pointed orange starfish had settled. Stephanie looked at the starfish and saw a severed hand.

And then Nicholas was swimming downward again, pulling her with him, down the bright coral arch of the reef. She saw the arch as a fire-rimmed mouth, as the red gate of hell . . .

And at its center, coiled around a rock and uncoiling up toward her, slithering dark green and slimy black, dancing like a snake in underwater waves—was an enormous moray eel. It must have been a foot thick. Its evil eye glared at Stephanie out of an anvil-shaped head, its giant jaw opened and closed, opened and closed, opened and closed to the rhythm of her own breathing. It was waiting to swallow her. . . .

She screamed through the regulator, jerked her hand free of Nicholas, and started swimming upward, upward, screaming for the surface, swimming faster than she had known she could swim—

She felt his hands tight around her ankle, trying to drag her back down again. She twisted and kicked at his face with her free foot, wanting to smash his face, to blind him, to get free! She twisted, and thrashed, and kicked, and clawed upward with her arms toward the surface. But he held on, and then his hands were on both of her ankles and he was pulling her back down again. He *did* want to kill her; he was killing her all over again. . . . Her chest was tight, she couldn't breathe, she had to hold on to her air. She felt her ankles squeezed into the vice of his groin; she had to breathe, she exhaled. . . . He clamped her ankles between his legs and his hands climbed her body. His hands were death claws; his hands were monsters feeling her and touching her everywhere. He was shoving her down between his legs, mounting her obscenely from the rear. . . .

His hands clutched at her waist, working the buckle of the strap that held the tank to her back, releasing it so that the tank floated only from her shoulders. His strong monster hands grabbed her breasts and pulled her against his chest; she tried desperately to push them off. And then she felt them on her shoulders, pulling her flailing arms down and behind her back as his thighs clamped around hers and their thighs were glued together, her knees touching the backs of his knees. She kicked frantically, but he forced his flippers between her calves, slid them down her calves, wrapped his ankles around her ankles and spread her legs far apart, like a frog's. He held her hands behind her back with one hand, and with his free arm pushed the water down and away, riding her, riding her as a conquering bullfrog rides the back of his croaking female mate—slowly to the surface.

○●

They hadn't spoken since they were back on the boat. There was too much between them that Stephanie didn't want to be between them, and Nicholas knew it. He helped her off with her tank without looking her in the eye, and she went to lie down on the faded blue cushions in the stern.

After a while she heard him start the engine, and then felt the boat moving toward the beach. She shouldn't have panicked, she thought. She had broken the rule about going up slowly, about following her bubbles. But that horrible moray eel. . . . And Nicholas had saved her. She was wrong to be suspicious of him; he had helped her save the little boy's life that morning, and then he had saved her. He was very strong and calm and competent in an emergency situation. She could trust him, after all. . . .

Except where her body was concerned. They'd been too close; he was too familiar with her body now. She'd have bruises on her arms, and she was sore from the way he pulled her legs apart—

The engine stopped, and she heard the anchor splash in the water, the rope sliding away. And then Nicholas was standing over her again. "I'm really sorry," he said. "I had no idea you would be so frightened."

She turned her head to look up at him.

"I'm really sorry, Stephanie," He was frowning and he sounded sincere. "I should have been more sensitive."

Was he really sympathetic, she wondered, or just selfishly disappointed? Those two emotions usually went together, like Jonathan when she'd been too pregnant to give him a decent game of tennis, or when she had had the flu and he had to take over the house and care for Angie and Kent. How solicitous he had been! He always waited on her hand and foot, overdoing the sympathy bit, rubbing the inconvenience of it in so sweetly. She had always felt guilty, in any case. Guilt was the companion of her ineptitude.

"Sorry I spoiled it for *you*," she said, smiling weakly up at Nicholas.

"Don't be silly. I can dive whenever I want, and the day's still young." His eyes took in the length of her body, and then returned to hers. "And at least we know each other better now."

Stephanie looked away, embarrassed and more aware of the stretched-out feeling between her legs.

"Anyway," Nicholas said, "here we are at our own private beach with cold wine, papayas, mangoes, and *ceviche* prepared by the hotel just for us. Shall we wade ashore, madam?"

The beach was small and isolated, a rim of fine white sand that curved around a lovely cove. The sand was fringed by towering palms and dominated by jungle cliffs that jutted out into the ocean at each end of the crescent beach.

After lunch she and Nicholas lay stretched out on their sides, facing one another on straw mats. The shadow of a large palm leaf played nervously on the sand that separated them.

"You haven't drunk much of this good Chablis," Nicholas said, and he leaned forward to pour more of it into her glass. His red-and-white striped suit was like a bright flag on the beach. "If you don't mind me saying so, you seem to find it hard to relax."

Stephanie said nothing, but took a sip of the wine.

"The silent *señora*." Nicholas smiled. "What more can I offer? Tropical sand and sun, a delicious lunch, a beautiful bay, and the sound of the ocean—"

"I'm sorry." She tried to smile. "But it's been quite a day for me. I don't usually spend my days helping save a child's life and then thinking I'm dying myself. And I'm sorry I panicked, out there. . . ." She looked at the ocean and shuddered.

"Want to try it again?"

"Oh, no. I don't think I'll ever go into the ocean again."

"Talk about a backfire." He was still smiling.

"What does it mean, to embolize?"

His smile vanished. "That's what I was afraid might happen to you out there, because you panicked and held your breath. There weren't any bubbles coming out of your regulator and you were going up too fast. I had to hold you back like that. . . ." He looked at her knowingly, forcing her to acknowledge their intimacy under the water.

Stephanie looked away from him and rolled over on her stomach. "But what happens?"

He rolled over next to her, moving closer, insisting on their intimacy by assuming a posture parallel to hers. "It's different from the bends, when you're down deep and have to follow the decompression tables. It's the fact that you've taken compressed air into your lungs below the surface, you see, and it expands in your lungs every thirty-three and a half feet as you rise. With the bends, the nitrogen bubbles that are in your blood stream expand faster than your system can absorb them and settle into your joints. It's very painful." He paused to sip his wine and then looked at her, his brow furrowed. "An embolism is fatal, no matter how deep you are. You can have an embolism in a swimming pool—with a tank on—if you hold your breath in a panic. Because the air you've taken in under pressure is driven out of your lungs and into your blood stream, and it expands there, blocking the circulation. An embolism is an air clot. You burst internally, so to speak."

"What a horrible way to die."

"Yes."

The shadow of the palm leaf on the sand quivered, and she felt the lingering heat of the sun burning into her bare back and the backs of her legs. The ocean whispered behind her, and the image of underwater death hung in the heavy air. She knew Nicholas saw it too: the twisting struggle, the flippers kicking, the body shuddering and then still. Was he seeing her body, or his? Would the body float to the surface or sink with the weight of the tank? He had saved her life. And yet death was everywhere around them on that beautiful private beach, the memory of Jonathan falling away from her, of the little boy lying on the beach, and the mental vision of her or Nicholas exploding internally underwater—

"How *do* you spend your days?" he asked, and turned over on his back.

"What?"

"Your days." He was squinting at the sky. "What are they like, normally?"

Stephanie frowned and had another sip of wine. "Oh, I don't know—"

"Are you a housewife?"

"Yes . . . yes. I'm a housewife." She reached for a handful of sand and let it sift slowly through her fingers. Not a housewife anymore, she thought. A housewidow. A housemother, now. Like the old maids in sorority and fraternity houses, the ones Fitz always mocked. But then Fitz mocked everything, didn't she? "You're in a rut, Stephie. A padded, quilted rut. Zipped up to your chin in a sleeping bag of security, snoring away . . . and holding status quo in your arms."

Lovable, nagging, obnoxious, best friend. . . .

Nicholas tried again. "Do you live right in the city?"

"Yes," Stephanie nodded. Right in the heart of the city, in Pacific Heights where the houses were full of living fathers.

Nicholas was waiting for her to continue. He turned his head to look at Stephanie, and she sensed that her remoteness was beginning to annoy him. She could see in his eyes the thought that she wasn't blending with his setting, with the mood of sensuality that their swimming suits, the heat, and the sound of the waves were supposed to create. But now was her chance; he was giving her the opportunity to talk about herself, to tell him she was a widow—

"You're unhappy about something," Nicholas said. "Would you like to talk to me about it? I mean, sometimes a stranger can be more helpful, more objective than a friend about things—"

She was getting confused, she realized. More confused than ever. She had come down here to be alone and to think things out, and now Nicholas was interfering with her memories of Jonathan and her suspicions about Fitz. She never should have become involved with him at all. And yet he was kind, attractive, and protective in a way—

"Won't you tell me about it?" he said.

"I'd . . . I'd like to talk about it, but I don't seem to be ready to, yet. Maybe it's because I don't feel I know you well enough."

He reached for his cigarettes. "The best way to know someone well enough is to talk about yourself."

"You sound almost like a shrink."

"Amateur." He grinned. There was a pause, and then he asked, "Have you ever been to one?"

"Good heavens, no!"

He was laughing at her reaction, but it seemed to Stephanie that his eyes had narrowed slightly. "It's not that I don't *want* to talk," she said quickly. "It's only that I came here to be totally alone, to figure things out for myself. After I've done that then maybe I can talk about it. So much has happened to me. . . ."

"You seem frightened of something," Nicholas said.

"I am!"

"What of?"

"I . . . I don't know. Something terrible has happened to me, and I think maybe my best friend—"

Nicholas leaned toward her.

She caught herself. "Never mind. I really can't talk

about it yet. I need to be alone and I need sleep; I didn't sleep well last night. What time is it? Please don't be offended, but I think I should go back now—"

"What terrible thing happened to you? I'd like to help."

Stephanie gazed out over the ocean, aware of his long legs stretched out next to hers, aware of the wine, the sand, the sun, the sleepy feeling that had suddenly invaded her—and a dilemma. She didn't want to tell him she was a widow because . . . because a recent widow shouldn't even have been there with him. Because she felt guilty, because Jonathan wouldn't understand. She shouldn't have come.

She looked again at Nicholas; he *was* handsome. "Thank you." She smiled. "But I'd like to go back and sleep now, Nicholas. You've been very kind—"

There was a long silence. He ground his cigarette out in the sand, buried it, drained the last of the wine in one gulp, sat up, and began repacking the picnic cooler. When the lid was closed he looked at her and said petulantly, "At least I've made some progress. That's the first time you've called me by my name."

"I'm sorry, I—"

"Please have dinner with me tonight."

"Dinner? I haven't thought about—"

"Please." He reached out and touched her arm.

His intensity was infectious, flattering, thrilling. She had no business responding to it; he couldn't honestly be that interested in her. She had no business returning the prolonged look in his heavy-lidded eyes. . . .

"All right," she said, returning the look.

He stood up, and as he offered her his hand she knew she had made a mistake. It had nothing to do with trusting him; it had to do with trusting herself.

Why had it taken her so long to realize it?

Someone had been in her room.

She knew that someone had been there as soon as Nicholas left her outside her *casita* and she went into the bedroom. Her room was too neat. It was too neat and her suitcase wasn't where she had left it, at the foot of the bed. The clock on her bedside table said 1:53. She ran for the closet and opened the door; her suitcase was closed and propped up against the closet wall, and all of her dresses had been hung up. A maid, of course . . . How foolish of her. They had finally sent a maid.

But something was wrong; something was missing from her room, something personal and very important to her.

The diary! Oh my God, she thought, *Jonathan's diary.* She grabbed her tan leather cosmetics case from the top of the dresser and rummaged frantically through the side pockets for the key to her green jewelry case. She found the key wrapped in a wad of kleenex, inserted it into the small lock, opened the case, lifted off the top shelf with her pearls and earrings—

The diary lay where she had left it—shiny black leather, not really a diary but an appointment-calendar book that Jonathan had received from their bank every New Year. She stroked the leather. Jonathan had kept a brief record of what he did each day, what they did each evening, how the children were progressing, how much mileage they covered in the car on vacations. She had nothing else he had written, no love letters to carry with her, not even any postcards. In seven years they had been apart for only two or three days.

Stephanie picked up the diary and held it to her chest. The police had been mildly interested in Jonathan's diary, at first. Lieutenant Brinton had thumbed through it casually the day after . . . the day after Jonathan fell. She remembered lying on their bed in a daze while strange men wandered around their bedroom, poking and snooping through their belongings, and she had told her mother to get them out of Jonathan's room, to get them the hell out. . . .

Mr. Sommers had asked for it, later. He said that it might help the insurance investigation, because if Jonathan had been depressed recently it might mean that he had taken his own life. And Stephanie had screamed at him, had screamed that Jonathan could never and would never do that to her or the children and that he should please leave her alone! Jonathan was not depressed; Jonathan was a happy, loving, wonderful husband who had no reason to be depressed! And anyone could see that it was an accident, a horrible accident!

"And everything was all right at his work?" Mr. Sommers had persisted.

"Everything was fine, I know. You can certainly ask his secretary and people at the office, if you insist—"

The next time he had asked for the diary Stephanie had hidden it well, at the bottom of the rag bin in the pantry. No one was going to take her only written remembrance of Jonathan away from her for any reason. She had answered Mr. Sommers's questions calmly and told him that she couldn't find it anywhere, that her mother must have misplaced it or accidentally thrown it away while she was in Stephanie's house, and that she was very sorry, that she, too, would like to have it. She told him that he was free to search the house. Lieutenant Brinton had also asked for the diary again, and she told him the same thing. It wouldn't have done them any good anyway.

She supposed she could have given it to them, she thought now. She *should* have given it to them, since there was nothing to hide. But it was an invasion of her privacy.

And she could have told them her suspicions about Fitz, but she hadn't. She was so unsure. . . . So she had answered all their questions about everything very calmly, without giving away her fears about Fitz. . . .

She bent Jonathan's book in her hand and watched the pages fall away under her thumb. She couldn't bear to read it yet, she realized, to see their life together described in such brief passages; it would make it seem even briefer. She put the diary back in the jewelry case, replaced the top shelf, and locked the box. Then she looked around the adobe room again. Something was still missing; she knew something was still missing from her room—

Her photograph, the small color snapshot of Angie and Kent that had been on the dressing table, propped up among her cosmetics. Her darling children with their sweet faces tilted upward into the sunlight. . . . Who would have taken it? She must have misplaced it, it must have been knocked off the table—

But no. The bare wooden floor was spotless, except for the waste-paper basket. It could have fallen into that, of course; that was where it had to be. Stephanie clutched the rim of the basket, lifted it into her arms. The picture had to be in it, smiling up at her, Kent's silly freckles and Angie's little round cheeks as smooth as peaches. . . . They had to be there; they must be there.

They were. Torn up in two pieces. My God, she thought, who would do such a thing, who would tear up her children? Who would want to torment her like that? It had to be an accident. A careless, stupid maid had probably ripped it accidentally and hoped that Stephanie wouldn't miss it. It couldn't have been Nicholas; he would have no reason, and he had been with her all day. . . .

Jonathan's face fell away from her: the open mouth and startled, staring eyes falling away. Fitz's shout, as she walked slowly toward him—

Fitz.

It couldn't have been Fitz. Fitz was thousands of miles away, back home in San Francisco, wasn't she? How could she have such thoughts, Stephanie asked herself. She was exhausted, she realized, desperately in need of sleep. It had to be the maid, some stupid fat peasant who was too dumb or too afraid to take the pieces away. That was the only possible explanation, of course. At least she had the pieces and could tape them back together.

She walked into the bathroom, took off her brown swimming suit, ran a tub of hot water, and sank listlessly into it. The water played over her body, pulling her down, sucking her into a grateful passivity, lifting her extended legs. She was a rubber doll, an elongated embryo floating in fluid.

A rubber doll . . .

She closed her eyes, remembering the rubber dolls she had had as a child, her lovely children with their organdy starched dresses, satin ribbons, and blond curls. She and Fitz had played with them for hours at a time, and Fitz had always done strange and wonderful things with her dolls, turning them into purple people or fascinating forest creatures who did poo-poo with twigs in it. . . . But then they had outgrown the dolls, hadn't they? And one day Stephanie's mother put them in a box and took them up to the attic. About that time she and Fitz began running away from home, escaping the world of duties and discipline as often as possible. Fleeing from the tyrannies of reality—

On roller skates; whirling away to the Nelson Art Gallery. Flying there, two prankish Hermeses in winged helmets, flying on the winged sandals of the God of Protection. (Fitz was reading mythology avariciously.) Flying in revenge, and to avenge their misunderstood childhood. Flying to preserve their innocence, their freedom, their imagination. . . .

Plotting: plotting how they would hide inside the protective armor of the fourteenth-century Knights. Or how they would settle deep into Egyptian sarcophagi, surrounded by basalt owls and onyx priestesses (where the humidity was just right for their preservation). Or maybe they would climb into four-armed Siva's lap on the third floor, and let him rock them to sleep before the sun sneaked in through the curves of his pagoda.

Their parents would be very worried about them, which would serve their parents right, but Stephanie and Fitz would be safe.

Escaping, fleeing, dreaming. . . . On their bicycles too, flying to the wide Missouri river with its endless possibilities: Howard Keel and Kathryn Grayson singing their way into the sunset on a silver showboat. Twin Aphrodites riding the turbulent waves of childhood, standing proud at the helms of their scalloped shells. (Stephie had liked that one best.) Two crocodiles basking in the sun-soaked mud; the Sirens singing to Odysseus; Aunt Polly and Becky Thatcher searching for Injun Joe. . . .

They never ran away after dark.

And Mansion-Snooping . . . real danger, Mansion-Snooping. They could get shot, if they got caught! The great houses of Mission Hills, perched high on sloping lawns and surrounded by giant watchful elms . . . "Happy Hunting Ground, Chief Sneakum-up-on-Secrets!" . . . "Ugum, Princess Keepum-Eyes-Alive!" Creeping up the sloping lawns, darting furtively in and out among the trees, crawling on their knees through thick hedges. Making their way stealthily, so stealthily, toward the Mansion-of-the-Many-Eyes, expecting Argus of the seven heads or the Hound of the Baskervilles to leap at them and tear out their throats . . . hearing a dog bark and running on sixteen legs back to their bikes, pedaling away on twelve wheels. . . .

Fitz was always the leader in their adventures, and she thought some of the normal things Stephie wanted to do were ridiculous, like being a Brownie Scout. All Stephie's other friends were Scouts, and her mother wanted her to be one, and she wanted to—

So Fitz became one with her because she was a loyal friend, but Fitz hated it. She really hated it. One day she tore out some pages of her manual and chewed them up in her mouth, then spat them into the toilet at Susie Bartlett's house. That was a weird thing for Fitz to do. . . .

○●

"Take off your panties, too," she commanded.
"I don't want to take them off!"
"You have to. They'll show."
Fitz was standing in the middle of the bathroom floor, holding one of Clarissa Borders's scarves between her teeth. The door was locked. A flowered silk scarf was tied around her slim waist, gaping open over her hips and barely covering the place where hair had started to grow.
"Hurry up!"
She had huge breasts. She had covered Stephie's mother's bra with a different scarf—a polka-dotted one—and stuffed it with hand towels until she bulged bigger than Maria Montez and Yvonne De Carlo, bigger than Marilyn Monroe. The painted lips were pouting.
She pointed to the panties. "Take them off!"
Stephie had turned her back to her, and obeyed. Fitz took hold of her waist and turned her around, slipping

the scarf between her legs as she dropped to her knees in front of Stephie and began to tie two corners of the scarf together over her left hip, tightly. She reached under Stephie's legs and pulled the scarf toward her.

"That feels funny!" Stephie had said.

"Be quiet, silly! It has to go in your crack. Your bare bottom has to show." She was holding most of the scarf in her right hand, in front of the place where Stephie's hair hadn't started to grow yet, and reaching for the pile of hand towels on the tile floor with her left hand. She picked one up and stuffed it into the scarf. It felt itchy.

"Don't wiggle!"

"Who am I?"

"Jon Hall of course, dummy." She was stuffing in another towel.

"I thought I was Turhan Bey. My thing is too big!"

"It's not big enough. It has to be huge. It doesn't matter which one you are, as long as it's huge and you like me. You can be Tarzan if you want."

"How can I be Tarzan if I won't be able to walk?"

"Someday," Fitz said, "I'm going to live in the jungle like Jane and Tarzan. Just you wait. Someday I'm going to live in the jungle for a long time. I'm going to do lots of things like that. Just you wait . . . ."

"Fitz, that's enough! And it's the wrong shape."

"Just one more," she said. "And I can change the shape of it. . . ."

○●

That was a strange thing for Fitz to do, too, Stephanie thought as she stepped out of the bathtub and reached for a large white towel—giving *her* a penis made out of towels. But she hadn't realized it at the time; it was only another naughty, wild adventure with Fitz, one of thousands of risky undertakings. . . .

But Fitz could never kill anyone, Stephanie thought. Never on purpose.

Still, she *was* strange, as a child. She'd always been strange, compared to everyone else. . . .

"I hate white houses," Fitz had said. "For God's sake don't paint that house white, please!"

They were sitting on the grass in Loose Park, not far from the Rose Garden and Summit Street, whose houses overlooked the park. It was a brisk and uncertain spring day; indecisive white clouds drifted in the still, blue sky. A large palette of watercolors rested on the grass between them; they had filled a plastic glass with water from the drinking fountain near the tennis courts.

"Why not?" Stephie had asked, looking around for something besides a white house to try. There was a lovely big elm down the hill—

"They're ordinary," Fitz said, "especially at night. Window shades and things." She swirled her wet brush over the black on the palette and squinted. "I especially hate the Dixon house."

"Mrs. Dixon? But she's our Scout leader!"

"*Your* Scout leader," Fitz said. "Not mine. Never." She was painting the corners of her white watercolor paper black. "Not since the first *big* meeting of the *big* Girl Scouts."

Stephie said nothing, and pushed her brush around in circles on the brown in the palette. She would start with an outline of the elm's trunk. . . .

"I was late," Fitz said. "I guess you were already there, sewing badges and all that stuff. I didn't want to go in. You know me. It was a cold night, and the light behind Mrs. Dixon's drawn window shades looked kind of secure, you know. But God, her house is ordinary! I couldn't hear all of you guys inside, but I knew you were there, eating Scout cookies and drinking hot chocolate. . . ."

Stephie wet her brush again and added more brown to it. She wanted to get the biggest branches first and then fill in the little ones later—

"It took me a long time to make up my mind," Fitz went on. She had turned the paper vertically. "Between that cold scary night and all the ordinary warmth inside. I guess you don't understand that."

"Come on, Fitz!"

"You don't."

"I do too!"

"Well anyway, I finally decided to go in. Be one of the gang. And do you know what happened? I'll tell you what happened. . . ." She was brushing the black in the corners toward the center of her paper, leaving the beginnings of a strange outline in the center, a blank. Stephie's tree was taking a nice shape.

"I decided to do it," Fitz said. "To go in and be one of the gang. And I felt sort of relieved, you know. Doing the right thing, what was expected of me for a change. I finally walked up to that big ugly old solid door of Mrs. Dixon's and knocked on it. I was feeling scared again. Like maybe I had waited too long. Maybe I wasn't loyal enough, or brave enough, or—what is it?—oh, yeah. Reverent enough."

Stephie stopped painting and looked at Fitz, who sat cross-legged, her head bent over her watercolor. The breeze blew her dark hair in her eyes. She kept on painting in black and talking.

"I knocked and knocked, and finally Mrs. Dixon opened the door. What a sweet face she has! It's like Aunt Bessie's face, grandmother's face. Dear old Mrs. Jackson who used to give us pennies. And the fourth-grade teacher we loved so much. . . . Mrs. Dixon's face is like all theirs, isn't it? She has a wonderful, kind, gentle face like hundreds of *dedicated* women." Fitz leaned hard on the word *dedicated,* and smiled. "It's the face of a perfect Girl Scout leader and a PTA president, a face you've got to follow, and believe, and obey. Aren't I right?"

She was looking at Stephie, challenging her.

Stephie nodded, wondering if Fitz was angry.

"Well," Fitz started painting again, fast strokes. "That sweet face peered at me, very courteously you know, through the dark. And then she recognized me." She dipped her brush in the water again; it was turning a muddy color.

"So what happened?"

"She slammed the door in my face."

"I don't believe it! Mrs. Dixon wouldn't do that!"

"She sure would. She did."

"No!" Stephie protested. "That can't be what happened—"

Fitz held her watercolor away from her face at arm's length, turned it, studied it. She smiled, and then showed it to Stephie.

It was a white house in the middle of a black background. A crude tall house with window shades for eyes and a door for its mouth and it had been squeezed in the middle, forced by broad strokes of black into an odd and yet familiar shape—

"I'm a bone!" Fitz laughed, and rolled over on the grass.

A bone, of course, Stephie realized. That was what the house looked like. "What an imagination," she said, and looked at her own painted tree.

Fitz stiffened on the grass. She straightened her arms along the length of her body and closed her eyes. "I'm a bone," she said again. "A thrown-away Girl Scout bone, instead of a cookie. Don't I look like a bone?"

"No," Stephie said. "Stop it, Fitz. It's not funny."

"Rejected. What's more rejected than an old bone?"

"Come off it, Fitz."

She sat up, smiling. "That damned Scout house is the bone," she said. "Not me. Fooled *you!* Old Mrs. Dixon never slammed any door in my face, I never gave her the chance! I refuse to be like everyone else!"

She should have known that Fitz would be a good painter someday. . . .

○●

Stephanie had to get some sleep. She lay on her side in the bed, with the coarse white sheet pulled up over her shoulders. The wooden shutters of the bedroom window were closed, and the large wooden fan overhead circled lazily around and around. Nothing moved quickly in Mexico. She rolled over on her back, and stared at the fan. Everyone else in this place was sleeping, she thought. The whole village, the whole resort. She had to get some sleep. She had to, or she'd never make it through dinner with Nicholas Hanson. That had been a bad decision, she never should have said yes to him. There was still something about him that frightened her.

She *knew* it was the wrong decision. . . .

The air was very cold and clear, and Fitz was wearing ear muffs. She was sheepishly aware that she looked silly in ear muffs; she hadn't worn them since she was a child in Kansas City, when she and Stephie used to go ice skating on the pond in Loose Park.

Everything around her and above her was a crisp, dark green. There were palm trees and pine trees, elm trees and great oaks covered with garlands of moss. A hodgepodge of trees. Fitz wasn't sure where she was exactly, but it felt like a friendly, familiar place in spite of the cold.

The sky began to darken above the bushy green branches. Fitz looked to the left and saw the outline of a gothic mansion whose turrets and gables were pointing at the blackening sky. Although it was much larger and grander then her grandmother's Victorian house, she knew suddenly that she was in her grandmother's garden and that the house was abandoned. She started walking toward it, slowly.

And then she saw the hand.

It was Stephanie's hand, sticking up through a bog that had once been her grandmother's fish pond. Fitz had loved the bright fish that used to swim there; for hours, as a child, she had lain on her stomach watching them flash back and forth. She could still see the rocks that had formed the curved border of the pond, but they were half-buried now under decayed moss and soggy brown leaves. The pond itself, her once bright world, was a stagnant sink of opaqueness out of which protruded Stephanie's hand, demanding her help.

Fitz grabbed the wrist. The frigid, rooted fingers sprouted into action, wrapping themselves around Fitz's wrist in desperation. She planted her feet in the semifrozen bog and pulled firmly, frantically. . . .

From the depths of the black quagmire came a solid, sucking sound. Stephanie's arm was emerging slowly in spite of strong resistance from the thick, coagulated mud. Fitz could almost see her elbow. Straining, with cold sweat streaming down her face, she tugged harder, harder . . . she was terrified! And then the black surface split with a dull groan and spat out Stephie's head.

Medusa's head. Stephie's hair was strands of caked black serpents. Her huge blue eyes implored Fitz.

And then outrageously, against all Fitz's power, she sank back down again into the muck, leaving only her grasping fingers. Again Fitz pulled; again the dull groan, the splitting surface, and the huge, imploring eyes. And once more she disappeared deep into the thick slop. Fitz pulled again; Stephie emerged, then was sucked down, down. Fitz pulled and pulled and pulled. Stephanie sank and sank and sank. . . .

○●

"Christ!" Fitz exclaimed out loud. "What made me remember that dream now?"

It was midafternoon; the sun had not yet started to slant through the northern windows of her studio. Far below her on Taylor Street the afternoon city traffic scurried and cable cars clanged, but she couldn't hear the noises; a Charles Ives Symphony was playing on her hi-fi.

She removed the three brushes that were placed between the fingers of her left hand and dropped them into a Yuban can full of turpentine, reached for the Saran Wrap on the shelf near her easel, and tore off a strip of it to cover the mounds of still fresh paint on her palette.

That frightening dream where she had no power, where she couldn't keep Stephanie out of the muck. . . . What had made her think of that now?

She stepped back from the easel and examined her large, half-completed painting. It must have been the darkness that reminded her of that dream, she thought. The sucking, swirling way she was painting the mouth. It was going to be damned good. More subtle and less bright than Van Gogh's night of swirling stars, but just as powerful and unique—

Ha! You conceited dreamer . . .

She sloshed the brushes back and forth in the turpentine can and picked up a cloth off the floor, wondering if Stephanie was in even more trouble, down in Mexico. She realized that it had been years since she had had that dream about the muck. But she used to have it often, and there was always a reason for it. When she was younger, she had had so many bad dreams. . . . They were, she thought, remainders of vulnerability that sneaked up on you in the night, treaded on the past, walked over your weaknesses, and prowled around forgotten fears. . . . Then they stalked off into the dawn, leaving behind them indelible footprints. Sole marks of old, abandoned shoes—

Like frustration. And anxiety.

And humiliation.

"We don't do things like that in this house." Stephen Borders had said.

Humiliation . . .

A rainy afternoon in November. She and Stephanie had done a skip-run dance all the way home from school, splashing in puddles and twirling imaginary umbrellas like Gene Kelly, not caring about their wet sneakers, singing and laughing. . . .

The Borders's house was a two-story, red-brick Georgian set back from Fifty-Seventh Terrace; the driveway went straight along the right side of the lawn to the red-brick garage. The front door granted access to a large, square entry hall with black and white diamonds on the floor. The living room and then the den opened to the left, and the dining room, breakfast room, and kitchen to the right. Upstairs, the four bedrooms were spacious; the house was a model-American, miniature replica of gracious English living. —A suburban pretension, Fitz thought, a subordination to former centuries.

Fitz disliked subordination. The girls skipped along

the driveway to the kitchen door and hung their yellow slickers up on a hook. Clarissa Borders had guests in the breakfast room, a bridge group.

"Heavens!" she called out to the kitchen. "You must be soaked to the skin! *Do* take care not to track!" Clarissa Borders, the lioness of luncheons, roaring her way through years of mediocrity.

"You look a fright," she said, smiling vaguely. "All gawky and wet and stringy-haired. But I suppose you'll grow out of this stage, eventually." She addressed her guests at large: "They *do* grow out of it, don't they, girls?" she scowled below her fading blond hair. "Now run along upstairs; I have a hand so gorgeous I must concentrate!"

Mother Clarissa, the half-benevolent queen, who belonged to three garden clubs and played bridge twice a week. The kindest and cruelest thing you could say about her was that she was typical.

Quite different from Fitz's mother, who was not typical at all.

They put a stack of Nat King Cole records on the phonograph in Stephie's room and tried to think about the first ten Amendments, which they had to memorize for homework. The freedom of worship, of speech, of the press, of assembly. The freedom of petition to the government for redress of grievances. The right to bear arms. Freedom from the quartering of soldiers. . . .

"I'm thirsty," Stephie said at about four-thirty. "Let's go get a Coke in the kitchen."

"Pepsi for me," Fitz said.

"Okay, Pepsi."

They avoided the breakfast room, entering the kitchen through the door from the dining room, and fixed themselves a tall glass of Pepsi-Cola. Back upstairs, they studied until Fitz announced that she had all ten Amendments down pat, and recited them flawlessly.

Stephie was slower, and Fitz had to prompt her three times.

"What a way to spend the afternoon!" Fitz grinned, and stood up to leave. "They should have given us the right to wear lipstick, and the freedom to petition teachers. And they should *force* us to quarter soldiers!"

"Don't go yet," Stephie said. "I don't want you to go."

"Poor single child," Fitz replied, and smiled at her. "You have to eat supper soon."

Fitz was not an only child; she had a handsome bratty older brother and a sister to keep her company. She lived in a less important neighborhood in a smaller house where there were astrology maps and two pianos instead of one and a thousand interesting things to look at and to do. And her parents usually talked to them about everything, including adolescent problems.

"Who Left This Ice Tray Out On The Counter?"

Stephen Borders stood in a navy-blue flannel suit in the doorway between the kitchen and the dining room. The bridge ladies had left, and Clarissa was emptying ashtrays in the breakfast room. She straightened up at the sound of her husband's anger.

"Who Left This Ice Tray Out On The Counter?" he repeated.

Pompous, superior, slick Stephen Borders, growling his authority and importance, hearing his own growl and loving the sound of it, but not really believing it. No wonder Stephie thought so little of herself.

Fitz stood motionless in the front hall, at the foot of the stairs.

"I . . . I did," she confessed.

"Sir." He scowled at her.

"Yes, sir."

He focused hard on her twelve-year-old knocked knees.

"I'm sorry, sir."

"We don't do things like that in *this* house."

"No, sir—"

We don't do things like that in this house. . . .

○●

There was a warm winter sun on the deck outside Fitz's studio. She bent over and spread two turpentined rags out to dry on the redwood. "We put things *away* after using them, in this house. We are orderly and well brought up, in this house. We do everything properly in this house. . . ."

Stephen Borders, Fitz thought, *I still hate you. I remember your fucking ice tray. No sir, yes sir, I'm sorry sir! I remember the social inferiority you tried to force on me, the stupid red humiliation. But I stuck it in the freezer along with your precious ice tray because you're a bourgeois nobody, you're not worthy of my hatred—*

It was that very night that Fitz had first had the scary dream about Stephanie in the muck. "Sometimes I wish you could come live with me," she had told her the next day.

And she had had the dream again two years later, when Stephie joined a high-school sorority. The sorority: sole arbiter of thought, action, and style. T-H-E-T-A, *Théta!* Honk, honk. Harpies in bobby socks, Fitz thought. Get-a-pin, compete for cashmere sweater sets, take your turn at accepting criticism, and never never never reveal the secret handshake! Be *accepted,* at any cost to your dignity. Dress up like Muriel, the Fine *Cigar,* for your invitation. How original. How literary! How very stimulating and creative! . . .

So Stephanie had gone from Muriel the Fine Cigar to Hannah the Happy Housewife.

But not because I didn't try, Fitz thought as she looked out over her view of the city. God knows she had tried to counterbalance her environment, grabbing Stephie on weekends and during the summer, playing the piano with her, painting with her in Loose Park, trying to get her to develop her potential. She hadn't wanted Stephie to sink into the common grave of ordinary minds. . . .

Fitz turned and walked back into the studio, folded up the newspapers on the floor around her easel, and climbed the stairs up to her bedroom and bath. It was time to prepare for a cocktail party, the kind of international party she loved, an eclectic gathering on a ferry boat down at Pier 5.

The bathroom was her favorite room in the studio. It was about nine feet square and papered in colorful posters covered with clear laquer. Posters of Fitz, of her golden eyes and creamy smile, her mane of dark hair. Fitz at the piano, Fitz's face alone, and posters of her paintings that had been made up for art shows. She stepped out of her jeans, smiling thinly at her own egotism. But why not? She'd worked damned hard and had often been lonely, to achieve success. So why not bathe in it? Stephie's bathroom was so gentle, so ordinary.

She reached for her shower cap, then changed her mind. Time to wash her hair; we must not have stringy hair, she thought; we must not have wet hair or look gawky, as Clarissa Borders said. She stepped out of her underwear and into the shower stall, then turned the faucet to *hot.*

For Christ's sake stop brooding about the Borderses, she told herself. But Stephanie had had such potential, when they were young . . . before that flimsy paper pattern—the dressmaker's design for social acceptance—was marked and pinned and tucked for fit, then pleated for style and finally slipped over her head. Before that happened, she could have become a real life-lover. But it was almost too late, now. The pattern fit; Stephanie wore the dress.

Almost too late, but not quite.

Not since Jonathan's death.

Fitz smiled and lifted her face to the full blast of the shower. Poor, dull Jonathan, she thought—sitting up there on the right hand of his bourgeois God, probably still worrying about the Dow Jones. He'd been no more than a mini-improvement over Stephen Borders, but he really hadn't deserved to die. Poor Jonathan. The timing had been all wrong. . . .

She twirled under the water, moved out from under it, and reached for her bottle of Earth Born shampoo. Jonathan's problem she knew was that he had had no real sense of humor. Oh, he would pull silly juvenile jokes sometimes, and laugh at other people, but never at himself. He had no sense of irony, either. No sense of the preposterous, the outrageous; he couldn't see that irony was everywhere, asking to be appreciated, like a child who deliberately put on a pair of mismatched socks and wanted it to be noticed. Fitz had forced irony on Jonathan, though, near the end. She began simply at first, insinuating it into his life simply by coming back at a time when he thought he had everything. Jonathan might have been ordinary, but at least he wasn't stupid; after a few weeks he had begun to understand the preposterous aspects of her return from Europe. He had known, near the end, that her intentions were centered on himself and Stephanie. . . .

And just before he died, in the last five minutes of his life, he had grasped the irony of her friendship with Stephanie. It flashed through him like black lightning; he finally understood irony.

But by then, it was too late.

Fitz closed her eyes and stepped back under the steaming shower. The white lather in her hair poured down over her face, her shoulders, her breasts.

I should have had more time with Jonathan, she thought.

More time to try to convert him to a more interesting life, for Stephanie's sake. She should have had more long hours to talk with Jonathan, more days to make violent, passionate love with him.

One long day and night of love with Jonathan was not enough.

12

A low, whirring sound penetrated Stephanie's consciousness—the continual humming of the wooden fan on the ceiling. And then the clicking of the clock on her bedside table. Had she slept? She opened her eyes. It was 3:25. She closed her eyes again and reached out across the sheets for Jonathan, moving her arm back and forth over the bed. There was nothing; she was alone.

Alone.

She lay on her right side for a long time. The fan whirred; the clock ticked.

She rolled over on her stomach. The coarse sheets rubbed against her breasts. Itchy, she thought. She felt itchy. Horny, Fitz would say, why don't you just say horny?

She turned onto her back. And suddenly her fingers were on her bare thigh, under the sheet. Her fingers were tracing a pattern on her thigh, circling upwards toward her groin. . . .

She couldn't do it, she realized, and pulled a pillow over her abdomen. She couldn't do it, wouldn't even think the word. It would be a travesty of her union with Jonathan, a grotesque parody. She could only lie here until the horny feeling was gone and the memory of how it had been with Jonathan had passed through her. It had been good—enough to keep her happy. . . .

Until Fitz.

○●

Fitz, a few days after her return from Europe, sitting on the edge of the bed, smoking and sipping a Fresca, watching her sort out the laundry. . . .

"So what's new in eroticaville?"

"Hmm?" Stephanie was sitting cross-legged on the floor, a large, dirty heap of clothing in front of her, spilling over into her lap.

"I'm asking about your love life."

"Fine," Stephie said.

Fitz tried again. "Are you having a love affair or anything?"

"Of course not. You should know me better than that."

"It's been a while, Stephie. You mean in seven years you've never had a lover?"

"I've never needed one. I have Jonathan." She began pulling white clothes from the pile of laundry.

"And that's enough?"

"Of course."

"Well, good for Jonathan," Fitz smiled. "He must be a fantastic lover."

"He's my husband." She pulled out a pair of Kent's polyester pants and started a new pile for the *Perma Press* cycle. She could almost sort the laundry blindfolded, by the feel of the fabric: Angie's flannel nightie for the *Colored Cotton* pile, Kent's navy sweater for the *Gentle* cycle, Jonathan's yellow pajamas for *Perma Press*—

Fitz had sprawled on her stomach across the bed and

was watching her closely. "How many times a week?" she asked. "And do you come in succession?"

"That's none of your damned business, best friend or not."

Fitz's eyes narrowed, but the smile lingered. Stephanie picked up a pair of Angie's underpants; they were sticky with clumps of brown glomp and would have to be rinsed by hand.

"I have the terrible feeling you haven't," Fitz said.

A pair of Jonathan's socks for the *Gentle* pile, a shirt for the corner Launder-Eze, a blue blouse. A child's white sock for the Chlorox, Angie's green dress for *Colored Cotton,* nylon underpants for *Normal-Gentle,* Kent's PJs for *Perma Press*—

"You haven't have you?" Fitz exclaimed. "Oh, Steph! I can tell! I know you've never even had an orgasm at all. My God, in this day and age, you poor thing—"

Stephanie looked at her. "You're beautiful, Fitz. More beautiful than ever, and exciting, and your life is truly enviable. But please get off my back and realize that I'm happy, that I love my life, my husband, my children. So stop trying to make me feel dissatisfied, okay?"

Fitz looked at her, purse-lipped, her eyes smoky. Then a smile broke through the smoke. "Your midwestern accent is showing," she grinned. "And you should know *me* better than that, dearie. . . ."

○●

Fitz, age fourteen. Shoving Stephie into Dickie Barnes's arms on the porch outside a party, whispering at her to let him French-kiss her or she'd be sorry, bawling her out for running, tail between her legs, back into the lighted safety of the kitchen and gulping down a glass of milk.

Fitz, age sixteen. Chiding her for never having petted, whispering its joys into her fascinated and frightened ear, sing-song-teasing her for being chicken.

Age seventeen. Chastising her *for* petting, for teasing the poor, drooling boys to distraction, giving them a French kiss here, a feely-breast there, doing as mommy says, never giving and never trusting, denying the physiological yearnings, resisting the natural desires, being old fashioned.

Age eighteen, nineteen, twenty . . . before Jonathan. Slightly superior at first, then sophisticated, and finally sarcastic and exasperated: "Choosy, aren't we, love? Choosy and chaste. How lovely, to watch the world go by that way, sitting on your cherry throne, preserving your dried-prune pussy! I wish you weren't so afraid of life. I wish you would try something new, just once. You might even start with a little sex—"

So now Fitz was near her again, and wanted her to take a lover.

○●

The slow, repetitious whirring of the fan sliced the silence in the adobe room of the Casa del Sol. Stephanie reached for a glass of water on her bedside table, took a long drink, and lay back down on her back. Maybe, she thought, maybe she should have begun right then, that day in her bedroom—to be wary of Fitz.

She didn't like these memories that were coming back. . . .

Had they been talking about sex, at dinner that last night? If only they hadn't drunk so much wine; if only she could remember. . . .

Jonathan slammed his napkin down on the table and stood up. Was he angry at me, or Fitz? He stalked into the living room and we followed him, we were all shouting. No. Fitz was shouting, and she followed him out onto the balcony. She was angry at him before *they went out onto the balcony!*

Oh, Christ, she thought. It was about sex.

She should have begun, that day in her bedroom right after Fitz came back—to fear for Jonathan. To fear for herself.

13

Nicholas Hanson sat in an awning-striped chair on the lanai of his *casita* and tapped his bare foot impatiently on the rattan rug. He lit another cigarette, his third in thirty minutes. He was wearing only white tennis shorts, no shirt; his hairless tanned chest glistened with sweat. The late afternoon heat was abominable, and his irritability was increasing with the temperature, the humidity, and the waiting. Where the hell was Gabriel anyway? He should have been there by four o'clock; he should have been there long before now. These goddamned easygoing Mexicans.

Maybe he had chosen the wrong man; maybe Gabriel had failed.

Pretty little thing, the widow McMillan. Good figure, too. He took a deep drag on his cigarette and stood up. She was frail-blond pretty and a lot sexier than she realized. It made the challenge even tastier; it would be a pleasure to kill two birds with one stone.

He looked out at the ocean, remembering how she had struggled against him under the water that morning, remembering how he had pinioned her and held her between his legs and how excited he had felt when he wrapped his legs around hers and held them apart. Hard to imagine Pinkie in that position! He grinned, thinking that Stephanie McMillan was the best kind of challenge, both sexual and professional. He'd get her, too. He almost always got the women he wanted.

The waiter Gabriel appeared around a bend in the path, carrying a tray. His white uniform was unbuttoned at the neck, and his pants need pressing, but his walk was brisk, given the heat. He was a young man, twenty-four or twenty-five years old, who came from Guadalajara and was saving his money to get married to a girl named Juanita—*muy bonita,* he had told Nicholas—from Mexico City. Nicholas had learned a lot about Gabriel during dinner the first night he arrived at the hotel. Money was very important to Gabriel.

Nicholas held the screen door open for him and told him to put the tray on the round glass table in front of the sofa. There was a bottle of Johnnie Walker Scotch, a bottle of Tanqueray gin, two glasses, and a cardboard ice bucket on the tin tray.

"Did you find the diary?" Nicholas asked him in Spanish.

"*Si, señor,*" Gabriel answered, his dark eyes smiling conspiratorially. His teeth were very even, but his nose was too broad; he was not handsome.

Nicholas opened the bottle of gin and poured some over two cubes of ice. "Did anyone see you?" he asked.

"*No, señor il inspector.* I was very careful." His chest swelled slightly and he smiled broadly.

"*Muy bueno,*" Nicholas said, and took a long drink of gin. "Where is it?"

"In the bottom of her jewelry case. It was locked, and I looked for a long time until I found the key in her little suitcase. I was very careful to put it back as I found it."

"*Excelente,* Gabriel. And you disturbed nothing?"

"No."

"My company is very grateful to you," Nicholas said. He smiled and pulled his wallet from the hip pocket of his white shorts. He counted out the five hundred-peso bills slowly, watching Gabriel's eyes grow larger. "In a few more days, I may ask you to return to the *señora*'s room and get the black book for me. Will you do that? It's most important."

"*Si, señor il inspector.*"

"And you will tell no one of this transaction."

"*No, señor.*"

"If you do, I'll have you fired," Nicholas said nonchalantly, and handed him the money. "Did you see anything else in the *señora*'s room, anything unusual?"

Gabriel folded the bills and put them in the pocket of his white, slightly wilted jacket. "*No, señor.*" Only that the maid had not yet been there, the room was messy, and the *señora* had not hung up all her clothes."

Nicholas took another drink of gin. "There was no photograph of a man in her room? A man with brown eyes, wavy hair, and a square jaw?"

Gabriel frowned. "No, I did not see one. But—"

"Yes?"

"But there was something, now I remember. Another photograph, of two children. It was torn in two and was on the floor. I did not disturb it."

"And the maid had not yet cleaned up the room?"

"No."

Nicholas frowned and stared into his glass. "Thank you, Gabriel. *Muchas gracias.*"

The waiter turned to leave, hesitated, then said: "The *señora,* she is not a bad lady? She is very nice."

Nicholas looked at him, then smiled. "No, Gabriel, the *señora* is not a bad lady, and she is very nice."

He took the drink into the bedroom, sat down on

the edge of his bed, and picked up the telephone to call Henry Sommers in San Francisco. He gave the operator the number, then waited calmly during the delay and the voices of three different operators. At last he heard the familiar gruff voice.

"Hello, Henry," he said. "Greetings from the sun to the fog. Or is it rain?"

"Hah hah. How goes it, Nicholas? Did you swing it yet?"

"I sure did. I'm taking her out to dinner tonight, and I know exactly where the diary is."

"Good. I knew she hadn't *misplaced* it."

"You sound angry," Nicholas said.

"I am. It's a goddamned expensive way to get information."

Nicholas grinned. "I'm enjoying it."

"I bet," Sommers growled. "At a hundred bucks a day you'd better be enjoying it. What do you think of her? Have you found out anything for our money?"

"Not much. She's a quiet one. I guess dull is the word. McMillan *might* have jumped off that balcony out of sheer boredom, but I doubt it. And the widow isn't enjoying her widowhood; she's a scared rabbit if I ever saw one. No sense of adventure. I took her scuba diving today to get to know her better, and she almost drowned from fear. She's scared of something—*life,* I think. But she's kinda curvy."

"Yeah. Well, try to restrain yourself. Anything else?"

"No photo of the late husband in the room and a torn one of her kids on the floor. But she's probably trying to forget him down here, and the kids' photo could have been an old one that fell out of her purse. Sorry, Henry, but that's about it."

"Well, it's still possible that McMillan could have killed himself. I'd sure like to prove it and save two hundred and fifty thousand bucks. Don't come back without that diary. Brinton was an ass not to have confiscated it in the first place."

"Yes, Henry, but a competent ass who's sure it was an accident. They were clowning around on the balcony, remember? And McMillan had had a lot to drink."

"Lieutenant Brinton can afford to accept stories and be sentimental over pretty women. Insurance investigators can't."

"You're the boss," Nicholas said. "I'll bring the diary back. Meanwhile I'll enjoy this sun and water and find out as much as I can. See you, Henry."

"Goodbye, Nicholas. Keep your eyes and ears open. I still don't trust the wife."

"I'll find out all her secrets," Nicholas said, and smiled to himself as he hung up the phone. All women had secrets, and especially quiet, shy women like Stephanie McMillan. He would pry them out of her, all right. He was an expert at it.

He reached for his copy of *Shōgun* and stretched out on the bed for a couple of hours of good reading.

Stephanie was walking on the beach, south of the hotel. She had remembered her straw hat this time; she was barefoot and wearing her new orange bikini again—like a danger flag on an abandoned railroad track, she had thought as she slipped into it, back in her *casita*. But she had bought it and she would wear it; she had to get away from her memories and out of that lonely room. . . .

It was even lonelier on the beach.

She wasn't certain how long she had been walking. Her thoughts were random, and she wasn't even certain what she had been looking at.

Suddenly her right foot touched something squishy—

It stared up at her. An eye that was a mouth, an open mouth that was an eye. A gruesome jellyfish, glaring at her through layers of slimy, milky mucus. It was a hideous blob, a flaccid, gelatinous, pus-filled pulp squatting on the sand. She had stepped on it, had touched her bare skin to a repulsive amoeba that had sneaked out of the sea. What business did it have, in the cycle of things?

She recoiled from it, muffling a scream, shuddering at the thought that she could have brushed against it that morning, when she was in the ocean with Nicholas. It was almost as frightening as that moray eel.

She walked gingerly around the jellyfish and continued down the beach, aware of the sun growing old over her right shoulder. The sun had a definite business in the cycle of things, she thought. Maybe it had lost its youth for one day, but tomorrow it would rise fresh with purpose; it would be given another chance.

And she never would.

Seventeen . . . eighteen . . . nineteen years old . . .

She kept walking along the water's edge, trying to remember what Stephanie Borders had been like. A baby rose, a fresh young thing. "You're the only girl I've seen for a long time that actually did look like something blooming," Dick Diver had told Rosemary in *Tender Is the Night*. And it must have applied to her, too. She was forever blossoming forth, openly and mindlessly turning her untried face to the future. And the future was no farther away than the next day's dawn.

The tide was going out. Lines of foamy bubbles sat on the wet sand and then sank into it slowly, leaving tiny holes like round mouths waiting to swallow tomorrow's sea. Stephanie stepped on some of the bubbles before they could disappear involuntarily.

She had been involuntary, hadn't she? Something bright and shiny had straddled each day's horizon, and the ultimate prize had been her shining knight and marriage. Marriage: the abstract ambition. The good life preordained, and nothing else. No trials, no preparations, no attempts at self-knowledge. What *was* self-knowledge? Who needed it at that age? She had read Great Literature. She had learned about Life. She had felt deeply for Jake and Lady Brett, for Anna Karenina, for Raskolnikov, for Benjy, for Emma Bovary, and for Isabel Archer.

But she understood nothing, and nothing applied to her. Identify with Rosemary? It never would have occurred to her. Rosemary's mother had plans for Rosemary; she was to become a movie star. Stephanie, on the other hand, was to get married. It would be love and babies and a pretty house for her. It would be housework and holidays and heaven. . . .

She stopped walking, and stared out at the ocean.

Who was she? What did she want for herself? She didn't seem to know, didn't seem to care. She simply took what had come along, when she was young. She had mimicked, sighed, agreed, and drifted her way through youth, mindless of everything except her manners and her virginity. She kept her nose clean and always did the proper thing—

A cold wave surprised her and squirmed through her bare toes. *Jonathan is dead now,* she thought. The wave lapped around her ankles. She was standing in a shallow pond of swirling murky water whose edges were receding. *Jonathan is dead now.*

She looked to her right, feeling tears beginning to form in her eyes. The beach curved away before her as smooth and bright and perfectly laid out as she had thought her life would be. Nature's lovely pattern. She brushed a tear from her cheek. Would she have done it any differently, if the future had been more than an abstract pattern? More than an undefined contentment that depended on someone else? On Jonathan—

And suddenly her cheeks were covered with tears. Suddenly, she was running back up the curved beach, trying to catch the curve of her life. . . .

And then she heard Fitz laughing at her. She heard Fitz's gentle, taunting, I-told-you-so laugh behind her on the beach, ahead of her on the beach. She ran faster and faster along the edge of the water, feeling her toes sink into the wet sand, hearing Fitz's nagging speeches eight years ago . . . ten years ago . . . twelve years ago: "Do something with your talent, Stephie! For Christ's sake, practice the piano more, or try to publish those poems! Show some pride in yourself! . . ."

She turned away from the water and ran across the drier sand toward the palm trees, in the direction of her *casita*. Young girls these days probably knew better, didn't they? They prepared for careers, they knew who they were, they took psychology courses—

The shadow of the palms ahead of her seemed far away; she looked small and frail on the empty beach. It was hard work running across the grainy, thick sand . . .

"Paint!" Fitz called out from the past. "You could be one helluva good painter! Do you want to end up like Emma Bovary?"

Stephanie's feet were dragging; she couldn't keep running at that pace. The palm trees were fifteen yards ahead of her, then ten yards. She couldn't believe she didn't belong to someone anymore. She couldn't believe it. Anna Karenina had thrown herself under a train. . . . "Don't get married young, travel! There's so much to learn, to experience, to contribute to the world!"

The hot sand was burning her feet; she ran faster

and saw her *casita* through the palms. When she reached their shade on the edge of the beach she slowed her pace. . . . Jonathan is dead and you have nothing valuable to take his place. Nothing at all for yourself.

She opened the screen door of her porch, ran through it into the cool bedroom, and threw herself down on the bed. Young Stephie died with Jonathan and there is nothing left for the older one. I told you so. . . .

Nothing left, except to be afraid of life, and to envy Fitz.

She lay on the bed, staring at the ceiling.

15

Pier 5 in San Francisco was on the northeast side of the elevated freeway that separated the waterfront from the Golden Gateway Development, a series of attractive townhouses, high-rise apartments, patioed shopping areas, and office buildings. For the most part, single people lived in the Golden Gateway. And many single people from all walks of life attended the occasional Friday-evening parties that industrial designer Walter Landor gave on his converted ferry boat at Pier 5.

Walter thoughtfully selected his guests for their variety of interests; there were single young executives, single-minded ambitious and successful people, single-in-spirit people, talented people. Advertising people and artists, writers and musicians; people who had used their potential; Pacific Heights society couples of all ages who had something to say or were wearing something chic to look at. People from distant cities and countries who were important and traveling through, often alone and single for the night. Walter's party was an "in" party, in San Francisco. The interior of his office on the boat was paneled in redwood, and it was beautiful.

"You're kind of a masterpiece, aren't you?" a man in beige gabardine pants and a blue blazer said to Fitz. His beard was neatly trimmed, but his eyes were too small. He offered her a cigarette. They were standing in the center of a large reception area in the boat's stern.

"Fifteenth-century," Fitz said, smiling. "Religious."

"Ah, so! Are you new in San Francisco? Haven't seen you at Walter's before."

"Sort of," Fitz answered. "I used to live here." She looked around; he didn't interest her because he was too interested in her. And why wouldn't he be? She knew she looked fantastic in the red Courreges dress she had bought only six weeks earlier in Paris. Well-tailored and yet revealing, 120,000 francs but worth it. Her gleaming hair was pulled back loosely in a pony tail; her almond-shaped eyes were searching. . . .

Several men returned the search. Passing glances darted back at her, and lingered. She smiled at the beard and took another drink of scotch. And then she saw the man she was after, one of the few who wasn't looking at her.

He was bored. Another man was talking to him, while he didn't even bother to nod, while he held his cocktail glass carelessly and stared out a window. The sea outside had captured him; no one at the party had managed that. He wore a pin-striped Savile Row business suit; he looked European. Gray sideburns, a fine-boned face—

"Hello," said a voice next to her. "Walter tells me you're an up-and-coming painter. My name is Frank Pascoe, and my admiring friend here is Bob Burnsides, if you can believe it. We're both admiring, actually."

Fitz smiled at the two of them. "Thank you—"

The man she had chosen looked around impatiently, missing her with his glance. A sensuous mouth, set hard in a strong jaw. He looked back out the window.

"What sort of things do you paint?" Frank asked.

Fitz forced herself to respond. "Portraits of apples and still lifes of people as Peter De Vries would say." She smiled again. "Actually, I paint abstract cowplop.

He was squinting at the bay. Broad shoulders, a beautifully cut suit. He looked so important and impatient. . . .

"What?" Bob said.

"This is Judy Teranian, and Dale Jergenson," Frank said, introducing two more people. A circle was slowly gathering around Fitz; the word was out as to who she was.

"Cowplop," Fitz repeated. "It's the only word one of his characters ever utters, practically."

"Whose characters?" Judy asked.

"Peter De Vries's. He's a very funny and very sad writer." Fitz took a long gulp of scotch. If only he would look her way, and want to join her group. But he wouldn't, she knew he wouldn't. "De Vries did a brilliant takeoff on Dylan Thomas," she continued. "Thomas had this thing about his teeth, you see. He was terrified of losing his teeth. And after I read *Reuben, Reuben* I dreamed that all my teeth were crumbling in my mouth, all night long. I kept chewing them and trying to spit them out!"

"How awful," Dale said.

"I'm sure you don't paint cowplop." Frank laughed.

"I've certainly heard of you, somewhere," Judy said. "And you live in Paris. Divine. This is Carol Shoenberg, by the way. And Jerry Baldwin. Oh, and Sue and Brad Courtland."

Fitz smiled at all of them, looked beyond them to

where he was now standing immobile with the cocktail glass held to his lips. The other man had stopped talking to him, and he was alone. "I'm talking about Dylan Thomas!" she wanted to call him. "I'm thinking about not going gentle into that good night. I *know* you already, I know you won't go gentle; you'll rage and rage. Why won't you look at me? . . ."

"—Must be nice to have all that talent," the girl named Carol was saying. "Mine takes me to L.A. and back twice a month. Big deal!" She laughed happily.

"They say Paris has changed—"

"All those high-rises—"

"Communism is slowly creeping in. Giscard is a flop—"

"Paris has never been more beautiful or more prosperous," Fitz said, interrupting. "It's a rich city now. Everything is clean and modern and the people look so much happier than they used to. I think it's wonderful! But I think their prosperity might make them susceptible to communism, even more so than poor Italy."

"How so?" It was Brad Courtland. Tall, good-looking, coming on with his eyes.

"Because there's less paranoia than there is in Italy, with its papier-mâché politics—"

Her man was only twenty feet away. Maybe he *had* noticed her, maybe he was biding his time. He was not as handsome as Brad Courtland but he had an arrogance about him, a lonely defiance.

"Another drink?" Brad Courtland asked, coming on stronger. "What can I get you?"

"That man over there," Fitz heard herself say. Brad's gray eyes took on a leaden look. "He seems so familiar. Do you know who he is?"

"Sorry," Brad said flatly. "Can't help you. Now what would you like to drink? Is this scotch and water?"

Fitz nodded.

"I'll be back," Brad told her. It was a warning.

Fitz was still staring at her man. He turned slowly toward her, she looked slowly away. A game—

"He is the most brilliant judge in Spain," someone said to Fitz in French. She turned, startled. A tanned woman in her late fifties—whose face was fascinating because of the intelligence, the humor, the self-knowledge she'd acquired from where her own sensuality had led her—was smiling at Fitz. She knew. She was wearing Peruvian jewelry. "Carlos is a loner," she continued without introducing herself. "A pessimist. A genius. He has seen too many things, made too many difficult decisions. You will succeed." Her French was guttural, an accent that Fitz couldn't identify: she touched the turquoise and silver creation that dripped into her bosom. "I know your paintings," she added. "He'll only be here until tomorrow."

"Tell me about him!" Fitz exclaimed in French, not trying to hide her eagerness.

"I don't think that will be necessary," the woman replied. "Look."

And he was walking toward Fitz, his eyes on her only, a force as strong as the way he walked—a challenge, a demand for the best things in life.

The tanned woman turned away.

"Would you care to join me outside?" he said, and that was all.

Europeans didn't bother with names.

○●

"I'm impressed by your paintings," he remarked, his voice soft and too controlled. "They are better than I'd expected. Especially the dark ones."

"My *Nights*," Fitz nodded. "My *Variations on a Theme from Nocturini*."

Carlos smiled. They were standing out on her balcony and speaking French because he preferred it to English. They had taken a short drive, and now the city and the bay sprawled lazily below them, turning pink and purple in the last light of a sun that still sat between the towers of the Golden Gate Bridge.

"Now tell me," Fitz said, "about the twilight. And why you want it so much."

The breeze did not ruffle his thick, graying hair. He arched an eyebrow in surprise and smiled at her sideways, a thin smile that showed he had understood her ironic tone and appreciated it. There was a melancholy strength in him that was still fighting experience—a sad and impatient dignity—and a repressed need that she sensed he was trying to hide now.

"Choose," he finally answered her, "between a wounded lion and a gladiator."

She looked at him, her golden eyes suddenly sad.

"Choose," he repeated.

There was a long silence. "How hard," she answered after a while, "to have them fighting each other inside you. Both prisoners—"

"Choose." His dark eyes were very impatient. And yet hopeful—

She shook her head slightly.

"The lion, or the gladiator?" He drummed his fingers on the railing.

Fitz gazed out over the panorama briefly, feeling her answer rise to his challenge, feeling a climactic self-confidence brought on by his intelligence.

She turned back to him, and replied tenderly. "But you know that I can't choose, because I am the arena."

They looked at one another for a long time. And then he took her gratefully in his arms. . . .

16

The tinkle of a small bell interrupted Stephanie's thoughts. A concave sound, a faint clamoring from the front door of her lanai. She started, feeling disoriented. The bell tinkled again; the clock said 7:30. Nicholas Hanson was at her front door, and she wasn't ready yet. She was sitting in her underwear at the dressing table and staring into the mirror.

"Stephanie?" Nicholas called.

Two dresses were laid out on the bed, and she didn't know which one to wear. The short yellow linen with a yoke neck that Jonathan had loved, or the long, pale-blue sheath in shimmery jersey that she had bought recently, which was very low-cut and not safe around Nicholas. She would wear the yellow one, to keep her mind on Jonathan.

"Are you there?" Nicholas asked.

After a fashion, she thought, and said: "Just a moment!"

Je Reviens, to help bring her back to the present. Je Reviens, a gift of perfume from Fitz to her, the flavor and smell of Paris, purchased at I. Magnin's on a rainy-day shopping spree a week after Fitz's return. She dabbed it behind her ears, on her neck, on her wrists.

Nicholas was standing outside the screen door, his face dark against the yellow glow of the setting sun, his jacket bright white against the bronzed background of palms. He held a bottle of gin in one hand, and a luxuriant branch of tropical flowers in the other.

I don't belong in this place, Stephanie thought.

"I come," Nicholas smiled, "bearing gifts."

"Then I should beware." She crossed the lanai and opened the door to him.

"My grand-daddy was Swedish, not Greek." He handed her the flowers. "One for each night of this week."

"They're . . . they're beautiful," Stephanie said. "But really, I shouldn't—"

"Why don't you put one in your hair? It would look great." He was breaking one flower off the branch.

"It's too short."

"What, the stem?"

"No, my hair."

"Nonsense." He gave her a kind, intimate look. "Be good now, and fetch a couple of bobby pins while I mix drinks. Is gin and tonic okay?" He was walking toward the door of her small kitchenette.

"My hair is too thin."

"That's ridiculous; your hair is lovely. Now go get the pins." She heard him opening the refrigerator door, and then the crinkling of an ice tray. It was a sound that Stephanie really didn't like.

She carried the flowers with her into the bedroom and picked up two bobby pins from the top of the dressing table, next to the torn pieces of Kent and Angie. She stood against the table for a moment, staring at the torn photograph, trying to overcome the feeling of having been invaded—like a robbery, or a rape.

Nicholas was waiting for her in the center of the lanai, holding two drinks in his hands. He set them down on the round glass table in front of the striped sofa and turned to her.

"Come here," he commanded. "Let me do it."

She handed him the pins and the flower, and stood

close to him, breathing the smell of his aftershave. It wasn't the same kind Jonathan had used; Jonathan's favorite had been Brut. Nicholas's shoulders were broader than Jonathan's, his body more powerful under the white jacket, and the feel of his fingers in her hair was as assured as if he had pinned hundreds of flowers in women's hair. Stephanie looked up at him.

"There," he said, not moving, looking down at her for interminable seconds. Then his fingertips brushed her cheek—

"I'm a widow!" she blurted out, "a very recent widow!"

Nicholas continued to look at her. Nothing moved in his face.

"So that's it," he finally said. "I didn't know. I'm sorry."

They stood facing one another while Stephanie bit her lips, fighting back self-pitying tears, and Nicholas lit a cigarette. Beyond him the palm leaves drooped and the rusty sun was setting. Soon it would slide down the horizon's silver throat, and the water would turn pewter gray and darken like unpolished hope into the iron black of night. . . .

Their eyes met and passed quickly. *I'll never have anything to hold on to again,* Stephanie realized.

"Let's talk about it," Nicholas said, and handed her a drink. "Come sit. Do you have any children?"

"Yes, two." She sat down next to him on the orange striped glider-sofa. It creaked under their weight.

"How old?"

"Six and three, a boy and a girl." And that's that, isn't it, Mr. Traveling Bachelor, she thought. Should she tell him how adorable they were? Should she describe their freckles and curls and peachy cheeks, their soft round bottoms? Their constant fighting and whining?

The four-bedroom house they all rattled around in, the view of the Bay? The dog, the bills? Should she unload the image of her life on him and every other single man she would meet in the future? Of course not; he had the picture already. . . .

Nicholas was watching her. "What a hell of a thing," he said. "How did it happen?"

"An . . . an accident, at night."

"What kind of accident?"

"I don't want to talk about it."

"You should talk about it, though. What kind of accident?"

"I . . . I can't talk about it. I'm sort of blocked."

"Blocked?"

"Yes. I can't really remember. Please."

"I think you need to unblock," Nicholas said. "Why can't you remember?"

"I . . . we . . . had a lot to drink."

"How did your husband die?"

"He fell. . . ."

"Fell? From where?"

"Our balcony."

"My God, how horrible. You said something this afternoon about your best friend."

"Yes. I—"

"Does she have something to do with it?"

"I . . . I don't know. I don't want to talk about it yet—"

"What's her name? Was she there at the time? Are you suspicious of her?"

"I don't know!" Stephanie almost shouted. "I don't want questions like this. What does it matter to you?"

Nicholas blinked, looking hurt. His green eyes were sympathetic. She didn't want him to be part of the questioning. He put his drink on the table and lit another cigarette. "It matters to me only because you're so unhappy and frightened, and I thought that talking about it might help. Don't you want to tell me about your friend?"

He was sitting on the edge of the sofa, leaning toward her expectantly. His forearms rested on his thigh; he held his drink between his knees. And suddenly Stephanie thought that his light, probing eyes were too eager. Why? Death shouldn't be so fascinating to people, and Fitz was none of his business. She looked out at the ocean and squinted at the last dying rays of sunlight. No, she didn't want to talk about Fitz yet, she couldn't cast suspicions on Fitz until she knew more in her own mind.

She finally answered. "The police said it was an accident."

"But you're not sure? You think she—"

"I don't know! Please stop these questions! I'm sick of questions!"

"Take it easy!" Nicholas exclaimed, reaching out to touch her arm. "I'm sorry, no more questions, I promise. But why don't you talk to me about Jonathan? Maybe it would help." His eyes were soft, compelling. He had saved her life, that morning. His eyes were casting a spell on her. . . .

She felt suddenly awake. "Jonathan," she said. "How did you know Jonathan's name? How do you know my husband's name?"

He paused only a moment before replying. "Because you registered under it, at the desk." He looked sheepish. "I know it was snoopy of me, but you talked so little last night, and since we're both from San Francisco, I was curious about where you lived. Please take it as a compliment. I thought you were probably getting a divorce." He took a drag on his cigarette, then ground it out in the ashtray. "Forgive me?"

Stephanie nodded. But she had touched something; for the transient tick of a second she had broken the glass-green spell of his eyes, and she felt nervous again—

"Come now," Nicholas said, and took hold of her hand. "Try to relax." His eyes smiled into hers.

He was right, she thought. She was all nerves; she should try to relax and talk about Jonathan—

"I'm not very good at defining people," she said, and took a long swallow of gin. "Jonathan was just a man. I mean he wasn't brilliant or exceptional or anything unusual but he was wonderful to me, he took good care of us and worked hard, he loved me and treated me well and was a good father to our children and we were as happy as—"

Nicholas leaned forward, frowning. *Slow down, Stephanie,* she warned herself. *You sound half-hysterical. He's still a stranger after all, and you don't want to go that far; you don't want to tell him that you and Jonathan were as happy as two people could be until Fitz came back, until Fitz—*

"Go on," Nicholas urged her. "I'm listening."

"Our wedding was beautiful."

Nicholas looked surprised, then smiled at her. She leaned back in the sofa. Could she tell him about all the beautiful gifts they had received—the George III silver tea set, the antique silver cruets, tea caddies, candelabra; the Lalique bowls, Wedgwood china, and Waterford decanters? Monogrammed towels and sheets? A brass waste-paper basket and a leather-bound atlas? About how she had displayed them on card tables in her apartment, before the wedding, about how thrilled she had been to have such magnificent possessions all her own because they represented fulfillment, they were silver and crystal symbols of security? No, no—Nicholas would think it inane of her to talk about objects that were worthless, compared to Jonathan himself, and he would be right. It had been stupid and insensitive of her to place so much value on them at the time—

"Stephanie?"

"Umm? Oh, sorry—"

"The idea is to talk, remember? How's your drink?"

"Fine."

Nicholas sat back and lit another cigarette, then closed his eyes and rested the back of his head on the couch.

"I know it sounds silly," Stephanie said, "but it was a fairy-tale wedding, every girl's dream. You know . . . a flourish of trumpets, the organ roaring . . . I had the organist play the third movement of Beethoven's Fifth. It was sort of a graduation cum laude, for me. I guess *men* don't understand that; they only want to live with you—"

Nicholas opened his eyes slightly and smiled sideways at her.

"Anyway, it was in Grace Cathedral and the reception was in a private club, my dress was Alençon lace and cost a fortune, I had six bridesmaids dressed in pink satin—"

He was nodding his head as though he had heard it all before. And of course he had, Stephanie realized. He'd probably been to hundreds of weddings just like it. There had really been nothing exceptional about it at all, except that her best friend hadn't been there and she hadn't thought about Fitz at all, didn't miss her on the most important day of her life. Why not?

Nicholas was looking at her with eyes as calm as the Aegean under smooth, overhanging cliffs. What incredible eyelids he had, she thought. But she'd never seen the Aegean, except on posters and in her imagination; she'd never been to Greece. Fitz had, though. The old jealousy; she didn't want to tell him about Fitz for other reasons. He would find her fascinating. . . .

"You must have been a lovely bride," Nicholas said.

"Thank you."

"And afterward?"

"Afterward? Well, afterward was a complete beginning, if you know what I mean—"

He smiled his turned-down smile and Stephanie felt annoyed. Why did everyone automatically think of sex?

"What I'm saying," she went on, toying with the silver bracelet on her wrist, "—is that I had never *projected* marriage, never imagined what an average day or evening living with Jonathan would be like. The *fact* of being married to him was what mattered, and the reality of it had been an abstraction in my head, so to speak."

"Are you given to abstracting things?"

She saw his eyes narrow again, almost imperceptibly, and wondered why he wasn't bored, wondered whether she *was* given to abstracting things, wondered what the difference was between abstraction and distraction, and knew she should know the difference.

"Yes," she said after a while, "I guess I am, in a way. But the *fact* of it was bliss. I whistled while I ironed his undershorts, if you can believe it! I spent my days painting and redecorating our first apartment on Green Street, making curtains, shopping for appliances. It was a whole new domestic world that women make fun of now—hours poking around ethnic markets for interesting meals. I couldn't wait for him to get home at night; I started getting ready for him at four o'clock every afternoon, showering and smearing lotion all over myself—"

She stopped. That was enough; she was getting too personal. She was being sucked in again, sucked in by Nicholas's green eyes, tricked into revealing too much, giving too much of herself. The way she had been sucked into the safe brown of Jonathan's eyes. But that had been different. . . .

"I switched to marketing at the Marina Safeway," she said flatly, "after the children were born."

Nicholas looked startled. Then he said, "Would you like another drink?"

"No," Stephanie answered. "Dinner, I think." *You certainly do make people come to you,* someone had told her once. Who was it? *You certainly do sit back and make people draw you out. . . .*

Nicholas stood up slowly, then offered her his hand. They walked silently down the stone path toward the terrace and the sound of mariachi music. He had drawn her out much too quickly, Stephanie thought as they walked, but why was that a threat?

They rounded a curve in the path, and the hotel terrace came into view: the candlelight from the lanterns, forms seated in shadow, and waiters moving around in soft warm light.

And then it came to Stephanie suddenly: the reason she had to be drawn out, the reason she resisted giving of herself. It whispered through her, a crystalizing chill in the tropical night air: ice in the oven.

There wasn't much left to give, she realized, because she had lost most of herself, the real Stephanie. She had lost and/or forgotten the real Stephanie little by little each day, each month, each year—in the safety of life with Jonathan. She had been pulled into security, abstracted into a daily convenience, starting from the first week of marriage. Exam time! Study Jonathan's habits, memorize them daily, cram for the exam and be a good student, a good wife. . . .

Newly married, she had cooked for him, cleaned for him, ironed for him while she blessed her good fortune and believed sincerely in her good fortune. She had clutched at his every word across the dinner table, his every opinion, watched his lips while she absorbed his ideas. Leaned on him, learned from him, denied her own opinions when they differed from his. She had taken up tennis seriously, wanted to sail, gone to the movies instead of dancing or to the opera or the theater, most of the time. . . .

"Let's take that table tonight," Nicholas said, pointing toward a corner table on the far side of the terrace.

Stephanie followed him obediently, thinking that she was not a women's libber, that she had been happy wanting to do what Jonathan wanted to do. And she had come to depend upon Jonathan more each year, to love him more every day. But she was absorbed into his secure world nonetheless, losing herself in the safety of his desires and his brown eyes. Both of the children had brown eyes, too.

Ice in the oven. . . . The making of children, the finalized giving. . . . The passive creation of their energy-melting bodies that had incubated inside her, then their energy-draining existence in her comfortable world. Stephanie had been sucked up even more into the brown of their dear little eyes.

But what had happened to the blue of hers?

"*Tostadas Compuestas*," Nicholas said to the waiter. "*Pollo con arroz.*"

So Fitz had been right, she thought. She had been right about Stephanie all along, and Stephanie must have known it. She must have agreed with Fitz, subconsciously. What else hadn't she admitted to herself?

Jonathan was angry at me as well as Fitz. And I was crying when we followed him into the living room. I was crying and Fitz was shouting at him, I couldn't stand to see them fighting—

"*Una botella de vino blanco,*" Nicholas said.

Jonathan was angry at me too, but he stopped shouting. He stopped shouting and was looking at Fitz in a strange way. I didn't like the way he was looking at Fitz while she shouted at him—

And there was something more. Something about

Fitz, something final and more frightening—twice as frightening—as Jonathan's death.

"Now tell me about your children," Nicholas said, and shadows passed across the light in his eyes. "What are their names?"

17

"Kent's growing up too fast," Stephanie had said to Fitz shortly after her return to San Francisco. "Can you believe he's already on a baseball team? At six years old?"

"That's America." Fitz shook her head, smiling. "What is it, the Itty-Bitty League? Good Lord."

"Oh well, you can't teach them too young, they say. It's good for his coordination. Teamwork, and all that—"

They were on the deck of Sam's Cafe in Tiburon, enjoying cheeseburgers on French bread and watching the seagulls circle and dip overhead. It was a windy, clear day, and whitecaps danced lightly on the heavy blue water around them. Rows of sailboats moored at the docks rolled with the waves; there were very few people sitting outside.

"Is he reading well?" Fitz had said.

"I'm afraid not. Too much TV."

"Speaking of children," Fitz said, "there's a book I just finished, by Simone de Beauvoir. *Les Belles Images.* It's sort of about children, and you've got to read it. . . ."

"I have," Stephanie replied, ignoring the surprised look on Fitz's face. "I didn't like it."

"Where's your conscience? How could you *not* like that book?"

"Life's not as complicated as she makes it." Stephanie pulled up the collar of her suede jacket.

"Yes it is!" Fitz exclaimed. "Your denial of it is the whole point of the novel! She's speaking to you and all the other mothers who lead your pretty lives in your pretty houses with your husbands and your pretty children, surrounded by pretty images. And your heads are buried deeper than an ostrich's in the sands of comfort. The real world of pain is an inconvenient enemy, isn't it?"

"You're oversimplifying it," Stephanie argued. "The real world is depressing, and I can't do anything *important* about it anyway, the starvation and suffering of others. Simone de Beauvoir dumps a heavy load of guilt on you, it's true. But I have my own problems, with two kids and barely enough time to make things run smoothly as it is—"

"I'm good at oversimplifying things that are too complicated," Fitz grinned.

"Okay, okay," Stephanie smiled. *"Touché."*

"What she is saying, as I see it, is that mothers naturally want to protect their children, and themselves—from unhappiness, from depression. The whole issue is a moral one, a question of what is really good for us—"

"You have the *time* to help others," Stephanie said. "And I don't." She took another bite of cheeseburger.

"Your conscience *is* showing! Won't you take a little time to give some of it to your children? Set an occasional example by allowing yourself time to feel, really feel, the misery that exists?"

"You're an artist, Fitz, and I'm not. You're more sensitive. And besides, I want my children to feel secure and happy. Once you start bleeding, it's hard to stop—"

"It hurts," Fitz said. "But it makes you feel alive. I could talk about that book for hours, how Laurence feels deadened by her comfort, by her surroundings. The intricacies of her feelings. How her child's sensitivity started the ball rolling. Didn't you identify with her at all?"

"All that psychology." Stephanie made a face. "You're a Freudian Santa Claus, dear Fitz. You always have been."

"And you think you're safe," Fitz replied. It sounded ominous, almost like a threat. She poured another glass of wine and returned the smile of an attractive bearded man in a green parka who sat a few tables away.

"If you had two small children and a big house," Stephanie said, "you wouldn't have time for charity work either."

"Lots of women do both. Why don't you come with me tomorrow? I'm reading to a blind man down in the Mission, a friend of a friend. He's delightful, and he likes me to read poetry. Please come see—"

"I can't," Stephanie said. "Tomorrow I have Kent's car pool and then Angie has a dentist appointment—"

"I really wasn't made to have children," Fitz remarked, and looked back at the bearded man. He was staring at her.

"You don't have to flaunt your availability so openly," Stephanie said, noticing the exchange of looks. "And you're right, you certainly weren't made to have children. . . ."

18

Fitz was sitting at an ordinary cafeteria table in the center of a bare, dingy, run-down restaurant somewhere in the heart of the San Francisco Tenderloin district. There were no murals, no pictures of any kind on the blank, chocolate-brown walls. Used paper napkins and rumpled cigarette packages were strewn over the spotted linoleum floor, and the only light in the large room came from behind an old bar in the dust-filled distance. The room was full of shadowy outlines, people seated in clusters around cafeteria tables. Worn-out, Daumier-like caricatures. Derelict humanity.

Fitz shuddered, and looked up at her best friend.

Stephanie was wearing a Lanz dress, a red-and-white striped, peasant-cut dress with little red and white hearts. It was a "cute" dress, something Fitz wouldn't be caught dead in. Stephanie was perched on top of an enormous ice-cream soda with a crown of maraschino cherries on her head—a magnificent, surreal ice-cream soda, made from mounds of strawberry ice cream piled six feet high in a giant crystal glass, and enveloped in a weightless fizzy-pink foam.

Stephanie sat cross-legged on top of the ice cream; the hem of her heart-dress sank slightly into its smoothness. In her right hand she held a large candy-striped straw which protruded from the glass. Fitz wondered if the soda was going to melt. Suddenly there was a shout from one of the dark corners of the room, and then a scuffling of bodies. Stephanie held out her hand and waved it imperiously, demanding silence; she was listening to something, Fitz realized, something inside her soda, something that was coming up through the straw. Fitz stood up and walked to the base of the glass, and the other vague forms in the room followed her. They stood around the base of the soda, listening.

What was it? What had Stephanie heard?

Fitz put her ear to the cold glass and heard a faint, high shout, then another. It was the voices of children, calling their mother: happy children laughing in the park, shouting at their mother to watch this! Watch that! Look, mommy, look! Unhappy children crying in pain; angry children fighting and screaming, demanding their mommys. . . .

"You don't remember me, do you?" a woman in the restaurant yelled up at Stephanie.

Stephanie looked down at her with blank blue eyes and took a long sip of pink fizz from her soda. The strawberry ice cream slipped and settled under her crossed legs and spread-out skirt.

"You don't want to remember me!" the woman shouted. Stephanie stared at her blankly.

"I hate you," the woman hissed. "You were born luckier than my daughter, and you could have helped her, but you don't even remember Cecily, do you? The girl with the brace on her leg, the limp. You avoid anything unpleasant or inconvenient, don't you?"

Stephanie wouldn't look at her. She took another sip from the straw, and the pillows of ice cream settled farther down into the glass. They were becoming gooey, melting rapidly. She was slowly sinking into the huge crystal glass.

"Vell, Stephanie, eet ees a pity," said a tall, elderly man as he emerged from the shadows. The vague forms parted to let him approach her, which he did boldly, his gray hair bristling. His pale eyes gleamed in anger.

He looked up at Stephanie. "Eet ees a shame, my dear, that you vill haf so leetle time for me. You vill dissipate your considerable ability. Your talents vill be vasted."

Stephanie's face remained placid, indifferent. She seemed unaware that she was sinking into the pink foam, that her head was now on a level with the rim of the giant glass. She clutched her straw tightly in her right hand and sipped loudly through it. Her children's voices rang louder and louder through the crystal.

124 ○●

The old man seized a chair and climbed up on it. A murmur of awe and dread spread through the room. He grabbed the rim of the glass with both hands and peered into Stephanie's eyes.

"You must find the time!" he shouted at her, and his demand caused havoc in the crowded, dark cafeteria. . . .

The mass of nebulous outlines that gathered around Stephanie's table now began to merge. They swelled toward her like a melancholy cloud brewing at the base of her crystal glass. And then suddenly they broke up into epileptic, blind, and palsied children; into senile, drooling old people; into sloe-eyed Indians with distended bellies, all clamoring for Stephanie.

"Find time for us!" they cried. "Find time for us!"

The gray-haired man wavered above them, his arms gesticulating wildly, his eyes half-mad now, his arms reaching down into the melting soda.

Who was he? *Cronus,* Fitz thought. Like the painting in her studio. Her wild, crazy Cronus, devourer of children . . .

Stephanie was sipping steadily on her straw, oblivious to the pandemonium around her, to the thin, wrinkled arms and the little trembling hands above her head, to the whines and pleading outside her crystal citadel. Her wide blue eyes never shifted as she sank down into the thick, pink puddle at the bottom of the glass, and the voices of her children rang through the room like the silver clanging of a great, gonging bell that drowned all other sound.

Her legs were starting to melt along with the ice cream, under the heart-shaped dress. Her legs and now her arms were becoming amorphous pink and white pudding, a mass that engulfed her, and her neck was sliding down into the collar of her dress. The features of her face were dissolving into a sweet foam as her disappearing mouth took a final, long sip from the candy-striped straw. The voices of Stephanie's children shouted triumphantly, and her empty red-and-white dress collapsed at the bottom of the huge crystal glass.

"You haven't heard a word I've been saying," Nicholas observed, and his voice came from far away.

Stephanie turned to look at him, and the present snapped into focus: the terrace of the Casa del Sol, flickering lights, empty tables all around them, their dinner finished. Two waiters were chatting quietly in the background.

"Have you?" Nicholas said.

The night air was soft, but over her left shoulder the hunched weight of the mountains hovered ominously. She hadn't been able to look at the mountains all evening; they had become a symbol to her, dark and mysterious reminders of that last horrible night—of Jonathan and Fitz embossed on the balcony against a background of black.

"Stephanie?"

And now there were Nicholas's hooded eyes, still interested in her despite her silence. He was really after her, she realized, and that he had to be an ironic, conciliatory twist on the part of Fate, because men never had looked at her twice before her tragedy, before Jonathan died.

"Shall we go?" Nicholas was standing up, pulling out her chair.

She didn't want to move, didn't want to face his sexual intensity or the mountains over her shoulder.

"Stephanie, don't you want to go back to your *casita?*" Nicholas tried to sound casual.

She looked slowly up at him, and found herself smiling. It was a resigned, inviting smile that came from nowhere, a "why not?" smile that she could feel on her face and see reflected in his eyes—a sudden, incomprehensible acceptance. She took his hand, stood up, and turned.

The mountains loomed above her. And suddenly they seemed to be alive, and moving. The mountains seemed to zoom in on her, to race at her, hunchbacked and hairy, to reach out for her with gargantuan arms. They reached out for her and then receded; her eyes were a camera gone crazy. The mountains reached out, receded, reached out again—like Fitz!

Fitz had reached out for Jonathan, high on the balcony.

Fitz had rushed toward him in the darkness, and their bodies had met in blackness high above the city. Fitz had blocked Jonathan from view for a moment; their bodies had been so close. . . .

The memory was expanding before Stephanie's eyes. She saw them together, too close, a horrible black memory, a dizzying vision.

She swayed, and then Nicholas's arms were around her, comforting her. He pressed her to his chest and said, "There, there, it's all right, you must try to forget, I'll help you forget." He put his arm around her waist, and led her off the terrace to the path that led to her *casita*.

Stephanie looked down at the stones of the path as they walked, trying to blot out the memory, thinking that each step she took on those stones was leading her closer and closer to Nicholas, farther and farther from Jonathan. Farther from Fitz—

No, she realized, not farther from Fitz. Closer to Fitz, closer to what she would do. Because she would have let Nicholas make love to her *last* night, if he had tried. She would have had sex with him without any guilt, without caring if she knew him better, with no sense of morality. Stephanie felt she was walking straight into Fitz's standards, and suddenly she loathed that idea. She hated the way Fitz had rushed at Jonathan, her arms outstretched, reaching for him to . . . to . . . to *what?* Oh God, if only she could remember whether Fitz had *kissed* him or pushed him!

They reached the door of Stephanie's porch. "Thank you, Nicholas," she said, and took his hand off her waist. "Thank you so much for being patient with me. I'm sorry, but I'd like to be alone now, and I'm sorry I've been so distracted. The dinner was—"

Nicholas opened the door to the lanai and walked in. She followed him nervously, suddenly realizing that he was too big and too broad-shouldered. "I really think you should go now," she said firmly.

He turned around slowly to face her. There was a vacant light behind the pearl-green of his eyes. His lips parted, lifting like a curtain above the footlights of his teeth, and then curved into the downturned smile. His eyes roamed over her neck and shoulders, lingered on her breasts, traveled down the length of her yellow dress and back up again, languorously, with unabashed insolence.

"Oh please," Stephanie murmured, "you have to go—"

His lips pressed down on hers, hurting. He was all around her; big, firm, hot, enfolding. A hand in her hair, an arm around her hips, a leg wrapped around hers, holding her breathless against the length of his body. Pulling her head back, forcing his tongue into her mouth, pressing his lips hard against hers, against her throat, her chest. . . .

"Nicholas," she whispered. "Oh please no—"

128 ◦●

His hand was on her breast, pulling it out of her dress, pushing it up to meet his lips. . . .

She wanted it. She wanted his tongue and teeth on her nipple, his wide mouth engulfing it, his hand molding it, his lips sucking at it. She wanted it, she wanted more. But she couldn't, she couldn't let him, it was wrong, it wasn't wrong, it was too soon, she wasn't ready yet, she needed more time, it felt so good—

He lifted her skirt, thrust his hand between her legs, clamped his fingers around her groin, and lifted her off the ground. He was picking her up to carry her to the bed, holding her between her legs. No one had ever, Jonathan had never held her that way.

Nicholas carried her past the glass-topped table, around the sofa, and to the door of the bedroom. He pushed it open with his foot. His index finger slipped under the elastic of her underpants and inside her; she moaned. His tongue flickered hard against hers; his eyes were pools of green greed as he carried her slowly into the room.

His pupils were dark mirrors moving closer to Stephanie, shimmering and swirling. He carried her to the edge of the bed. His pupils were black concentric circles that filled her vision, carrying her into blackness, carrying her backward into time and space and the black memory of that last night. She couldn't do this, she couldn't let Fitz win. Fitz would gloat over her if she made love to a stranger. . . .

Nicholas lowered her to the bed, following her down, releasing nothing. She looked into his glazed pupils and could see only the blackness of that last moment on the balcony, of Fitz rushing at Jonathan, arms open, of her body crushing against his.

But Fitz couldn't win anything, now. She couldn't gloat any more, could she?

Nicholas sucked on her tongue, and the black circles

●○ 129

of his eyes swallowed Stephanie, sucked her into their centers. His finger probed and pounded inside her. There was blackness everywhere, pounding, pounding, a bright blackness descending over her. Nicholas's glazed and vacant pupils gulped her; they were the cold ebony of the sky—where Jonathan fell and Fitz fell with him.

Jonathan fell and Fitz fell with him.

She had remembered everything the wrong way. She had blocked out the fact that Fitz was dead. Fitz had died with Jonathan, hadn't she?

And then it was a fuzzy blackness, a stampeding formless cloud that blanketed Stephanie's eyes and smashed her brain into exploding black stars.

"Stephanie?" Nicholas said. "Stephanie, are you all right now?" He was sitting on the edge of her bed, holding her hand.

His outline was a blur. The white walls of the room were an empty, snowy horizon gliding and slipping into focus. Shredded ghosts swirled around her, and she heard whispers overlapping: *Fitz can't be dead. I couldn't have done such a thing; they can't both be dead.*

"Stephanie, look at me now."

His voice was distant. Was he her judge?

"Listen," Nicholas said. "It's okay now. You fainted, that's all. You're fine." He smiled weakly. "And that has to be the least successful and yet most powerful effect I've ever had on a woman."

His voice was dark in tone, but light in inflection. He couldn't be too strict a judge. But she couldn't look at him.

"Stephanie," Nicholas said softly. "Listen to me, look at me. Please. I'm sorry; it's all my fault for rushing you—"

She turned her face away.

"There's no need to feel guilty about this," he said. "It was a natural thing to happen."

"Nothing is natural for me anymore."

"Of course it is." He reached out and touched her cheek, turning her face toward his. "For God's sake don't look so guilty! You're going to be fine if you give yourself more time. And I'll try not to tempt you again." He took his hand away from her face, stood up, and sat down farther away from her, at the foot of the bed.

Was her dress pulled down? She lifted her hips and smoothed the wrinkled yellow linen down over her thighs, running her hands flat over the telltale creases. Nicholas smiled ruefully.

"Would you like some water?" He stood up and walked to the bathroom; the faucet squeaked when he turned it on. He filled a glass for Stephanie, then stopped in the doorway and looked at her. "Is Fitz the name of your best friend?" he asked. "You kept mumbling that name."

She couldn't tell him about Fitz. He'd think she killed her.

"Yes," she said. "Fitz is my best friend."

"I see." Nicholas handed her the glass of water, and she sipped it slowly.

No, he didn't see anything, she thought. He didn't see that Fitz was dead, that she fell with Jonathan and that Stephanie couldn't have done such a thing. She knew she was incapable of it, no matter how angry or drunk or frightened she had been. But he wouldn't believe her, and who would? She had been alone with them. . . .

The police. The police had believed her, they decided it was an accident, they closed the case. She had to remember the police. Thank God for the police. . . . She missed Angie and Kent; she wanted Angie and Kent. Her precious, darling, peach-cheeked children. What had happened to their poor mommy, to her life? Everything was taken from her now except for them. Oh God, she prayed, please don't let her beautiful children ever know a living nightmare like this—

"Don't cry!" Nicholas said. "Stephanie, for God's sake don't cry like that. I feel responsible. Here, have some water. Please stop that crying."

"I . . . I can't remember it," she sobbed. "It was night and I drank too much and I can't remember what happened—"

"Hey, slow down," Nicholas said, and took her hand again. "Take a deep breath; that's right. I know you can't remember. But now's the time to try, now's the time to talk about it."

She looked at him through her tears and his eyes were more than sympathy, they were depths of relief waiting for her plunge. "We drank too much red wine," she started out. "We drank too much and talked too seriously instead of being happy. We talked about me; I remember that much. And Jonathan was worried about me, and then annoyed with me, and Fitz was picking on me too, and then on Jonathan—"

"Your friend Fitz was there that night?" Nicholas leaned forward, his voice calm. But his eyes were full of light, eager curiosity.

Morbid curiosity, Stephanie realized. *Don't tell him, he won't believe you—* "Yes," she said. "And then she left. That's all I can remember."

"What's Fitz's last name? Do you think she might have pushed your husband?"

"No, she couldn't have . . . I don't know!"

"But you think she might have, don't you?"

"No! I don't remember, please—"

"What's her last name?"

"I don't know anything! Please stop questioning me like this! Why do you care, anyway? Jonathan is dead and that's all that matters. . . ."

"What's your friend's last name, Stephanie?" Nicholas said. "I'm very interested in your friend Fitz—"

"I don't *want* you to be interested in her!" Stephanie sobbed. "I don't want you to be interested in me! I want to be left alone!"

Nicholas stood above her, looking worried. She looked back at him through watery blue eyes and wanted to tell him that his worry was phony, that his concern was minor, worthless and expendable compared to the doubt and fear she was feeling—mostly the fear. It filled the silent room with its corpulence: it was the Big Daddy now. And Big Daddy swallowed little baby worries, gobbled them up like Cronus, like Fitz's horrible painting. . . .

"I don't think I should leave you," Nicholas said. "You really don't look well. I'll sit here until you relax more, and maybe I can help you remember. You have to, because this thing is eating you up. Your friend Fitz, for instance. Why did she leave? Was she angry or did she threaten you? Why don't you want to tell me her last name?"

"Because I'm not sure of anything! Stop all these questions! Please, just leave me alone. I need to sleep."

A thin silence floated back and forth between their eyes, and she realized that he didn't want to give up. Why? His eagerness gnawed at her nerves; his eyes changed too often.

"Okay, sure," he finally sighed. "Anything I can do to help you end this ordeal." He started to give her his sexy smile, then stopped. "See you in the morning?"

"I don't know."

"You must, Stephanie. I still feel responsible for all this." He waved his hand through the air behind him—through her crying and fainting, and back farther, through his passionate kisses and pounding fingers and the moment she saw Fitz and Jonathan falling in the black pupils of his eyes. She was still afraid of his eyes.

And I was afraid of Fitz, she thought. *It was a fear that grew, and grew. . . .*

"Stephanie?"

"You're not responsible, Nicholas. But please go now." She turned her head away from him, waiting for him to leave, willing him to leave.

In a few moments she heard the screen door of her lanai closing with a subdued hiss.

21

Nicholas walked quickly back to his *casita* and headed for the door of his refrigerator, eager for a strong drink. The interior of the small, ancient Maytag was dark; a slow, dripping sound had replaced the usual noisy hum. He opened the freezer door and pulled out the single ice tray; tepid water splashed over his hands and onto his plaid slacks. He swore, slammed the door, and poured himself a straight scotch from a bottle on the counter of the kitchenette. The whisky burned his throat.

He went into his bedroom and took a long yellow legal pad and pencil from his brief case, then sat down on the edge of the bed and began to write. After a few minutes he picked up the telephone and waited for the operator at the hotel to answer. It was a long wait; at close to midnight, he knew, he would be lucky if anyone was on duty at the desk. At last a male voice answered.

"I want to send a cable to the United States," Nicholas said in English. "Can you get it to Western Union for me? It's urgent."

"*Si, señor,*" the man replied. "Tomorrow."

"Not tonight?"

"No, it is impossible."

"Very well," he sighed. "First thing tomorrow morning. Send it to Mr. Henry Sommers, Mutual International, Three-forty-two Montgomery Street, San Francisco. Have you got that?" He reached for his drink and took another gulp of scotch.

"*Si, señor.*"

"Good. Here it is: 'Check all sources for name and info . . . re female McMillan friend. Stop. Fitz only name available. Stop . . . Repeat Fitz. Stop. Urgent call me ASAP . . . with results.' Sign it 'Nicholas.' Did you get that? Read it back to me, please."

The man did so, and Nicholas smiled at his pronunciation of ASAP as if it were a Japanese word. After hanging up he lit a cigarette and sat smoking it with short, impatient puffs, contemplating the recent development. If he could confront Stephanie with her friend's name she might be shocked into talking about her. Or willing to talk about her. But he couldn't do that without giving himself away.

He was getting nowhere; there had to be another way. Gabriel could get the diary for him, but she was never away from her *casita* long enough, alone, for him to read it, and if she missed it it would blow the lid off. God knows she was unsettled enough already. He ground out his cigarette and stood up to undress, hanging his jacket carefully on a wooden hanger. He should have contacted his private-investigator friend Hal Lipset in San Francisco before he came down, and gotten hold of a Psychological Stress Evaluator, that marvelous way of giving a lie-detector test without strapping anyone to a polygraph. Stephanie wouldn't have to know he'd even done it unless he wanted her to know. If she saw the results, it might help her to remember what had happened, and he could find out if the friend Fitz had left or not.

Henry was right, Nicholas thought. There was something about Stephanie he didn't trust.

He hung up his shirt and bent over to take off his shoes, which were tied with a double knot. He always tied everything with a double knot. If only he could get hold of a PSE. But in this remote place . . .

Acapulco. Acapulco was only a forty-minute flight away, and the police or someone there would have the set-up. Hal Lipset might know someone in Acapulco. . . .

He stopped in the process of unbuckling his belt and turned to stare at the telephone. Of course; he would call Hal early in the morning! And if it could be arranged he would go there tomorrow. Better yet, he would talk Stephanie into going with him on the pretense of a change of scenery, and trick her into taking the lie-detector test. He'd make a game out of it. Control questions first, then a few zingers—

He finished undressing rapidly and went into the white-tiled bathroom to brush his teeth. He grinned at his own reflection in the mirror, turned on the tap water, and studied himself again with concentration. So what if he hadn't made it with her tonight? There were several days

left, and tomorrow he would persuade her to go to Acapulco with him. It was a brilliant idea. He would find out
about this little domestic triangle. Could it be a *ménage à
trois?* No. Stephanie McMillan hardly seemed the type.

He switched off the light, got into bed, and fell into
a satisfying reverie in which she lay next to him in the
darkness, telling him exactly what had happened the
night of McMillan's death, while he caressed her. . . .

Just before he drifted off into sleep, he made the
decision to send Gabriel after the diary, anyway.

22

The night was very still. There were no insects clicking in
the stillness, only the clock in Stephanie's room. No
crickets or cicadas or whatever they were that had clicked
through the summer nights of her childhood. She never
knew what anything was, specifically; she had never bothered to ask about anything except for the whippoorwill.
She had lain in bed in her grandmother's Victorian house
in the country and listened to the whippoorwill in the
early dawn, the whippoorwill and the long forlorn whistle
of a train in the distance, fading away into the future.

She could take all the Seconal pills.

She could drink them all from the bottle and wash
them down with that glass of water that Nicholas had
brought her. The children would live with Jonathan's
brother and family in Connecticut. They would have
other children their own age to play with, and a Saint Ber-
nard. All children love Saint Bernards. . . . They would

have cold winters; they could build snowmen in their front yards and stick carrots in for noses. They would have hot summers, and lemonade, and a nice aunt and uncle who cared about them and loved them. . . .

No. She couldn't take all the Seconal pills; she couldn't desert Angie and Kent. She would have to fight this nightmare and dissolve it, escape it with a clean conscience for Kent's sake, for Angie's sake—so that they would grow up secure and well-adjusted in spite of what had happened to her, and to their father.

And to Fitz.

I didn't like the way Jonathan was looking at her when she rushed toward him. I thought it was anger in his eyes but it could have been lust. Or it could have been fear but I didn't like it, I saw it and I was afraid of Fitz. . . .

I was afraid of Fitz from the first day she came back.

The clock clicked loudly in the stillness of the room. Tick, click. Tick. She would force herself to remember. She would unwind her memories back through the last two months, coil them up like the spring of her tightly wound clock, and then tick off in her mind each crucial moment, until that fatal night. Tick, click . . .

Why had Fitz come back, after all those years? And why was she afraid of her?

Oh God, *why* had Fitz ever come back?

23

"Nervous?" Piero Luigi had asked.

Fitz was lighting a cigarette. She shook her head, exhaled, and leaned back in the seat of the taxi. She was excited, but not really nervous; everything had gone beautifully at the opening of her show last week, and everything would go beautifully tonight. The taxi darted like a gnat through the swarm of traffic in Rome's Piazza del Popolo. They were on their way to a fashionable party in a villa on the Via di San Filippo Martire; the marchese who owned the villa had bought one of her paintings and was giving the party in her honor.

Why *wouldn't* she be excited? Her paintings were a huge success with the critics, and all but two had sold the first night. A photograph of one of them, and a picture of her standing next to a famous movie director had appeared in two Rome newspapers the next day. She was finally making it big! Not bad for a girl from Kansas City. The man sitting next to her, handsome Piero Luigi Doravini, was a well-known music critic and composer who had shown her a wonderful, exotic, erotic time in Rome. . . .

And tonight, dressed in a deep pink chiffon gown by Madame Grès, Fitz knew she looked beautiful. Like a full-blooming rose.

The party was sensational. They were greeted by a *maggiordòmo* at the door to the villa, and shown into a magnificent courtyard where the guests had gathered. There were faded frescoes on the walls, and columns two stories high, and bas-reliefs of Carrvera marble; it was like something out of *Anthony and Cleopatra* or *Spartacus*. Fitz had never seen so many beautiful people. The wealthy Italian women, she decided on the spot, were the most glamorous and well-dressed in the world, and she would learn to make up her eyes the way they did, with that dark accent on the lower lashes. Everyone was marvelous to her; the champagne flowed freely. The food was fabulous: cherry tomatoes stuffed with caviar, purple grapes filled and decorated with a delicious creamy cheese, oysters and clams on the half shell, smoked salmon shaped like stars.

At one point the marchese took Fitz and several other guests upstairs to his drawing room, where her large painting hung on an impressive wall, between two Palladian windows. It was of a double-dawn, tilted diagonally across the canvas: delicate explosions of pale light sprayed irregularly from its brilliant, split center—toward twin horizons at the edge. Opposite her painting, a Bronzino family portrait graced the marchese's drawing-room wall. Her work was in illustrious company; she really *had* made it—

"*Scusa*," a man on her right said. "I would like to present Signora Christina di San Giorgino—"

Fitz started. The woman smiling shyly at her was of the delicate, pale blond genre of Italian women depicted by Botticelli, although not as beautiful. Below the smile, her chin was a little weak, and her nose a touch too prominent. But her eyes were eyes that Fitz knew. They were wide-set, clear blue, and searching for something in Fitz's face. They were Stephanie McMillan's eyes.

"*Enchantée*," she said to Fitz in French. "I'm sorry, but I don't speak English."

"*Et moi*, I don't speak much Italian!" Fitz answered with a smile. "But French is fine."

"I wanted to tell you," the Italian said softly, "how much I admire—"

Fitz barely listened to her words of praise. She couldn't get over it; it was as though she was talking to Stephanie, after all these years in Europe! It was uncanny: this woman was no prettier than Stephanie, but her familiar eyes were elegantly made up, and she was exquisitely dressed in a low-cut blue silk that had to be a Dior, or whatever. . . . And her jewels were splendid. Stephanie could have looked like that, could have looked even more stunning, Fitz thought. What *did* she look like now? It had been so long. . . .

"—And your paintings," the Italian woman was say-

140 ◦●

ing, "speak to something, how does one say it . . . un-spoken, is that the word? Yes, something unspoken inside of me. Your work is . . . almost an answer. I am sorry, I am not very eloquent—"

"*Au contraire,*" Fitz smiled at her. "That is the most eloquent thing anyone has said to me tonight. It makes me very happy. . . ."

The blue eyes gave her a grateful, intimate look. It really *was* uncanny, the resemblance. Suddenly, Fitz missed Stephie, wished that Stephie was there to share this evening with her, this triumph in Rome. What was *her* life like, now? She had hardly had time to give Stephie much thought, over the last seven years; she was completely out of touch with her. What a shame. . . .

"So, *mia bella,*" Piero Luigi said at her elbow. "Don't you think it's about time to go?"

"Oh," Fitz said, "not quite yet, please. I'm having such a ball; let me enjoy my night of nights just a little longer? . . ."

They stayed until shortly before midnight. Then a group of them went to a disco on the Via Veneto, and it was almost three o'clock in the morning before Piero Luigi took her back to his apartment and made love to her.

She couldn't sleep, afterward. She lay awake in his arms, reliving the fabulous evening. And wondering what Stephie Borders McMillan's life was really like, so far away. . . .

○●

"Gimmee!" Angie was shouting. "Gimmee, gimmee! Mommeeeee!"

"She hit me first!"

"Yuk, yuk, yuk," said Huckleberry Hound. "That thar's a real nice place you got. Yuk, yuk."

"Children," Stephanie said. "Please?"

It was a miserable Thursday morning in early January. She wondered if her mood was an extension of the weather, or if she was aware of nature's foulness only after it mirrored her disposition. Stephanie didn't know; all she knew was that it had been rainy and foggy for ten straight days or longer, while Kent was home from school for the Christmas holidays, mostly fighting with Angie. And he was home again with a sore throat now, battling with Angie once more over the blare of the TV. Those horrible cartoons one after another all day long, hammering her children's psyches into a thousand animated fragments. . . .

"Shucks," said Huckleberry Hound. "I ain't never seen nothin' so nice. Yup, real nice—"

"Mommeee!"

"Shut up!" Kent shouted.

"It's mine! You know it's mine!"

"What *is* it, children?" Stephanie turned away from her desk, banging her knee on its inside edge. Damn it, she thought. "What is it *this* time?"

"He took my Pentel!"

"It's not hers, it's mine!" Kent's voice was a croak.

"Well," Stephanie sighed, "please give it back to her if she was using it."

"That's no fair!"

"Settle down, Kent. You have to rest your voice, honey. And you can see that I'm trying to work."

"Whar in the world didja ever seen such a purty thing?" asked Huckleberry Hound, as he slammed his club down on whatever it was that was so purty. Angie squealed happily.

It occured to Stephanie that she was a terrible mother; she should be taking them to the zoo or a museum, or making papier-mâché villages with them—

She turned back to her desk work. Bills in the left

pile, note cards for Christmas thank-you notes on the right. She'd been alternating, to alleviate the tedium: bill, thank you, bill, thank you, bill, thank you. . . .

"Duh," Yogi Bear enunciated. "Duh. duh. I dunno what I'm gonna do. I jest dunno."

"Sit down!" growled Kent. Angie wandered over to Stephanie and pulled at her sleeve. "I'm hungry, mommy." She was sucking her thumb and her dirty pink security blanket at the same time. That blanket absolutely had to go into the next wash, Stephanie thought. "It's too early for lunch, sweetheart," she said. "Now sit back down and wait a little."

Their gas bill was much too high, as a result of all that cold weather. But $87.50 was outrageous; she'd have to call and complain about it—

"Get down!" Kent gargled.

"I'm hungry!" whined Angie.

"Duh," said Yogi Bear. "Duh, duh . . . doncha feel jest great?"

"All right!" Stephanie shouted. "You win! Lunch it is. I can't stand this noise another minute!" She stood up and switched off the television.

"No!" Kent rumbled like lightweight thunder. "I wanna watch Yogi Bear and Huckleberry Hound! I wanna watch the rest!"

"Okay, okay!" Stephanie sighed. "Anything to keep the peace. I'll get lunch. How does a grilled cheese sandwich and hot soup sound?"

"Yeah," he said, absorbed again in Yogi and Huck the Hound. Duh, duh, yeah, yeah, yuk, yuk . . .

"No!" bawled Angie. "I don't like grilled cheese!"

"Tough, chickadee. You'll eat what I fix."

"I ain't never!" Huckleberry declared ecstatically, and danced around waving his club. "I ain't never gonna git to live in sech a real nice place as thisun. . . ."

●○ 143

Why the paroxysms of joy? Stephanie wondered irritably. It's nothing but a crummy cave.

○●

Fitz had muttered in her sleep, rolled over in Piero Luigi's bed, and touched his thigh. But she wasn't in his bed; she was back in the art gallery, on the opening night of her show—only the art gallery looked like the courtyard in the marchese's villa. She was in the marchese's villa-gallery-courtyard again, surrounded by her paintings and by rich, famous people. They all toasted to her success, to her beauty, to her gaiety. Champagne sprinkled down on her head, she was radiant, this was the *first* of her "night of nights!" "I'll rent a larger studio in Paris," she was saying to the crowd of admirers. "Or maybe in the country . . ."

Suddenly the people around her gasped. The crowd screamed, parted, scattered! They left her alone in the center of the large courtyard. Unprotected.

A beast stood in the corner, under a palm tree.

It was a huge dog wearing a yellow Brooks Brothers shirt and a brown felt hat. It was a human-sized mutt who held a tennis racket in one paw, doffed his brown hat with the other, and smiled charmingly at Fitz. His whole body was covered with short, wavy brown hair. He replaced his hat and walked on his hind legs over to one of Fitz's paintings hanging on the courtyard wall.

Fitz couldn't move. The dog looked her painting over quickly, then smiled at Fitz again. He had an erection. Fitz stood petrified. The mutt turned back to her painting. She felt a surge of relief. The huge mutt lifted his tennis racket triumphantly over his head, grabbed his penis in his other paw, and urinated all over her painting.

Then he started toward her.

She looked around. She was completely alone; the

villa was empty and as quiet as death. The mutt ambled toward her, grinning hideously. She still could not move. He reached out and grabbed her around the waist with his hairy paw; she screamed! The dog pulled her closer, smiling and showing the crow's feet around his soft deep-set brown eyes.

Jonathan McMillan's eyes.

Fitz screamed and screamed. . . .

The next night he came after her again. She had had a marvelous day in Rome: lunch with Piero Luigi and some of his friends, a stroll through the Borghese gardens, then two hours alone in the Sistine Chapel with Michelangelo's masterpieces. She had sat on a bench on the left side of the chapel, her head back, gazing in awe at the ceiling, wondering if myths *should* be made so real, marveling that they *could* be made so indelibly powerful. Did it matter if it was myths, or dreams, or fantasies that one painted? As long as they were as powerful on canvas as they were in real life. . . .

Piero Luigi had taken her out to dinner at Mario's, one of the best restaurants in Rome, and then said *addio* to her for over two hours with passionate and tender caresses. The mutt followed her with a gun this time. He was much bigger and hairier, and wearing only a narrow, striped tie. He chased her from the bright light of St. Peter's piazza into the darkness of the enormous basilica, and the slap of her feet on the marble floor echoed through its cavernous nave. She ran and ran, terrified, aware of the huge dog always behind her. . . .

He cornered her in a chapel.

He lumbered toward her with a stubby black gun in his hairy paw, pointed at her heart. And a sick, smug smile on his face.

The next day Fitz flew back to Paris. It was cold, gray, and raining there; in the taxi she felt lonely and let down, missing the sun of Rome. It had been an exhilarating two weeks. Back in her studio near the Boulevard Montparnasse she ate some cheese and part of a stale *baguette,* drank a glass of red wine, and went to bed early to catch up on her sleep.

The dog came after her again, when she was lying, in her dream—as she had lain two summers earlier—on the hot white sand of a small private beach on Mykonos. She was naked on her stomach while the cool waves of the Aegean licked at her ankles, and a tongue traveled down her back slowly, in little circles. It was a special tongue that belonged to her friend Anna, an artist whose skin was smoother than anything Fitz had ever touched. Or known. Fitz turned to look at her, to thank her. She looked at Anna and saw hair on her soft white breasts. She saw hair on Anna's stomach, on her thighs, her arms, her shoulders. Short, dark, wavy brown hair all over Anna's beautiful body . . .

The next morning, Fitz made the decision to leave Paris for a while and return to San Francisco. She had to get Jonathan the Dog off her back.

A week later she was on an Air France 747, crossing the Atlantic. During the long flight she made an attempt to read, but found herself staring out the window, trying to imagine what Stephanie's life with Jonathan was like. What would she see, if she could peer into their house on a given day? What was Jonathan really like? If she could know her enemy, then she could try to look at him objectively. And she needed to know him; he was haunting her nightly . . . for a reason. Dreams always told the truth.

Actually, she thought, closing the book on her lap . . . actually, their life probably wasn't hard to imagine. She almost *knew* what she would see if she looked into their window. She glanced at her watch: eight o'clock in the evening, Paris time. That would make it six o'clock in the morning in San Francisco, the start of another day for the McMillans. The alarm would have just gone off and Stephie would be awake, but not up. She would be lying on her back in bed, staring at the ceiling. . . .

It really wasn't hard to imagine at all: Jonathan would sit up, swing his legs over the edge of the bed, stand, stretch his arms sleepily over his head. His pajamas would be unsexy; why didn't he sleep nude? He was touching his toes now, Fitz thought. Five times, ten times, fifteen times . . . He walked around the bed, switched on Stephie's bedside lamp, bent over to give her a kiss on the cheek. Why didn't they make love? Because they were married and it was Never on Monday, Tuesday, Wednesday, Thursday, or Friday mornings, when you're married. Stephie was making an early-morning attempt to smile at her hubby now—a duty smile. . . .

Jonathan went to the closet door, slipped on his robe, walked into the bathroom. He peed, washed his hand like a good clean boy, and started shaving. He was fond enough of himself in the mirror, all right. . . .

I'm sure Stephie is still lying in bed and staring at the ceiling, Fitz thought. I hear you Stephie. You've been through it all before, haven't you? Hundreds of times. You do what I'm seeing every morning, and every day. Breakfast, kids dressed, breakfast dishes, housework. It's always the same, isn't it? Your life is nothing more than a patterned abstraction of the present, I bet. A straight-line drawing executed in boredom, and complacency. . . .

Fitz lit a cigarette and pulled out the ashtray in the arm of her airplane seat. She shouldn't feel so angry. Maybe she was all wrong; maybe their life was idyllic. But how could it be?

Stephie had gone downstairs to fix breakfast now, and Jonathan was dressing. Fitz knew what he looked like; he was probably thickening around the waist by this time.

He wore those droopy boxer undershorts, and a white shirt, a tie, a conservative suit. She knew the type. He would examine himself in the mirror, when he was ready. He would run his index finger under his nose, contemplating a mustache, then dismiss that idea as too far-out. Tomorrow he would contemplate a clipped beard and dismiss that idea, too. Every day he would contemplate something new, but he would always dismiss it. Going out to dinner or buying a Neil Diamond record was undoubtedly his idea of something different. . . .

The top of his chest of drawers would be in perfect order: a manicure set in a leather case, a wallet, keys, a photo of Stephie with the children sitting on her lap, and *Time* magazine. Perfect. Order . . . This was a waste of time! Fitz thought. She could imagine Jonathan the rest of the day but it would lead her nowhere. It would only lead her downtown and into his stockbroker's office building— one of those big spaces scattered with squares, a crummy cubist painting. Spaces broken up into little office boxes, rows of squares. They were all alike: Danish-modern desks with black leather tops, and swivel chairs for the aesthetic curve. Office buildings like Jonathan's were cages of fluorescent light, stories and stories of glass-lined cages. . . .

Kennels for giant dogs.

Jonathan in his brown suit would talk to other brown suits, today and every other day. He would talk to secretaries; he would talk on the phone to brown suits in New York, arranging his tiny square corner of his tiny square world—

The monotony of the man, the lassitude of his life— those would be the real enemy. Fitz didn't want to have anything to do with them.

She returned the smile of a stewardess who walked past her in the aisle. She loved flying; travel still excited her as much as it had when she had first flown away from Kansas City with Stephanie—dear Stephanie, the house-wife. . . . She would concentrate on Stephie, instead of Jonathan! Of course. It was obvious that Stephie needed her, wasn't it? Married to a man like that. *Hold on, Stephie,* she said to herself. *It's really for you that I'm coming back! Just like the old days—*

She would get even with the dog that way, by con-centrating on Stephanie.

Before the dog got her.

And Stephanie.

Again.

24

Stephanie sat on the creaky sofa on her lanai, staring into the tropical darkness. She wore a yellow robe and held a glass of gin and ice in her hand. Vague pearl-drops of moonlight dripped on the silver screen of the porch; the round glass tabletop in front of her reflected the moon's residue.

It was three o'clock in the morning, again. The hour of the dead who walked the night. All Souls' Hour. Some-one had written that it was always three o'clock in the morning in the darkness of the soul.

She took a sip of gin, thinking that there was an order to the night outside and a breadth to its blackness unlike the claustrophobic chaos of her bedroom and her mind. It was a different quality of darkness. The round glass table in front of her had its place in the order of things, too; it was like a shimmering oasis, an island of muted light floating in the dark night. . . .

An island. Like the island of order and calm that Baudelaire had written about. How did it go? She wished she could remember the French; it was so much more beautiful in French. . . . *"La, tout n'est qu'ordre et beauté, luxe, calme, et volupté."* Something like that . . .

She put her bare feet up on the table, suddenly wanting to bridge the gap to that island, feeling the need for its order, its calm, and its beauty. She felt the need as Baudelaire must have felt it, cooped up in his rooms on the Ile St. Louis and smoking opium, hating the ugliness of the world and conquering it in his own way with beautiful visions, beautiful words. Stephanie could see his island, could picture herself on it with Jonathan.

My God, she thought, what arrogance! She took another long swallow of gin and listened to it slide down her throat. She was up to her old tricks again. She may have been a frightened, miserable, suffering widow, but she was also only an average housewife, a nonhelpful nonentity who didn't give a damn about the ugliness and suffering in the outside world. And there she sat, trying to feel for herself with the passion that Baudelaire had felt for the world.

How typical, she thought. She'd always done that, hadn't she? Always perpetuated the hoax of experiencing other people's feelings. . . .

And yet she could have been a decent poet. The truth was that she had never done anything well unless Fitz was with her, prodding her to get good grades in class, to speak up, to express what she felt. She had never done anything without Fitz except to become a dull housewife and mother.

Stephanie had taken her feet off the table and now sat with them on the sofa, her knees forming a high mound under the yellow robe. She rested her chin on her knees, hugged her legs, and continued to stare into the darkness outside. One frond on a palm tree moved. She saw its jagged silhouette stir briefly above the sculpted trunk, and then freeze again into the high-relief of chiseled leaves. Was anything up there? She thought of the vaulted arches of medieval cathedrals, of saw-toothed gargoyles grinning down from stone jungles. Behind the trees, the dark night was a flat background for frozen leaves and stars.

And moments like the one when Jonathan fell and Fitz fell with him.

Stephanie rattled the ice in her glass. Why couldn't she focus on the other important moments too, the ones that also mattered? She would *have* to, if she was to remember everything, if she was to glue together the fragmented pieces of her memory and come up with an answer. She should do it chronologically and precisely, she thought. She should start with the moment—a very happy moment—when she had looked up and seen Fitz standing near her after all those years. . . .

○●

It had finally stopped raining. Kent's sore throat was better, although he still had a runny nose. But Angie was sick with a fever of 102 degrees. Stephanie had been up with her for most of the night, and now they had to go back to the pediatrician's office for the third time in two weeks.

"Hi again!" the receptionist had said. "Which one today?"

"Angie, I'm afraid," Stephanie smiled feebly.

"Okay, Mrs. McMillan. Please take a seat, and Dr. Hortiner will be right with you. . . ."

Right with you, my eye, Stephanie thought. She knew

●○ 151

the routine. And of course there were no empty seats in the waiting room. There was everything else: Leggo sets and jigsaw puzzles scattered over the floor, shredded *Playschool* and *Family Health* magazines, rubber balls, plastic dolls, twelve children, ten mothers and one father, who didn't offer Stephanie his seat. A teenager staring at his toes; a fern that looked healthy despite the streptococci and staphylococci and pneumococci floating invisibly through the air. She knew the names of all the germs; she was sick of the place. She leaned against the doorway, holding Angie in her arms.

A nurse finally came and called Mrs. Driscoll. Stephanie took Mrs. Driscoll's seat; Angie was getting very heavy.

"What is there to do, mom?" Kent asked.

"Look at books, honey. Here's a Kleenex for your nose." He'll get sick all over again, she thought.

"I don't wanna look at more old books!"

"Of course you do. There's a beautiful book on horses, over there—"

"I wanna see!" Angie shifted her weight on Stephanie's lap and kicked her in the shin.

"Oow! Angie, sit still—"

"That's *my* book," a little girl said, reaching for it.

"No, you don't!" Kent cried.

"Now children, I'm sure—"

"Me!" Angie yelled. . . .

At the drug store an hour later Angie was feeling better. She wanted an ice-cream cone; Kent insisted on an ice-cream cone; Stephanie said no. They would have a nice hot lunch at home, she told them, hot broth that was good for their tummies and throats.

Back home she gave Angie her medicine and a children's aspirin, but there was no broth or soup left in the cupboard. Hell, she would have to make peanut-butter-

and-jelly sandwiches again, and she'd have to go to the market; they were almost out of milk and eggs. She poured herself a glass of sherry, which was not her habit before lunch, and thought that she should have been fixing a good meal for the children, not PB&J again. She used to spend time on their meals. Now she would have to drag them both out to the market after lunch. . . .

Angie sat in the grocery cart chewing on a dirty doll's ear while Stephanie pushed her around, while the cart grew heavier and heavier, and while Kent tugged harder and harder at her skirt. "Twinkies, mommy?" he said. "I want Hostess Twinkies. And Zingers. Can I have Zingers? And popcorn. Will you buy popcorn?"

"Peanuts? Popcorn? *Cracker Jacks?*" she yelled at him. Kent looked startled; she felt guilty. "Sure honey, anything you want; you're still my sick boy."

She dropped the third grocery bag on the third trip into the house. She dropped it half on the sidewalk, half on her foot—the one with the eggs, of course. Eggs and grape jelly and apple sauce. Why, oh why, hadn't she bought it in a can instead of a jar?

"Goodie!" Angie squealed happily. "Jelly!" She stuck her hand into the broken jar. . . .

Stephanie looked up from the mess and saw Fitz standing behind her, on the sidewalk. Seven years had passed. Seven long years.

"Greetings and salutations, mama!" Fitz said, grinning. "Long time no see." Her eyes were laughing and there was a sprinkle of mockery in her voice.

Stephanie was surprised, stunned! She felt a surge of relief; Fitz was back. Relief, and then a panicky flash of humiliation. She started to cry.

"To market, to market, to buy a fat pig!" Fitz laughed gaily. "Home again, home again, jiggety-jig! You look great to me sore old eyes, dear heart. But I must admit that seeing you like this does remind me a bit of Zorba and his full catastrophe! Anyhow, dry your tears. I've come back to stay for a while. Aren't you happy? . . ."

After the mess had been cleaned up and Angie and Kent were out of their hair—settled again in front of the television upstairs—they went into the living room. Fitz sat on a leather sofa, admiring the view of the bay. Stephanie had almost forgotten how beautiful her golden eyes were, her hair, her body.

Fitz lit a cigarette, smiled at her, and looked around. "Big room," she conceded. "It would make a great studio, wouldn't it?"

"Yes, I guess it would. Funny, but that never occurred to me. You look fantastic, Fitz! You can't imagine how happy I am to have you back."

"Oh yes I can." She smiled. "I can imagine everything, remember?"

Stephanie smiled back conspiratorially. It *was* exciting; Fitz couldn't have picked a better day to return.

"For instance," Fitz said, taking a long drag on her cigarette, "I can imagine sitting here and watching the ships coming and going on the bay, day after day—moving links to the rest of the world. I'm afraid that would be hard on me. Isn't it hard on you, dear Steph?"

"Not really," Stephanie replied. The defensive forces were marshaling in her stomach, so soon. "I'm so busy most of the time—"

"That's good," Fitz smiled. "I'm glad it doesn't bother you. But I'd go *folle* watching them. It's just not in me to live in the same place all the time. How can you say you've really known life, without traveling and experiencing as much of it as you can? TV and the movies just don't do it, love."

"I have my compensations," Stephanie said. "I have Jonathan and—"

"You have Jonathan."

"I have Jonathan."

Fitz smiled. "Living in one place and monogamy may work for you, dear heart," she said, "but I'd blow a fuse."

○●

A faint breeze was blowing in from the black space where the ocean rolled, out there beyond the palms. It seemed to Stephanie that the stars were restless, and the vague moonlight was gone from her island table; it didn't glow any longer.

She had felt the excitement of Fitz, that first day as they went into the kitchen to unpack the groceries. And she had felt envy and defensiveness, up to that point. But anger and guilt were yet to come—and then fear. Especially the fear.

Stephanie's feet were cold, and she wanted another drink. She stood up and went to fix herself one, then returned to the sofa, knowing that she should try to sleep instead. But the memories were returning fast now, and she had to face them. . . .

○●

Fitz had stopped at the Steinway on the way into the kitchen, and run her fingers lightly over the keyboard.

"It's out of tune," she declared. "You don't play anymore at all, do you?"

"I can't seem to find the time or the inclination."

"What a shame. How about your painting?"

The old inquisition, Stephanie thought; she should have known it would be this way. "Once in a while," she said. "I have an easel in the hall closet. But it makes such a mess, and the children get into the paints." She led Fitz through the dining room and into the kitchen. "Now tell me everything about *you!* It's been so—"

"Have you written any more poetry?" Fitz asked. "I

mean what have you been doing with yourself, Steph? Lunching with the ladies? It looks to me as though you're not giving yourself a chance at life. If you were, you could do—"

Stephanie whirled on her angrily. "Come off it, Fitz! I've *given* life, which is more than I can say for you!"

"Ah-ha!" Fitz said, smiling. "Mama Cat fights back with curled lip and hisses! Mama Cat and Mama House-Mouse. Mama Cow and Mama Sow, munching straw. Warm, swollen tits drooping toward open baby mouths. Fine, dear heart; that's just beautiful. The world needs mamas, I love mamas. . . ." She frowned, looking concerned. "But what about time for yourself? Doesn't Jonathan encourage you to do *something* for yourself? Don't *you* want to love yourself, too?"

Stephanie felt it then, the first stirring of fear. "You've always expected too much of me," she said.

"Not too much. Something."

"You've always pushed me."

"Not far enough."

"You won't leave me alone about all that?"

"Not again. That was a mistake."

"But you're supposed to love me; you're my best friend!"

"That's why," Fitz said.

"Can't you see that I'm not special, like you?"

"Everyone is special. Most people only use a tenth of their potential, Stephie. Only one-tenth!"

"No!" Stephanie whispered. "I'm not special. I'm just an ordinary, untalented housewife and always will be."

"I don't think so," Fitz said. "Because I'm going to have a lot to say about that, now." The light from the kitchen windows played on her golden eyes; the pupils were miniscule. She closed her eyes slowly, with satisfaction, wrinkled her nose playfully, and then opened her eyes again quickly and very wide. They were the facial movements of a cat, Stephanie thought, watching her. She would play with her, play with her domestic ball of yarn as a kitten plays, gleefully unraveling her long string of wound-up securities. She would pounce on her rolled-up ego.

Stephanie turned away from Fitz and began unloading the groceries, taking them from their brown bags and putting them onto the maple counter. Bread, Hostess Twinkies, English muffins. Her arms were trembling. Cherry yogurt, spiced apple yogurt, two cans of Campbell's Chunky Beef soup . . .

"You've been married over seven years," Fitz stated from behind her. "That's a long time. A very long time."

A bunch of bananas, a head of lettuce, a pound of onions, a large bottle of Heinz catsup. "A lifetime is not too long for us," Stephanie said. Jonathan insisted on Heinz and no other brand; it was a family joke—

Fitz made a whistling sound, and Stephanie faced her. Fitz's eyebrows were up.

"You don't know anything about it!" Stephanie blurted out. "You breeze through life giving away your talents and your body like glorious gifts of providence, without ever committing yourself to anyone! I think you're too selfish to take care of anyone but yourself. You don't believe in devotion to others; you'll never understand the power of an emotional bond—"

"I believe in butterflies."

"What!?"

"Butterflies," Fitz smiled. "Among other things. The beauty of butterflies, escaped from the chrysalis." Stephie's attack hadn't fazed her. "You've forgotten about them, Steph. The ones in your stomach—the ones you used to feel fluttering in there every time Jonathan walked into the room, remember? The prickly, itchy, alive expectations. It's a theory of mine, the law of diminishing returns—"

"Bully for your theories." Stephanie turned back to her groceries.

"It applies to things as well as people," Fitz went on. "The more you commit yourself emotionally—the more dependent you become on someone else, on a set routine, even on a room in a house—the less interior excitement you feel. Everything flattens out, doesn't it?"

Baked beans, tortillas, two packages of chicken thighs, a rump roast—

"Don't you agree that there's something incongruous about the physical diminishing as the emotional dependency increases?"

Frozen peas, a bunch of broccoli, Tuna Helper—

"Being physical is being alive!" Fitz insisted. "I like my butterflies still fluttering."

"And I love Jonathan. That's still the most important thing. But, I. . . ."

"But what?"

Frozen corn, two quarts of chocolate ice cream. "But . . . but I guess you're right, about the butterflies."

Fitz smiled a victorious smile that was more chilling than the puff of cold air Stephanie felt as she opened the freezer door. She knew that Fitz was already on her way to corrupting something inside her. On the first day back. No wonder she was frightened. . . .

And it was only the beginning.

25

Jonathan was actually a very attractive man. Fitz was surprised. He hadn't thickened much around the middle because he played tennis often; he wasn't losing his hair, he was in good shape for a man in his late thirties. His large biceps were visible when he wore tennis shirts; Fitz thought biceps were a turn-on—and calf muscles, and strong muscles in the thighs. Jonathan's legs were really quite good. He moved well, he danced well, he could be a good lover. She was sure he could be a superb lover, given the proper inspiration.

It was a week later, and Fitz had settled into her still-sparse studio; her paintings and other important belongings would soon arrive from Paris. She had what she needed most: an easel, paints, and a bed; a leather sofa would be delivered tomorrow. It had been great fun, shopping with Stephanie. . . .

Jonathan had charm. It was a damn shame his job and his life were so stultifying, that he had made such unimaginative choices and forced them on Stephanie. Their life was as dull as dog shit.

She walked into the kitchen and poured herself a Courvoisier. What Jonathan needed, for Stephie's sake, was inspiration. Attacking him and their marriage and their lifestyle weren't really working so far; Stephanie obviously depended on him too much and still lacked faith in herself. He was totally inadequate as a partner. But he could change his life, he could learn. . . .

She had to seduce him.

She had to make him her ally instead of her enemy. . . get the sweetest kind of revenge, winning him over, for Stephie's sake. Stephie wouldn't be hurt because she'd never know. And it would be lovely to have power, again. For their own good.

26

Stephanie shook her head, ran her fingers through her short streaked hair, and looked up.

A sickly gray, wavering light was stealing through the darkness, weaving through the grove of palm trees like the diffused flashlight rays of a thief. Dawn, again. The light-fingered prowler that crept up on your subconscious, bumped carelessly into it, and then absconded with your peace, your privacy, and your imagination. She was beginning to dread the dawn as much as everything else—as much as her memories, and Fitz, and even Nicholas Hanson and all his questions.

But she had nothing to fear from the memory of Jonathan himself, she knew. He was blameless. There was too much consolation for her in his innocence, in his sturdy reliability, in his motionless principles that would never have betrayed her. No one could take away his devotion to her; Fitz couldn't take it away from her, even now. He had to be the same after death as he was before. . . .

○●

Jonathan was sitting in his favorite leather chair during the cocktail hour, ten days after Fitz had returned. He had showered and changed into brown knit slacks and a yellow cardigan, with a paisley ascot at his neck, He looked fresh, smooth-faced, casual. Stephanie loved the way his still-wet hair was slowly dipping down over his forehead, descending as it dried.

"Change our lifestyle, darling?" he had asked in reply to her question. "Whatever for?"

Stephanie looked out the living-room window; a large dark freighter with a red, white, and blue smoke-stack was steaming toward the Golden Gate. "I don't know," she said. "Maybe just to do something different?"

Jonathan eyed her over the rim of his martini glass, then took a sip and replaced the glass carefully on a coaster. He usually did everything carefully. "You mean change just for the sake of change? Hell no, honey. I don't believe in that."

"It was just a thought—"

"Well, it's a crazy thought to me, when you look at what I've got! A gorgeous wife, two cute kids, a good job. Too many bills, it's true. . . . But this is a great house in one of the most desirable cities in the world. Why would I want to change anything?" He took another sip of his martini and grinned at her.

"I know it doesn't make much sense," Stephanie said. "But doesn't it ever bother you to see your whole life laid out before you? To shave every morning and know what you'll be doing every day? Approximately?" She knew that sounded stupid, and she buried her nose in her glass of bourbon and soda.

Jonathan's smile was tolerant; he'd had a good day. "We never know, of course. But no, it doesn't bother me at all, maybe only once in a while. I consider myself lucky, all things considered."

"That's redundant," she said, and smiled.

"Is it? Sorry, teach." He stuck his tongue out at her, stood up, and walked across the room to pour himself one more drink.

Stephanie spoke to his back; "But wouldn't you like to try something else? I mean, aren't you curious to know what it would be like to be an explorer in Africa? Or a photographer traveling all over the place? An English teacher in Europe, maybe. You could do that; there are so many things you could do with your intelligence, and we have enough money, don't we? You could take the whole family and go anywhere, try anything. . . ."

"What's got into you?" He turned to face her, frowning. "For Christ's sake be practical, honey! Think of the kids' schooling, their health, their stability. Suppose I grabbed you all up and went gallivanting off in search of some dream, something new. I'd need training, first of all. And what if I failed, then what would we do? No job to come home to, and it would probably screw up a good marriage." He waved his hand in dismissal.

"Tell me honestly, Jonathan—" Stephanie looked out the window again. "Haven't you ever wanted other women?"

"What the hell has that got to do with it?" His voice was sharp, for Jonathan. "Sure. What man hasn't?" She looked at him; he smiled. "I'm only normal, darling. But playing around isn't my bag, and you know it. It's not worth the gamble of losing you." He walked over to her and kissed her on the forehead, then sat down again and crossed his ankles. "Nothing is worth gambling away what we have, believe me."

Stephanie had nodded her head in agreement. . . .

○●

She could see the palm trees clearly now. They stood at attention on a field of sand, outlined against the gray haze of dawn. Their formation was irregular and their fronded helmets askew; a general would never have approved. But they stood stoically prepared for battle, nonetheless—for battle with another day.

She was wearing down, Stephanie realized. She was losing the will to fight. If it weren't for the children. . . .

How many times over the years, and in how many

different moods, had she said, "If it weren't for the children?" Too many, too many. Perhaps she *had* begun to
change a little, listening to Fitz. But Jonathan never had.
She was sure that nothing could have happened between
Jonathan and Fitz, no matter how hard Fitz had tried.

Something began to uncoil inside Stephanie, a cobra
preparing to strike.

How did she know that Fitz had tried?

*"You should have listened to me!" Fitz screamed at Jon-
athan in the living room. Jonathan was backing away from her.
"You should have listened! I gave you my time and energy and
love and you should have listened!"*

So they had been alone together, Stephanie realized.
When?
How often?

27

Exterior light, interior shadow.

Perfect, Fitz had thought. Perfect for this preliminary occasion.

She was sitting in front of her easel. Morning light
entered through the balcony doors, and shadows cast by
her Mexican shower tree dappled the blankness of her
large canvas. A palette dotted with mounds of oil paints
was balanced across her thighs; her eyes glowed in anticipation.

There was nothing like the excitement of a bare canvas, no agitation, no challenge as great as the knowledge
that she could create her own world on it. She could

change that blank whiteness into anything she desired: into any place she wanted to be, into any state of mind or body, into any person she wanted to be—or wanted to possess.

She dipped her brush into burnt sienna. Fitz was quick and agile with her brush; within minutes she had sketched a side view of Jonathan's brain. Then she sectioned it correctly; she had checked a copy of *Gray's Anatomy* out of the library and studied the brain carefully, over the last few days. She knew the medial surface of the left cerebral hemisphere by heart—the cingulate gyrus, the precuneus, and paracentral lobule. The side view of Jonathan's brain floated alone on the large canvas; she topped it loosely with a frontal view of his wavy brown hair.

It was a large brain, four feet across by two feet high. In its center she painted Jonathan's soft brown eyes.

It took her over an hour to get the eyes just right, and then she began to work on his brain. She painted red and blue poker chips and a deck of cards inside the superior frontal gyrus. Jonathan had to be taught to gamble, figuratively speaking. Next she placed a globe of the world in the center of the paracentral lobule, and painted its background a sky blue; Jonathan should want work that involved travel. Then the precuneus was meticulously filled with a small typewriter, a T-square, scuba gear, a camera, a sextant, and an archeologist's kit. The background for that section of his brain was bright yellow.

All those details took her until noon, and by then she was thirsty. She put her brushes into turpentine, stood up and stretched, and went to the kitchen for a Pepsi. The phone rang but she ignored it; she didn't want to lose her concentration. . . .

Red—she would use a deep passionate red for the corpus callosum at the center of his brain, she thought.

She sat back down and in that section painted a small Stephanie, naked and surrounded by three, four, five other naked women whom Jonathan would want, and have. So that Stephanie could have three, or four, or five men. . . .

But Jonathan would have Fitz, first. And in the middle of the cingulate gyrus she painted a larger image of herself, reclining seductively in space.

The brain was completed—a multicolored, disembodied brain that floated before her, with Jonathan's eyes in the center. They looked directly into hers.

"I need your hands now," she said aloud, smiling. "And of course your cock."

She raised the level of her easel bar so that the canvas was higher. It was difficult, doing hands; the larger they were the harder it was to paint them. And Jonathan's hands had to be very large. Fitz placed them beneath the brain and on either side of it, very low on the canvas. When she had finished, his fingers reached out to her, grasping at space, as adrift as the opened head above them. Then she started on his genitals. Just for the fun of it she made his testicles somewhat hairy, in contrast to the underside of his smooth, erect penis that jutted up in the center of the portrait. An exercise in textures; her flesh tones were excellent. . . .

It was fun, making love to Jonathan that way.

Fitz glanced at her watch; it was almost four o'clock. She stepped back from the canvas and examined Jonathan's portrait. It would work. It would work beautifully, for what she had in mind, the brain was filled with exactly the right stimuli, the right associations. And Jonathan's genitals and hands were the perfect size and proportion. He would need to use more than his brain, if he was to become a life-lover.

All this preliminary business was great fun—until

she got her hands on the real Jonathan, tonight. Of course she wouldn't show him the portrait; maybe later, when she had won him over.

But that would take time. . . .

Starting tonight.

○●

"You're . . . incredible," Jonathan had said.

Lighted candles were placed on tables around the studio, and an orange pink fire spread feathers of fanlight over the brick chimney. Fitz lay like a pagan princess on the leather sofa, her arms stretched above her head. Her skin glowed through the diaphanous folds of her hetaera's toga.

"You're . . . exquisite," Jonathan murmured. He was sitting opposite her in an armchair. "I really have to go now—"

Fitz smiled, and placed her hands on her breasts.

"Don't," he said.

She played with her breasts, and ran her hands down her thighs.

"Please—"

Fitz pulled at the filmy fabric of her toga, so that it crept slowly up her bare brown legs.

"Stop it." Jonathan's voice was a husky whisper. He stood.

She pulled the toga higher up her thighs, revealing her pale, untanned triangle.

Jonathan stood above her, watching.

Fitz spread her legs.

"Oh, Christ," Jonathan groaned, and knelt down to her offering. "I'm sorry, Stephanie. . . ."

28

Nicholas Hanson was sitting on the low stone wall of the terrace, smoking a cigarette and looking at Stephanie as she walked toward him. Jonathan hadn't looked at her that way for years.

The first other man.

"Hello," he said, smiling. "How was your night?" His eyes were the color of the ocean close to shore; they made her feel uneasy after what had happened the prior night.

"I didn't sleep much," she replied, and looked away. "I'm having trouble separating my dreams from my memories." *Don't do that,* she said to herself. *Don't tell him even that much.*

"That's natural," Nicholas said, nodding, "when your nerves are frazzled." He pointed to a table in the corner of the terrace. "Let's sit here this morning."

The tablecloths were pink again; Stephanie was wearing white slacks and a cotton shirt almost the same shade of pink. As Nicholas pulled out her chair for her she wondered how they did the laundry in such a remote place. Some poor peasant woman probably washed it in a stream, scrubbed it on rocks and then laid it out to dry over the same rocks. It was this kind of view of the "real" world that Fitz wanted for her.

Nicholas was studying the menu; his handsome face was becoming too familiar. It wasn't the real world, though; she had to remember that it wasn't and never could be. She looked up at the mountains; they seemed less threatening in the morning sunlight.

Nicholas cleared his throat and smiled at her again. "I thought about you all night."

The waiter was pouring coffee, and their eyes locked over his white-coated arm. It seemed to Stephanie that it took forever to pour the coffee. Nicholas would not let go of her eyes.

"I dreamed about you," he whispered.

"Last night," she said. "You promised—"

"To try."

"You're not trying very hard."

"I know."

"Listen, Nicholas, I—"

"I want to know everything about you, every inch of you—"

"Oh, please—"

"*Por favor,*" the waiter grinned.

Good Lord, Stephanie thought—all this in front of a waiter. . . .

"*Huevos rancheros,*" Nicholas said to him, with his eyes still on her. "*Dos, y dos papavas, gracias.*" The waiter disappeared. "I had fantastic dreams about you."

"Don't," she murmured.

"We came so close." He leaned forward, collecting the tension between them.

"I'm afraid," Stephanie said. "I shouldn't be talking about this; it's out of the question." Was it? she asked herself. If Jonathan really had betrayed her with Fitz. . . .

"I'll kiss away your fear," Nicholas said.

"No!"

"We'll spend the day together. I have a great idea—"

"I'm not even sure I want to go on living!"

His face hung suspended before her; she thought his eyes were trying to echo her own dismay. But something else was registered in them—surprise at first, and then anger. "Christ," he muttered, "don't be ridiculous.

You have too much to live for. I'm taking you into Acapulco today."

"What?"

"Acapulco. It's only a forty-minute flight, and the
change of scenery will do you good."

○●

The new jet airport of Zihautenejo was in the jungle
behind the village; two enormous concrete slabs sliced
through the greenery like machetes. Stephanie noticed
that the plane they were boarding was a Boeing 727, and
thought that she hadn't noticed things like that before.
She wished it were a decrepit, battered machine that
might shudder and split in midair and be lost along with
her memories on a ridge of the Sierra Madre del Sur, and
the children would live in Connecticut with a Saint Ber-
nard after all. . . .

"Are you sure you won't let me pay for my ticket?"
she heard herself say.

Nicholas shook his head and maneuvered her into a
window seat. There was something facetious in his evasion
of that subject, as if he felt she was incapable of doing
anything for him or for herself. It bothered her that he
thought of her that way.

"The reason there are so few people on the plane,"
Nicholas explained, while casually eying the stewardess
who walked past them smilingly, "is that this whole development is so new. They're spending seventeen million
dollars at Ixtapa, a little to the north. By the way—"

The engines started, and the captain's voice came
over the speaker; they listened while Nicholas fastened his
seat belt and checked hers. "As I was saying," he went on,
"I'd like to take you up to the Catalina for drinks and dinner tonight. It's the oldest hotel here, and the view is spec-
tacular."

"I don't know," Stephanie said in a low voice. "I—"

"I first came here in the late fifties," Nicholas continued, ignoring her. The plane was taxiing down the runway. "I wish they'd leave the whole area alone and not destroy it like Puerto Vallarta has been destroyed by all those San Franciscans and jet-setters who build houses there. The ethnic flavor's gone, the foreign remoteness that we still have here. Vallarta's become a playground for socialites, ever since Liz and Burton. They fly down for the usual rounds of Christmas and Easter parties with the usual people and drink margaritas instead of the usual martinis. Jesus. I won't ever go back to Vallarta; I liked the fishing village and the Oceano, the only hotel there. Now there are twenty high-rises that I can't afford and don't want to stay in."

Stephanie knew some of the San Franciscans he was referring to. She had been to occasional parties with them, and she envied them.

"They've even changed the name of the beach at Vallarta," Nicholas remarked, releasing his seat belt and lighting a cigarette as the plane climbed up and out over the bay, circling southward. "*Los Muertos* wasn't good for the *tourista* business."

"*Los Muertos?*" Stephanie asked, "What does that mean?"

"The dead," Nicholas answered, then frowned. "I'm sorry—"

He took her hand and she looked out the window at the diminishing coastline, remembering Jonathan. Everything was a hazy blue and lumpy green outside her window. Jonathan and parties. The appeal of travel *was* in the remoteness, the sense of being truly away. . . . Parties. . . . There was one party in particular, shortly after Fitz had come back. . . .

"I'd like to sleep a little," she said. "I'm so tired."

"Of course." Nicholas squeezed her hand; a long, muscle in his tanned forearm tensed briefly.

She leaned back and closed her eyes; the engines purred. That party had been important, she remembered. It was a party at Jack and Carol Simpson's, and it was the night that Fitz had really *moved in on her.* She had always secretly hated parties, but she hid her dread behind a forced smile. She had hated all parties until Fitz came back, until that night at the Simpsons'. . . .

○●

The beige living room was stuffed like the hot mushrooms that were passed on silver trays. It seemed to Stephanie that the room was filled with human hors d'oeuvres: celery-stalk females choreographing poise, small clusters of carrot-stick males, a few plump olives eying the whole scene. . . . Here we go again, she thought, as Jonathan removed her coat. Pressure, pretensions, camouflaged comparisons—

Carol Simpson: black velvet, pearls, straight brown hair, straight nose. "Stephanie! Jonathan! Marvelous to see you both! Where have you been hiding, Stephanie? I never see you, I don't think I've seen you since where was it? Was it at Walter Landor's?"

"I don't think so," Stephanie said, not wanting to admit that they had never been invited to Walter Landon's ferry boat. "I can't remember—"

"You know Barbara, don't you?" Carol asked. "And Bill Perkins, and Melinda Barlow. . . ."

Barbara Norstrom: basic brown, circular gold pin on the shoulder, thin face, the ripple of a bosom under the basic brown. Smith College incarnate. "Hello, Stephanie. I was just telling Bill here about the exhibit at the Focus Gallery. Have you seen it? No? Well my *dear,* you simply must! This man Morrell is simply *divine* with a camera.

I'm surprised you haven't heard about him. He takes—"

Bill Perkins: big, bored, soft, an aquiline nose disappearing between puffy cheeks, prematurely fortyish. He was kind; he smiled at her with patient pink-rimmed eyes.

Melinda Barlow: tall, tanned, hazel-eyed, gregarious. Object of envy, traveler to Puerto Vallarta.

Sandy Winters: organizer. Short, dark, and bossy, hiding her envy of more attactive women behind beady brown eyes, shoving her worth around in front of her. Invulnerable, on the surface.

Jonathan: at her side as usual, handing her a drink.

A brunette: languid, purple-jerseyed, doe-eyed, sharp nosed. Sidling up to Jonathan, smiling at him heavily, offering him mauve finger tips.

". . . Of course it was expensive," Melinda Barlow was saying, "but it was one of the most exciting things I've ever done! When that helicopter dipped, my heart dipped with it—right over the edge of that first cliff, down four thousand feet to the valley floor and back up again. It was incredible; the beauty, the wildness, the two-thousand-foot free-fall waterfall. *"NaPali,"* the natives call them." She turned to Stephanie. "Have you ever been to the islands?" Her hazel eyes sparkled.

Stephanie hated to dull them. "No," she answered, smiling her forced smile. "We usually take the children to Santa Barbara on vacations."

"Oh? Well, that's lovely, of course." Melinda's eyes were still friendly, but a quick, blank look had flitted through them. "If you ever get a chance, though—"

She was so plain, compared to Melinda.

"How are my two favorite *frauleins?*" someone said at Stephanie's elbow. She turned; Jack Simpson was smiling at her with friendly politeness. How long, she suddenly wondered, had she wanted *more* than friendly politeness in the eyes of other men?

"I can't stand to see two women talking together at my parties," Jack said. "It's a form of crime and punishment." He winked at her, waiting for an answer, and then turned to Melinda. Of course; she hadn't come up with an answer. He was attractive and charming and had grown a mustache that enhanced his profile. She watched him talk to Melinda, not hearing the words, thinking that the profile would be all she would get of him the rest of the evening.

She looked at Jonathan. He was lighting the brunette's cigarette.

"Who are your choices for the school board?" It was Sandy Winters, a woman who couldn't ask a question without accusing Stephanie, without challenging her to provide the correct answer.

"I haven't decided," Stephanie said. Not true: she didn't even know who was running. She hadn't read enough about the election yet. "Whom do you recommend?" She watched her grammar, with Sandy.

Sandy Winters started to talk, grateful for an audience, feeling worthwhile. Her husband was on the far side of the room. Sandy's husband was always on the far side of the room.

But so was Jonathan, sitting down on a window seat with the brunette in purple jersey, who draped herself next to him.

"—sense of responsibility," Sandy was expounding. "With two children going into the system, Stephanie, you *should* take a big interest in the problems. It's your duty. You have to agree that—"

Help! Help! Help!, Stephanie thought. She didn't have to agree to anything. She didn't have to stand there being lectured to; she didn't even have to be at this party. . . .

She looked up and saw Fitz entering the room, drifting toward her. Fitz's tall beauty was a standout even in the crowded room, but people were so busy invading and avoiding one another at the same time that no one seemed to notice her. Sandy was still prattling; Jonathan and the brunette were warming up together in rapt conversation, her hand resting gracefully on his arm. . . .

"Pep up!" Fitz whispered in Stephanie's ear. "You look like a drowning rat."

How did Fitz always know, Stephanie thought, always show up when Stephie didn't feel like fighting? It was as if she had never been gone all those years. Stephie smiled sweetly and blankly at Sandy Winters, then turned away from her in the middle of her illuminating sentence. Sandy muffled a protest.

"That dress is fabulous on you," Fitz said. "You're the most gorgeous woman in the room—next to me, of course. So act it!"

The dress was fabulous because Fitz had picked it out for her two days earlier, in the lingerie department of Saks. She would never tell Jonathan it had come from lingerie; he would have been shocked. It was clinging bright blue and very low cut, but apparently he preferred purple jersey. . . .

"It's okay about Jonathan," Fitz said, smiling. "You'll see."

"How can you say that? He's been with her since we arrived—"

"Shh! Look, it's time to go in for dinner. I'll meet you in the powder-piss place right afterward, and then we'll hash this out. Now chin up!"

The powder room was papered in shiny gold and bronze squares like oriental tiles, and one entire wall above the basin was a mirror. Fitz was sitting on the toilet with the lid down. Stephanie had locked the door. "The world is alive," Fitz said, "with the sound of music . . . tra la la la la. . . ."

"Shut up, Fitz," Stephanie said. "It's not funny."

"Pull yourself together, love. A whole new world is about to start rotating on your axis. I think we can even swing it without Esalen or est!"

"What in God's name are you blathering about? Melinda thinks I'm dull, and she's right. Sandy is convinced I'm an uncommitted idiot, and she's right. And Jonathan is talking to that brunette again now! I bet he could hardly wait to get through dinner to talk to her some more!"

"I know he is, dear heart. But you're about to discover how exciting and scintillating little Stephie Borders can be, because you're going to rise to the occasion with all stops out. You're going to corner Melinda and tell her that by next month you'll be in Mexico or Machu Picchu; you haven't decided which. And you're going to tell Sandy that you've been so busy organizing an in-school opera program for the schools that you've no time to read pamphlets. Don't look so startled. I'll help you do it."

"Fitz, I—"

"And you're really going to open up when it comes to the men, sweetheart. It'll be easy, you'll see. This challenge, this jealousy, is good for you. Who knows? One of these days you may even bring yourself to suck cock." She smiled sweetly.

"Oh God, I *hate* your vulgarity!" Stephanie exploded. "If you think *that's* what it takes for me to hold on, you're sadly mistaken. We have a good sex life. Jonathan would be shocked if I suddenly—"

"I doubt that."

Fitz's smile was enigmatic, as if she knew something about Jonathan that Stephie didn't know. Stephanie wondered what it was.

"But *revenons à nos moutons, chérie,*" Fitz said. "First of all, not one glance in Jonathan's direction, okay? No octopus for a wifie, that's a no-no. Secondly, come on strong to the sexiest man out there—that would be Jack Simpson or Tony Barlow—and wow him, baby! Dazzle him with your wit! Look deep into his eyes! Stare at his balls if you have to—"

"I can't. I'm no good at flirting. Jonathan—"

"He's busy, baby. Remember?" Fitz grinned. "What are you fighting for, anyway?"

"I'm not sure—"

There was a knock on the door. "Anyone in there?" someone asked. Stephanie leaned past Fitz and flushed the toilet. "Be right out!" she called.

Fitz winked. "Remember you're the best looking, smartest broad in the whole room. You'll have Jonathan drinking out of your slipper. Now go to it, Cinderella."

Stephanie put on lipstick, smoothed her hair, and opened the door to a pinched-face Joanie Perkins. She hoped Fitz would get off the can for Joanie; it would be just like Fitz, Stephanie thought, to sit there on her throne until Joanie wet her pants. . . .

○●

She had worked on Jack Simpson and she had won. She had drunk two brandies quickly and then walked up to him and watched him melt slowly along with her own reserve. She teased him casually about his mustache and toyed with her pearls, dipping them in and out of her bodice. She asked him about his job; she listened with her eyes. It was invigorating to use her attractiveness on another man, to use it with a purpose. She began to talk about herself, and the more she talked the more Jack's dark eyes probed hers, strayed to her shoulders, her chest, and back up into her eyes. . . .

"You did what?" Jack asked, returning from a distracted cruise along her neck and throat.

"I dedicated it to Dag Hammarskjöld, because I felt sorry for him," she said. "They actually printed it in the *Paris Review,* and in *Le Canard Enchainé,* in translation. Can you imagine?"

"I'm beginning to imagine lots of things. What does *Le Canard Enchainé* mean, anyway?" His eyes were on her mouth.

"It's an idiom for a trapped misconception, or falsehood. But I always called it a tongue-tied quack, which was more appropriate in the case of my poem."

Jack smiled. His teeth were very white, and it occurred to Stephanie that he probably didn't nibble like Jonathan when *he* kissed; he probably kissed with strength, and brutality. Maybe she had made a mistake to know only one man in her life—

"I hate to break this up," Jonathan said affably, showing his crow's feet, "but everyone's leaving, and I think we should too, darling."

She looked around; the brunette was gone. For how long? She didn't really care.

"Oh, no, please stay!" Jack said. "Let's have a nightcap together—"

"Thanks, Jack." Jonathan smiled. "But we really must go. The kids will wake up early tomorrow, per usual. Lovely, marvelous party—"

They were both silent on the drive home. Stephanie was thinking about Jack Simpson's white teeth, and about how happy she was that Fitz was back. . . .

"What a lifeless, proper lot your friends are for the most part," Fitz had said the next day. "Going . . . going . . . *gone!* Easy, uncluttered lives. Blah. I'd love to pluck them out of their sorority-fraternity, club-club, glub-glub mentality and heat up their asses!"

She exaggerated, she always exaggerated everything. Fitz *was* exaggeration personified. So why did Stephanie listen to Fitz? Because Fitz was fun and amusing and right about a lot of things. . . .

○●

The engines dropped a tone and the plane dipped slightly; Stephanie opened her eyes and looked at Nicholas, her guardian Lochinvar who regarded her avidly the way Jack Simpson had looked at her. Only Fitz wasn't there to prompt her; Fitz was gone from her life, and she didn't know what had happened to her. . . .

"There's Acapulco," Nicholas said and pointed out the window. "We'll land south of it. That's Sunset Beach directly below us."

"It *is* beautiful," she remarked as the plane tilted toward the huge bay. The distinction between mountains and gardens, between mass and movement, between white hotels and pink houses and automobiles and people grew sharper as they descended upon them, until reality rose to meet them and the wheels of the plane bounced on hard concrete.

○●

She and Nicholas had been having a lovely day until they ran into his friend Charlie. She had almost forgotten about Jonathan and Fitz, and even the children for the first time in a month. She had been having a truly good time with Nicholas. On their way in from the airport the taxi had stopped at Las Brissas, the famous hotel at the south end of the bay, where the guests had private bungalows that sprawled down the mountain, and each bungalow had a private swimming pool and even a private jeep if the guests wanted it. In the lobby Nicholas had laughed and spoken in Spanish with the man behind the desk, who had eyed her with eyebrows that jumped up and down like Groucho Marx's until she laughed out of embarrassment, not knowing that Nicholas was telling him about her. Nicholas had said that it was good to see her laugh and blush, and then they had had cocktails and lunch in the German restaurant at the top of the hotel, high above the ocean, looking out over everything. It was the most beautiful site for a hotel she had ever seen.

After a delicious lunch and wine and liqueurs they went walking around the Zocalo, or main square, in the indigenous part of Acapulco, a block away from the Costera Miguel Aleman, the big street that ran along the ocean. Nicholas taught her silly phrases in Spanish, like "poor horse" and "sunny sidewalk" and "one hundred hands" and "dizzy blonds," and she forgot that she had ever been afraid or suspicious of him. . . .

"You mustn't be angry with me, Stephanie," Nicholas said later, in his friend's small office. "Don't be angry, please. It occurred to me suddenly, as soon as I looked over Charlie's place here and saw the PSE set-up that it might be a way to help you remember. . . ."

His arm had been around her shoulder as they crossed a street off the Zocalo, and he had been laughing at the way she was trying to remember *encanecer*—which means to get gray-headed—when Charlie tapped Nicholas on the shoulder. He was a small man with dusty shoes and narrow eyes and an ingratiating smile that she didn't like. Charlie had done the "long-time-no-see" routine with Nicholas and smiled at her and invited them to his office-apartment three blocks away for wine and cheese.

"Nice place you've got here," Nicholas said to him. "Been here long?"

It *wasn't* a nice place, Stephanie thought. The living room was small, hot, and crowded with brown wicker furniture stuffed with old colored cushions that looked as if they needed to be aired and puffed. They had wine and cheese there, and then Charlie asked her the first innocent questions.

"Where are you from?" Charlie said, when there was still cheese in his mouth.

That was called a control question, Nicholas explained to her later. He told her that he had had the idea when they had walked through Charlie's office to get to the living room, and while she was in the bathroom he had asked Charlie to set up a hidden microphone in the living room. They must have set it up very fast, she thought.

"Great city, San Francisco," Charlie said. "Were you born there?"

Control question number two, she learned afterward. "No," she answered. "Kansas City, Missouri." She had always added the "Missouri."

"And where did you meet old Nicholas here?" Charlie took a casual sip of wine to wash down more cheese.

Old Nicholas; Old Saint Nicholas, Stephanie thought now. "In Zihautenejo," she had answered, smiling at Nicholas, who was stroking a large gray cat curled up in his lap. She didn't like cats; Nicholas's eyes were much prettier than the cat's eyes. "Only two days ago."

"Tell him how madly attracted to me you are," Nicholas said.

"Are you madly attracted to Nicholas?" Charlie spread more cheese on a cracker and smiled his cloying smile.

"I don't know him well enough," she said.

"Stephanie's a recent widow, Charlie. We shouldn't press her on that one." There was something slightly condenscending in his tone. The fantasy of Las Brissas and the Zocalo was beginning to disintegrate; she wished they had never seen Charlie.

"I'm sorry," Charlie said. "Do you have any kids?"

180 ○●

"Two."

"How old?"

"Six and three."

"What are their names?"

"Kent and Angela." She drained half a glass of red wine that tasted somewhat sour. She wanted to leave.

"I'm sorry," Charlie said again. "Excuse me a minute, will you?" He stood up suddenly and walked out of the room.

"Where's he gone?" she asked Nicholas.

"Probably to the john. You're not enjoying this much, are you?"

"Not really. But if he's an old friend of yours—"

"Say no more," he said, and smiled. "I'll get us out of here. I thought today would help you forget Fitz."

"Fitz? Why do you mention her, all of a sudden?" She was sick of that small, hot room. "You promised me no more questions!"

"I'm sorry," Nicholas said, and he pulled a package of cigarettes out of his pocket. The cat jumped down from his lap. "I'm just so curious about whether she really left that night. I only want to help you remember."

"I told you Fitz left," she said flatly. "I want to go now."

"So she didn't kill Jonathan."

"No, she didn't kill Jonathan! No one killed Jonathan. Jonathan fell off the balcony accidentally."

"And you didn't push him?"

She stared at Nicholas. His eyebrows shot up; he looked as surprised as she was at his own question, as numbed by the possibility of its implication as she felt. She stood, knocking her glass of wine off the table with her purse. He sat motionless, an unlit cigarette held stiffly between his fingers.

"The idea that that could even occur to you makes

me sick to my stomach," she said, feeling nauseated. "I could never have killed Jonathan. I loved him. I want to go home."

The cigarette twitched between his fingers. "I'm sorry," he said. "I don't know what came over me. Of course we'll go. Please stay here a minute while I make our apologies to Charlie."

The door of the office closed behind him and she stood weakly in the center of that hot, dusty room, hating it, hating Charlie, hating the cat that stared at her from a dusty colored cushion, hating Nicholas for the dissolution of the day's happy dream, glad she had spilled red wine on Charlie's rug. Whatever she and Nicholas had shared earlier was gone with his question. Half of the Acapulco day was dead, like half of her life.

She heard their voices whispering in the office; she knew they were whispering. What was taking so long? She had to get out of there. She pushed open the door to the office, and heard her own voice: *Kent and Angela.*

Her own voice. *Kent . . . and . . . Angela. . . .* Drawn out, very slow, very steady. *Kent and Angela. . . . Where's he gone?* And then Nicholas's voice: *Probably to the john.* Very slow, very drawn out.

"Normally," Charlie said, smiling his sickening smile at her, "—normally, I would retranscribe only *your* voice onto the graph. But we didn't have time for that. I'm afraid you'll have to put up with Nicholas's voice also."

"Charlie's an expert at this," Nicholas said. "Please sit down, Stephanie. . . ."

The Psychological Stress Evaluator, she learned, was a relatively new system for detecting lies. It consisted of a microphone, a tape recorder, a moving strip chart of graph paper, and a pen that you couldn't see attached to a sensor device, all of which were contained in a black attaché case. The attaché case sat on Charlie's desk in that hot office; the two reels of tape were in the lid, turning around slowly and repeating her voice:

You promised me no more questions!

"The PSE is the most accurate, versatile, probing, and effective method of "Lie Detection" ever developed," the brochure said. Nicholas had given her the brochure. "The tape recording preserves the speech pattern containing the voluntarily formed words. The PSE-1, by using electronic filtering and frequency discrimination techniques, detects, measures, and graphically displays on a moving strip chart certain stress-related components of the human voice. Superimposed on audible voice frequencies are inaudible frequency modulations (FM) whose strength and pattern relate inversely to the degree of psychological stress in the speaker."

I told you she left. I want to leave now.

"The instrument measures 3 parameters: cardiovascular and respiratory activities of the auto-nervous system, and the micro-muscle tremor (physiological tremor) of the central nervous system. The voice acts as the carrier of these physiological reactions to psychological stimuli."

No, she didn't kill Jonathan! No one killed Jonathan. Jonathan fell off the balcony accidentally.

"Stress, induced by fear, guilt, anxiety, or conflict facilitates detection of attempted deception."

And you didn't push him?

The voice is recorded at 7½ inches per second and played back at $^{15}/_{16}$ths of an inch per second—"

The idea that that could even occur to you makes me sick to my stomach. I could never have killed Jonathan. I loved him. I want to go home.

They were hunched like two vultures over the bones of her voice. She wanted to go home. Thank God, thank God he hadn't asked her where Fitz was; he hadn't asked her if Fitz was alive or dead. She missed Angie and Kent; she wanted them there with her, sitting on her lap. . . .

"Come here, Stephanie," Nicholas said. "I think you should see this." He was looking at her strangely. She was right to have mistrusted him; he was not her friend.

"You've been protecting your friend Fitz," he said. Charlie smiled at her as if he'd swallowed a canary.

"Look what this graph does when you say that Fitz didn't kill Jonathan," Nicholas said. Charlie rewound the tape.

"I think you should see the whole thing," Nicholas said. He turned to Charlie: "Start where you ask her if she's madly attracted to me." He spoke to her softly. "I only did it to help you, Stephanie. I wanted you to take this test to help you remember. Now you know something definite, and maybe it will all come back to you. Please don't be angry with me. . . ."

The black scratches on the chart were thick and dark and shot back and forth when she said she didn't know Nicholas well enough to be attracted to him. He looked at her with a trace of victory in his eyes. The black scratches were steady and very even when she was talking about her children and said she was not enjoying herself very much, and then they thickened and shot back and forth again when she said *Fitz? Why do you mention her all of a sudden? You promised me no more questions!* She didn't want to see what came next. . . .

The black scratches went haywire. They shot out to both edges of the graph chart. They ran fast and thick and dark across the page while her voice repeated, *She didn't kill Jonathan. No one killed Jonathan. Jonathan fell off the balcony accidentally.*

She was lying. She knew she was lying but she didn't want to lie. Why had Fitz done this to her? Oh God, she missed Angie and Kent.

The idea that that could even occur to you makes me sick to my stomach. I could never have killed Jonathan. I loved him. I want to go home.

Her voice was very low, very drawn out, very slow, very steady. The scratches on the graph were doing something different, and Charlie was smiling. The scratches were not shooting back and forth, but they were very thick and fast. "You were obviously under a great deal of stress here," Charlie said. "I'd have to study it more carefully of course," he said to Nicholas, "but it looks on the surface as if there's no deliberate attempt at deception in those last remarks."

Nicholas smiled at her in triumph. "Of course not. I knew that all along, but I felt I had to ask the question."

She felt dizzy and ill; she might faint again. . . .

29

Nicholas pumped her about Fitz all the way back from Acapulco to the door of her *casita*, where he told her he would pick her up at six-thirty for drinks and dinner at the Catalina. She shouldn't have agreed. She didn't trust him now; he was after her openly. . . .

The sky was almost white and the ocean was much rougher that afternoon. It pounded on the beach where she stood alone in her orange bikini, staring out and remembering more, more details that had come back as she told Nicholas about Fitz and herself, about their childhood together, their sharing, what Fitz looked like, how beautiful she was, what a good friend she had always been, how she had been gone for seven years, that she didn't know why Fitz had killed Jonathan, although she was trying to remember. . . .

But she hadn't told Nicholas that Fitz was dead, that she had died with Jonathan. Because she was trying to remember, and she knew she was innocent of Fitz's death. She couldn't have killed her; she was not a murderer. Fitz was the murderer. She knew that now, and she had been right to be afraid of Fitz. Jonathan *must* have pulled her off the balcony with him, when she pushed him. Oh Jonathan. . . .

Total loneliness enveloped her as she gazed at the ocean. She had never expected to be without Jonathan. God knows that she had never expected to be without him, and if she could have foreseen it then she never would have listened to Fitz. Damn Fitz! She would have spent her days with Jonathan showing him her love, showing him that he and the children meant more to her than anything else. . . .

She wouldn't have spoiled her last two weeks with Jonathan by feeling dissatisfied.

She looked up at the gray white sky, remembering the morning after the Simpsons' party. She and Jonathan had been sitting at the kitchen table in their robes, just finishing breakfast. Sunlight glittered through the window; the counter was covered with dirty dishes, and Kent lay sprawled on the floor trying to read the Sunday funnies. Angie was upstairs, already watching television.

"*You* certainly had a good time last night," Jonathan had said. His face was hidden from her by the green sports section of the *Examiner,* but the staccato challenge in his voice seemed to perforate its pages.

She shifted in her chair. "It *was* a good party."

"You and Jack certainly had a nice long chin-chin."

"Yes, we did." That was the second time he'd said *certainly,* she thought. She rose to clear more dishes and felt his eyes following her.

"I guess I brought you home too early."

"Not at all, darling."

"Be honest with me, Stephanie."

"Honest?" She had turned to face him. "What do you mean?" She saw the hurt little-boy look, the soft brown eyes searching for reassurance.

"You find him very attractive, don't you?"

"Who—Jack?" She was trying too hard to sound casual. "Of course, darling. He's very attractive."

Jonathan folded the pages of the paper neatly, automatically. "I think we should talk about it, don't you?"

"Talk about what? There's nothing to talk about."

"Oh yes there is."

"Darling," she said, smiling, "I do believe you're jealous! I should think you'd know better, for Pete's sake. Want some more coffee?"

"Thanks." He put his hand on her arm as she poured. "Maybe so, but I'll never take you for granted; you're too pretty. And last night you were different, so animated. It's just that you seemed changed to me, and that scared me a little." He tightened his grip on her arm.

"I probably just had too much wine. Forget it, darling." She stood up and kissed him on the forehead. "Finish reading your paper."

Jonathan bent over the pink section; she picked up the main one. FIRST HIT AND RUN OF THE YEAR, it said, and showed a photo of a child sprawled in the street. Stephanie turned the page quickly. She had loved flirting with Jack, putting her best foot forward. Why couldn't she tell Jonathan that? RAPIST APPREHENDED. It had nothing to do with loving Jonathan; she simply liked being on stage. It was exciting. . . . So what? If they were really secure about each other, they could flirt all they liked and enjoy it. . . .

"Jonathan?" she said.

"Umm?"

"What do you know about open marriages?" Lord! She hadn't meant to ask that, at all!

He looked up quickly.

"I . . . I don't mean I'm considering it or anything, darling! I was only wondering if you know anything about it, or how it works. You know, people are writing so much about that stuff these days. . . ."

Jonathan stared at her. "Kent," he said slowly. "I think you'd better leave the room now."

"Aw, daddy—"

"Go on, upstairs! You can take the funnies with you."

They looked at one another while Kent scrambled to his knees, gathered up the funnies, and skipped out of the room. He had never obeyed *her* that quickly. Jonathan said nothing.

"I'm just curious about it," she ventured.

"I thought we were happy."

"Oh, darling, of course we are! It's nothing to do with that, honestly. It's only that some of my friends have been talking about these new books, and I wondered. . . ."

What had she seen in his eyes? If he had really betrayed her with Fitz she would have seen guilt or fear, or defensiveness—she knew she would have seen it. But no; only sensitivity and concern were reflected in his brown eyes. She couldn't explain, she couldn't tell him what she was feeling. Jonathan's love was too valuable and too necessary. How could she explain her sudden greed for flirting, for adventure, the need to be swept off her feet? Or her fear that mad excitement might escape her completely? She wanted too much, because of Fitz's propaganda. . . . She wanted what was beyond his capacity, and hers. Jonathan could only feel frustrated and angry that all he had given her was not enough, and he would be right. She couldn't hurt him that way.

He was watching her closely. "I still think," he said, "that it's Jack Simpson."

"No, darling, not at all. I promise. If you want to know, it's that I was jealous of you last night. Of you and that purple-jerseyed bitch. Is that silly?"

Jonathan grinned with relief. "It sure as hell is! She works for the government, you know. In Washington. We were talking about the economic mess all that time. I guess we were both being silly?"

"I guess we were." They'd made a pact; everything was settled. Stephanie tried to smile.

"Something *is* wrong," he said. "What is it, Steph?"

How incredibly dear he was, how trusting, and kind, and gentle! How handsome, with his hair all rumpled and the curly hairs sticking out of his robe. She wanted to bury her head against his chest, under the robe. . . .

"I think I'm housebound. Bored with the daily routine, I guess." She loved his frown, his thoughtfulness. She knew he would take care of her.

"Well, why didn't you say so, honey?" he said. "We can fix that. There must be lots of things we can do about that. Would you like to get a job? I think we could work that out—"

"What could I do? I'd hate being a receptionist somewhere, or having a dull office job, and I'm not qualified for anything else."

Jonathan took another sip of coffee. "How about your music? I'll pay for full-time lessons if you want to start studying again. Or your painting. You could go to those classes at the DeYoung Museum, or whatever—"

"It's hard with Angie still home, and I'm not really good enough, anyway. It would only be a waste of your money. I mean, I could never be a professional, and there's always so much to do around the house. . . ."

He drummed his fingers on the table, the impatient

executive. "Well, hell. You said you needed a change. I don't know what else to suggest."

"Of course, darling." She smiled at him. "You're right. I'll take a couple of classes at the DeYoung. It'll be good for me to get out of the house more. Thanks, sweetheart. You're an angel—"

He really *was* an angel.

It wasn't much; it really wasn't nearly enough. But at least it was a start in the right direction. . . .

○●

It wasn't enough because Fitz said it wasn't enough, and I listened to her. Goddamn her.

Like Stephanie's memories, the far-off horizon was separating. Its upper half of dry-white sky was turning darker in the distance, pulling away from and yet pushing down on the gray white ocean. She stared at the distant, contrasting colors of the horizon for a while, and then she continued walking down the beach.

Was her envy of Fitz turning into an insidious challenge? No, that was not her nature, and yet she felt *afraid* again. Suddenly she remembered Angie and Kent and thought that she must call them when she got back to the *casita;* she felt so guilty about not calling her children. "Hello, darlings," she would say—

There was a large patch of seaweed floating off shore, to her right—a dark, ugly blot on the ocean's surface. Stephanie knew what lay beneath its bloated bellies, those hard bronze bubbles that the children loved to burst when they went to Stinson Beach, back home. She couldn't see the tangled mass of tentacles underneath, but she knew they were there, reaching out—

Angie woke up when it happened. Angie came down the stairs crying and I held her on my lap but she didn't see it. She couldn't have seen what happened. I held her in my arms in front of the fireplace.

Stephanie closed her eyes and rocked silently back and forth on her heels in the sand. Maybe she should tell Nicholas Hanson that Fitz was dead and get it off her chest. The police had said it was an accident, hadn't they? Maybe talking more about Fitz to Nicholas would help her remember that last struggle in detail; maybe it would help her define all the mixed emotions she felt about Fitz then and still felt—her love for Fitz, the fear, the pride in her, the anger, the envy, yes. . . .

The insidious envy of Fitz.

○●

Fitz was radiant in Oscar de la Renta evening pajamas of purple and white peau de soie. She sat relaxed and smiling in a low chair out on her deck, surrounded by the social and artistic elite of San Francisco. The big names, the successes. They crowded her studio and deck, drinking and laughing, commenting on her fabulous paintings.

Stephanie had stood on the balcony not far from Fitz, watching her throw back her head and laugh at a joke, watching her charm everyone, watching her flirt with a tall man who had dust-blond hair and striking light eyes. . . .

At that moment Fitz had turned to smile at Stephanie, and it seemed to Stephanie that her smile held in its tipped-up lips every grace, every assurance, every fluid ounce of sweet pride in the world. "My cup runneth over," that smile seemed to say. "My cup runneth over, and see how much excess spills out? Don't you wish *you* had some of it?"

Stephanie had hated her, then. Stephanie had hated Fitz and feared her own hatred.

And then Fitz had done the strangest thing: she had stood up and walked toward Stephanie with her tongue sticking out. A child's spiteful tongue.

A lover's tongue, curling and uncurling.

○●

A bank of bruised clouds was swelling on the horizon. The tide had turned; Stephanie was now walking on a narrow strip of sand close to the southern point of the beach. She stared at the bony arm of rocks that reached out into the ocean, shuddered, and turned back in the opposite direction.

She couldn't have allowed Fitz to love her physically! She could never have betrayed Jonathan with Fitz, and yet her memory had betrayed *her,* had cheated her and stolen from her, but she knew that she could never have hurt Jonathan that way . . . she wouldn't have allowed Fitz to love her more than Jonathan loved her! She couldn't have—

Walk faster. . . . If only I weren't so confused. She had to get away from the ocean, from that foreign beach. . . . *Did I let Fitz love me?* She had to walk faster along the water, hurry back to the *casita,* to Nicholas, to someone who could help. . . .

Oh God, I couldn't have let her love me more than Jonathan, and yet I was changing; she was pushing me.

Stephanie broke into a run, along the water's edge, feeling her feet spanking the sand. Jonathan hadn't done anything wrong; Jonathan was so good, so vulnerable, and yet so blind. . . . She ran faster, feeling the air turn hotter, feeling her body running away, feeling her head grow colder and colder rushing against the air, feeling her brain freezing. . . . She would keep on running forever—

She couldn't keep it up, she hadn't the strength, her

legs wouldn't go on, her brain wouldn't stop. The sky swirled above her; the sand was hard and wet where she lay, sprawled on her back.

I think I let Fitz love me.

○●

A fire in the fireplace on a cold San Francisco evening, needlepoint spread across her lap. Jonathan on his knees, his broad back sagging under the weight of both children. Kent squealing with delight, Angie's small brow furrowed nervously. . . .

"Most of the time, darling," Stephanie had said, "I feel a warm glow when I watch you playing with the children. But sometimes, like right now, I feel consumed with such a scalding rush of love for the three of you that I'm afraid I might disintegrate, you know . . . burn up in my own fire. It's hard to explain—"

"That's very poetic, honey." Jonathan had smiled up at her, then wiggled his fanny. Kent shouted with glee, his eyes shining, waiting for Jonathan to rear up and buck him off.

"It's all so perfect, isn't it?" Stephanie had sighed. "It's so beautiful that I'm afraid it will be taken from me, that I can't be this lucky forever." Why couldn't she express it more forcefully, with both the hot tenderness and cold defenselessness that were welling up inside her? She wanted Jonathan to share her thoughts.

"Aieeee!" Kent screamed, as Jonathan sat back on his heels, spilling both children to the floor. Angie's eyes widened in terror, then squeezed shut as she bounced to the carpet. *She's so much like me,* Stephanie reflected.

"It's the Puritan ethic in you," Jonathan said. "You can't have the good without expecting the bad."

Was that when it had started to go wrong, she wondered—with his pragmatic dismissal of her emotions? Was that how it had happened? She had jabbed at the needle-point canvas and missed the mark. Why did there always have to be an explanation for everything? Why couldn't she just describe her feelings, instead of eternally explaining them!

"I suppose so," she had answered Jonathan. "Bedtime, kids. Up to bed, now! Brush your teeth, and I'll be up in a minute to tuck you in. Kiss daddy goodnight."

They hugged and kissed. But all trace of her intensity had vanished, had disappeared with her inadequate depiction of it—and with Jonathan's practical explanation. Was she tiring of practicality? She should have relished her intensity alone, feared it alone. That was what Fitz did. . . .

"You look beautiful." Jonathan was standing in front of her.

"Do I?"

"Very."

His eyes asked for a return of the feeling, but she knew it had gone from her. "Thank you, darling."

"Shall we go to bed early? As soon as you've tucked in the kids?" He put a question mark at the end of it, as all husbands did, she supposed. But she never felt that it was a question; she knew it was expected.

Yes, she thought, they should go to bed early, as soon as she had tucked in the kids. They should undress in a dim light and lie on the bed together, wrapped in a cocoon of love and gratitude, safe in their nice house while their children slept close by. That was how it had always been, and always should be. . . .

Wasn't that what had happened? Her memory told her that that was what happened. . . .

No. It hadn't worked that way; her memory had lied again. It hadn't worked that way because her intensity had disappeared and she had made a mistake: she had tried again to share with Jonathan. . . .

194 ○●

"I'm . . . I'm wondering how often you sacrifice your real thoughts for the sake of our harmony," she had asked him. He was a threat to her honesty, didn't he see? The bedroom light that had clicked on in his eyes was a threat to her sincerity, because what she had felt was gone.

"I don't quite follow." Jonathan looked into the fire. He had stood before her asking for easy love and had received words instead.

"It's hard to share your most private feelings," she said, "or lack of them, without wounding someone else. Because of social training, I think. Because society demands polite dishonesty of us in order to be liked, and loved, and to please others."

"Look, Stephanie. If you don't feel like screwing tonight, just say so." He stared into the fire, wounded and angry. Uncomprehending.

"It isn't that, at all! I only want to be *me* completely! To share my feelings with you as well as my body, because we're best friends. I want us to share our innermost thoughts without fear or guilt, and without hurting one another. I want us to accept each other for what we really are—"

"I've always accepted you." Jonathan pouted. "That's not fair."

"I'm not accusing you of anything! I only wanted to talk about me, about my fear of losing intensity, and being alone in my fear! And about your feelings, too. About both of us not playing roles when we don't feel like it—"

"Well, you certainly don't feel like it tonight. I think I'll put the kids to bed."

It was her turn to stare into the fire while she listened to his footsteps on the stairs behind her. Whose fault was it, his or hers? It didn't matter, but she had hurt him; she would have to go up to him soon and make things right again. Betrayal. Betrayal of both of them. No, not betrayal at all; only compromise, mediocrity, acceptance of the way things were. Love. Marriage.

There was a low bench in front of their fireplace, next to the marble hearth. From where Stephanie sat it obscured the last burning log, but she could see the reflection of the flames burning in the marble—a rosy square of moving light, set in beige marble. The repetitive flickering of flames rushed downward, glowing translucent inside the marble's shining surface; a fire contained within its own perimeter. Tongue upon tongue of flame overlapped; layer upon layer of rosy orange light rushed steadily downward—in the wrong direction.

She would have to go upstairs, and make it all right again.

But Jonathan should have been willing to talk more, she thought; he should have listened to her. Because she was trying to block out Fitz's influence.

○●

Stephanie sat up and brushed wet sand off her shoulders and arms. She decided she would fight her memory calmly, now. She would sit there on the sand and watch the ocean recede and return, then recede again. She would study what it deposited on the sand: the dead wood, the empty shells, the slimy jellyfish. She would dissect her memory as she would cut up a frog. How funny for her to think of that; she could never dissect anything, she had always gagged in biology class, and turned away from Kent's trapped moths and segmented worms—

Her nights and her days were not what her memory had said they were, those last two weeks. She had remembered lying safely asleep in Jonathan's arms at night, but her memory was wrong. Her memory had been wrong about everything. . . .

She hadn't been able to sleep. The clock on Jon-

196 ○●

athan's bedside table read 1:17 A.M. He lay on his side, turned away from her. She tried to fit her knees against the backs of his and slipped her arm over his waist. She tried to fall asleep pressed close to Jonathan. The clock ticked loudly; he felt warm. She should have made a list of everything she had to do the next day. She *would* have made a list a week earlier; she had always made lists. But her organization was on strike, rebellious. It had chosen to picket her at night, now. The list would read:

1) Carpool for Kent
2) Sort laundry
3) Take Jonathan's shirts
4) Pick up reheeled shoes, Mrs. Hayes
5) Art class 10:30
6) Petrini's on way back—Meat, tomatoes
7) Order thyroid at Agnew's
8) Call plasterer
9) Change Angie's dentist appt.
10) Get gas, more burnt sienna

Jonathan rolled over on his stomach and reached out for her with his left arm. When had it become not enough, to lie there next to him? Or when had it become too much, with not enough left over? Which was it, too much or not enough. . . .

11) Soak Kent's parka in Biz
12) Green peppers for meatloaf
13) Pick up Jonathan's shirts

If only she felt more important.

Why did she think she heard the phone ringing each time she stepped into the shower? What made her feel, standing under the shower's hot steam, that the phone was ringing in the bedroom, that the outside world knew her, wanted her, needed her?

She *was* important.

To Jonathan and the children. They couldn't get along without her, could they?

○●

"Stephanie? Stephanie!"

It was the next day, and Jonathan's voice had boomeranged down the stairway, curved sharply through the dining room, and caught her off guard in the kitchen, where she was distractedly stirring avocado soup.

"Yes, darling?" she had called.

"Where the hell are my shirts?"

Oh, no. She had forgotten to pick them up again. Why? Because of her busy day, the list, all those damned chores . . . No. Because of the chores and Fitz, because Fitz had taken her to lunch with some crazy people from the museum, and then they had gone shopping together. . . .

"Stephanie?"

She shouldn't have forgotten his shirts. Now he was angry with her, and she'd have to deal with that awful, guilty fear of his anger.

"Stephanie!"

The little-girl, first-married fear that raced back and forth between her head and her solar plexus. (Was the rhubarb pie as good as his mother's? Did his friends really like her?) The guilty, little-girl married fear that came next. (Should she tell him she had put celery down the disposal? Or had broken a wine glass?) Then the angry married fear. (So *what* if she'd dented a fender?) The silly, stupid fear that squeezed her hard and held on. . . .

She smoothed her hair and walked through the dining room, out to the foot of the stairs. Jonathan was leaning out over the banister; his set jaw hung heavily over her upturned eyes.

"I'm terribly, terribly sorry, darling," she said. "I had such a busy day that I forgot to pick them up."

"You forgot them last week too, damn it."

"I . . . I know. I'm really sorry. I promise it won't happen again."

"I hope it won't," Jonathan said, as his head disappeared beyond the banister. The doorbell buzzed loudly in her ear, momentarily shattering her guilt. Angie and Kent stood on the front porch, covered with dirt, grinning up at her. . . .

She struck Kent across the face.

Her *days* were not what she had remembered.

She had slapped Kent's little cheek hard, leaving an ugly red mark on it. "You're the oldest!" she had screeched at him. "How many times have I told you not to ring the goddamned doorbell! How many times? It drives me crazy! The door is unlocked, Kent, *unlocked!*" He was crying. "Get upstairs!" she had shouted. "Both of you! I want a little peace and quiet for a change!"

Children were not to be slapped. Children were to be cuddled, and fed, and appreciated, and molded, and bathed, and helped, and loved. She had never before slapped a child on the face. She needed a quiet Chopin prelude. The calm and beautiful Thirteenth Prelude. She sat down at the Steinway and began to play, to create her own peace of mind. . . .

The meatloaf. She would have to put the miserable meatloaf in the oven, or it wouldn't be ready in time for dinner.

Jonathan came down the stairs at the very moment when she had stuck the meatloaf in the oven and was heading back to the piano. He poured a drink for both of them in silence. She couldn't play Chopin; she would have to talk to him, or the whole evening would be shot again. She shouldn't have forgotten his shirts.

Two o'clock in the morning, following that same day. Her kitchen was a quiet, calm place, where only the refrigerator hummed in her ear. The crumbs were gone from the table, the floor was swept, the pots and pans put away until morning. And the electric clock did not tick in the kitchen. Stephanie took a saucepan from the cupboard and turned it upside down on the counter, next to the sink. Her yellow rubber gloves were in the left drawer, next to the dishwasher; the jar of Metal-Eze and a clean cloth were under the sink. She opened the drawer, removed the gloves, bent over to pick up the Metal-Eze and the cloth. She polished the bottom of the saucepan carefully, rubbing in little circles, over and over, rinsing it in hot water, rubbing again over and over in little circles, rinsing again. The kitchen was a quiet, clean place.

She rubbed and rinsed, rubbed and rinsed, rubbed and rinsed.

After a while she turned on the burner to *simmer,* placed the clean pan carefully on it, opened the refrigerator door, extracted a carton of milk, and poured carefully into the saucepan. She must not spill the milk on burner; it made an unpleasant smell. She replaced the milk, pulled three more pans out of the cupboard, and polished them carefully, rubbing over and over in little circles, rinsing, rubbing again, rinsing again. Her nights were not what she had remembered. She polished all the pans in the kitchen; her nights were not what she had remembered.

She peeled off the yellow gloves, replaced the pots and pans in the cupboard carefully, and poured herself a mug of hot milk. It had not stuck to the bottom of the pan; there was no unpleasant smell. She sat down at the maple-topped table and doodled on a memo pad while she sipped the sweet, warm milk. She drew her face on the memo pad, and then drew a line through her face and wrote words instead. "I was once . . . Once I was crimson. . . ." and then:

I am a once-crimson crab shell
Since cracked by rocks
In an untimely tide
Split now, and
Spilling soft innards
That melt and ooze
Over family and friends
I shift
Unsure in stronger sands
And suffer the moon's
Whim
To wash me out. Again
Unusable
In Time

The meter's lousy she thought. *I need work; I'm completely out of practice.*

○●

Stephanie opened her eyes. The ocean was splashing around her ankles, cold and blue-white gray. A veiled sun hung high over the horizon, and she had been wrong about the dark clouds there; they were not gathering after all. But her nights were not what she had remembered. Her nights had changed after that, hadn't they? And she had spent the rest of them with Fitz, until the murder.

I know I let her seduce me.

"Forgive me, Jonathan," she whispered to no one. "Oh, please! Forgive me for letting Fitz court me, for allowing her to tear me away from you and the children and the house. Forgive the mad shopping sprees and the hundreds of dollars I spent and didn't tell you about, hundreds of dollars for crazy jewelry and clothes that are still hidden in my closet. Fitz *wooed* me, Jonathan. She took me to museums, to lunch with her wild, funny friends during the day. I neglected you and the children and tried to conceal it. I was a terrible mother. I abandoned little Angie to Mrs. Hayes almost every day or sent her over to friends' houses. . . .

"She lured me away from you at night while you were sleeping. You didn't know that, did you? She lured me to her studio while you were sleeping, and we painted together, laughed together, played together; she cheered me up. She told me I was beautiful and that I should let my hair grow long and stop streaking it, that I was naturally beautiful. She told me that I was too smart, too sensitive to spend my time rolling your socks and cleaning house. And then she touched me, Jonathan, and I let her."

I let her fondle me; I let her lovely long fingers play with me and do things to me that he had never done. . . .

Stephanie squirmed as the ocean splashed around her, darting between her legs and spraying her shoulders. The rushing waves swirled around her, pushing and pulling at her from every direction, preparing to suck her into their vacuum. "I didn't understand, Jonathan," she said out loud. "At first I didn't understand what she was doing to me, to us. . . ."

Jonathan wanted to leave. He got up from the table angrily because he was drunk and said he was leaving me. He didn't go into the living room. He went to the hall closet to get a suitcase and then came back into the living room where Fitz started shouting at him. . . .

She had to get away from this beach; she had to get up, get back to her *casita* or the waves would swallow her as Fitz had. With her impossible demands Fitz had cut her off from Jonathan little by little. She hated Fitz! *Oh Jona* *than!* Stephanie thought. *I hated and feared Fitz, but I let her love me anyway. . . .*

It was all coming back to her now. The helpless fear, the real memories and the helpless fear of Fitz were riding in on these terror waves. *What was Fitz doing to me?*

Fitz had tossed and turned on her bed, not quite asleep, watching a shadowy crowd. Thousands of dark forms swayed back and forth, moaning in a low, slow, endless drone. . . . .

Suddenly the dream burst open inside her: a Technicolor pageant, a vast panorama of brown-skinned foreign bodies, of turbans and veils bobbing under the dazzling blue of an alien sky. Jonathan was there in the center of the crowd, carrying Kent on his shoulders and holding Angela in his arms. He swayed and chanted with the rest of the crowd, taller than most, swaying and chanting eagerly, as though he were riding on the crest of their noisy, ominous wave.

Fitz heard drums pounding, pounding. The crowd swelled in a great slow undulating motion, and then split open with a gutteral roar to reveal six skinny, withered little men whose loins were swathed in dirty white muslin. Their bare, bony chests and shriveled thighs shone with sweat; she could smell the sticky odor of fear. The moving cortege of wasted brown flesh was carrying a sedan chair on which sat a beautiful naked woman.

It was Stephanie.

Over the low, expectant humming and the pounding of the drums, the crowd hissed at Stephanie and wished for her blood. They carried her to a raised platform and manacled her wrists and ankles to a crude wooden altar. She lay there—Fitz's beautiful Stephanie—white with fear. Jonathan remained in the crowd, which was silent now, and made no move to help Stephanie. Fitz thrashed in her sleep. She *couldn't* help Stephie, because she herself wasn't there; she wasn't a part of that blood-begging crowd. . . .

The drums pounded, pounded. Their volume increased with the volume of Fitz's terror . . . and the sacrifice began.

The drums never stopped pounding throughout the entire dismemberment.

The shriveled brown men started with the little toe of Stephanie's left foot. They chopped it off neatly, and the drums failed to drown out her screams. Then they cut off the little finger of her right hand. Next the little toe of her right foot, and the little finger of her left hand. One finger after another, one toe after another, but Stephanie would not faint! Fitz prayed that she would faint. Stephanie's screams rent the air, but she would not faint.

The little men severed her feet next, with swift blows of their curved knives, and then the bloody stumps of her hands. Then they cut off her legs below the knees, and her arms below the elbows. Still Stephanie screamed. Her arms at the shoulders, her legs at the hips . . . Fitz begged to wake up! Blood spurted everywhere; Stephanie screamed through a thick mask of her own blood. They disemboweled her then, and cut off one breast at a time. Fitz couldn't stand it, but she *could not* wake up! She kept screaming, screaming, until they cut off Stephanie's head.

But Stephanie's heart was still beating. They threw the rest of her on the floor and left only her heart on the altar. It would not stop beating, thumping. All alone on the blood-soaked altar it continued to thump louder to the rhythm of the drums, growing larger. It swelled and covered the altar. Stephanie's still-beating heart expanded, blotted out the crowd, pounded louder and louder until it filled Fitz's vision and was pounding deafeningly, indistinguishably. . . . Along with the rhythm of Fitz's own terror-filled heart.

Their two hearts beat as one, only Stephanie was dead.

And Fitz was alive.

31

Nicholas Hanson was sitting on the edge of his bed. He hung up the telephone, let out a long whistling sigh, and smiled. He had dressed for dinner and was ready to leave for Stephanie's *casita* when Henry Sommers had phoned from San Francisco to confirm what Jonathan McMillan's diary had already revealed.

He reached for the small black book lying next to him on the bed, which Gabriel had brought to him an hour earlier. He thumbed through the pages one final time, concentrating. . . . February 26, 27, 28 . . .

He closed the diary and sat staring at it. Jesus Christ, he thought—who would have believed it? The friend Fitz was the missing link, all right. And if his guess was accurate. . . .

But he had to be sure. That was the only reason he hadn't told Henry what the diary said, wasn't it? He had to be sure. He grinned again, put the diary in his brief case, stuck a package of cigarettes in his shirt pocket, and left his *casita*.

It would all come to a head tonight.

He rounded a curve in the path and saw Stephanie's bungalow in front of him and to the left, not crammed as close to the other cabins as his was. How would he time it, and how would she react to his information? Would she be secretive, or sly, or coy and seductive? Angry? Frightened? It was hard to tell about her. . . . .

At first he thought her lanai was deserted. A tin wind chime tinkled next to the door; nothing else moved behind the screened-in façade of her cabin. The inside door to the kitchen was open, but the bedroom door was closed. She was probably changing or taking a shower. He decided to mix drinks for them while he waited.

Afterward—when he thought about it later, when he realized the exact moment of awareness, of seeing her lying there on the striped couch—he could not remember whether he had noticed the dangling leg first, or the dangling arm, or her body as a whole—a slim, seductive body clad only in a brief orange bikini.

Her face was turned away from him, buried in the corner of the couch, covered by her disheveled hair. She didn't move when he opened the door and stepped inside. It hit him then. She had killed herself. Oh Jesus Christ, he thought, she couldn't have. . . . Her body was sprinkled with sand, smudged with patches of sand. . . . He ran toward her and reached for her dangling wrist, for her lifeless pulse. . . .

She turned her face up to him, unsmiling. She looked at him through half-closed eyes, through long dark lashes that fluttered faintly. There was high color in her cheeks; she was still all right. He would have time to save her. Thank God for that. . . .

She opened her eyes. They were bright blue, and

flecked with a strange golden light that beckoned to him from some other place. Then she smiled, and reached her arms up to him, and as she pulled his face down to hers he felt her body arch in desire and her legs move far apart.

"I'm sorry," she said, pulling out from underneath his long kiss, sitting up abruptly, and pushing away from him. "I must have fallen asleep and thought you were Jonathan."

"Don't play games with me, Stephanie," he said angrily. "Don't play the fuck any more games with me. I've got your number." He reached out for her small round breast under the shimmery orange bikini, but she pulled away from him wide-eyed, her posture a paradox: She sat huddled like a frightened child in the corner of the couch, her blue eyes innocent, her arms clasped around her knees and protecting her breasts from him. But her feet were apart, the orange triangle between her legs a deliberate temptation.

"You want me and you know it," he said. "No matter how screwed up you are about your husband you still want me."

"I'm not screwed up about Jonathan, and I don't trust you," she said in a low voice, pushing her messy hair away from him wide-eyed, her posture a paradox: she sat her mouth was smiling a sensual and contradictory message, a lingering sexual invitation. "I don't trust you," she said again.

Nicholas looked from her mouth to her eyes, from her frightened eyes back to her inviting mouth, and felt his desire for her increasing along with the certainty that he must be right about her mixed inclinations. And he would prove it. "Why not?" he asked smoothly. "Why don't you 'trust me,' as you put it? You know I was attracted to you the first moment I saw you."

"What happened at Charlie's today," she said. "I think that was planned."

"Of course it wasn't. Pure coincidence."

"I don't believe you."

"Aren't you glad about it, though? Now you *know* what you couldn't remember about Fitz. I feel good about helping you, no matter how painful it must be." He put his hand on her thigh.

"None of it's your business!" she exclaimed, infuriated. But she didn't pull away from him this time. "You don't know anything about Fitz or Jonathan, do you? So why do you care?"

"No." He smiled, wishing this conversation could be delayed. "I don't know anything. So tell me more about the grown-up Fitz."

Her eyes changed. He couldn't define the change; a flicker of that golden light seemed to darken their color, a quick flash of light receded into her pupils and then returned abruptly. "Fitz is talented and famous now. And more beautiful than ever. And she killed my husband."

"As beautiful and sexy as you?"

"I'm not sexy," she said in a flat voice, but her thighs moved farther apart and she slowly lowered her hands, uncrossing her arms from in front of her breasts.

"Let me be the judge of that," he said. "Has Fitz led an exciting life?"

She looked away from him, frowning.

"I'm going diving again tomorrow," Nicholas smiled. "And you're going with me."

"No!"

"You want to, you wanted to yesterday. You liked it, liked the way I held you underwater."

"No. . . . Yes. I—"

"You liked the sense of adventure, of danger. Behind that scared little-girl act you're hot for some excitement in your life, aren't you? I bet you want to try diving again and conquer that fear. And you're hot for me."

"No, I'm not," she said in the same low voice. "I loved my husband, and I still love him."

"I believe you," Nicholas said, and reached out again to run his fingers lightly around the rim of her bikini top. "I believe a lot of things about you." His fingers crept inside her suit, then quickly he clasped her breast in his hand. She didn't move, but her eyes were still frightened.

"Your friend Fitz isn't married, is she?" he asked, fingering her nipple.

"No—"

"Has she known lots of men? Has she had many lovers?" He was leaning over her, his face an inch from hers, pressing her against the sofa. He pinched her nipple slightly, and she moaned weakly. "Has she told you how exciting it is to have passionate lovers like me?"

"No! Yes . . ."

"Did you like it when she told you? Did you want to have lovers too?" He pressed his mouth to hers, but she turned her face away and closed her eyes.

"Why do you want to know so much about Fitz?" she asked. "I hated her—"

"You don't hate her," Nicholas said, kissing her neck. "And after I've made love to you for hours, I'll tell you why."

She jerked her frightened eyes back to his.

"I think I know why Fitz killed Jonathan," he said. "It was *his* fault."

"Oh God, tell me—"

"Later," he said, putting his arm around her bare waist. "Later. Let's forget about all that for a while." He kissed her again. "I'll tell you what I think afterward." He picked her up to carry her into the bedroom, and as he lowered her onto the white bedspread and pulled off her orange bikini, first the top and then the bottom, he felt the smug triumph of a dual success.

32

So Fitz's amorality had won out after all, she thought. Nicholas's hands and lips glided over her, soothed her, violated her. After more than two hours his hands and lips were still gliding over her while she sank deeper and deeper into betrayal of Jonathan. She lay there sinking into the white semen sheets while Nicholas's body and her guilt comingled.

"Good," Nicholas murmured. "Oh, yes—"

At least she had put off finding out for a while; at least she was able to forget everything. She supposed she would feel less guilty if she weren't enjoying it so much. . . .

"Roll over," Nicholas commanded. "That's right, good—"

No, it wouldn't matter. What mattered was that she had betrayed Jonathan and Fitz had won, irrevocably. She had done things tonight that she was always afraid to do with her husband. And she was still doing them, so Fitz had won, and won, and won, and won, and won!

"Oh Jesus," Nicholas groaned, "you're fantastic. . . ."

○●

Stephanie slept a short sleep of obliteration. When she awakened, it was dark in her room, and rain was falling somewhere in a square of light. No, she realized, not rain; it was her shower. In her shower, a strange man who knew her body was washing off the residue of unfeeling passion, the remains of giving and taking without commitment. She had diminished the pleasure of giving and the gratitude of receiving by having sex that animal way, without devotion. She shouldn't have done it.

Now she was left alone with guilt, and with her memories of Jonathan. . . .

Jonathan—her dear and honest Jonathan . . . his smiling crow's feet, his soft eyes, his trust in her. The way he had liked his eggs basted in bacon fat, and rhubarb pie, and Heinz catsup, and his socks rolled. The day he had given her an old-fashioned wooden darning egg, and was all puffed up with pleasure at having found it in an antique store. His habit of picking at the skin on his left thumb when he was nervous. She used to worry about skin cancer; that seemed ridiculous, now. . . . His delight in good meals, his muted ambitions. And the way he had always lost his nail clippers! He would rant and rave about his nail clippers and ballpoint pens always disappearing and accuse the children of stealing them, and she would tell him over and over again not to worry, that they were around, that they would turn up somewhere, and they *would* always turn up. And one day he said that when they were old, and he died, and someone asked her where he was, she would say not to worry, that Jonathan was around, and that one of these days he would turn up.

And she had laughed, and laughed. . . . But he wouldn't turn up.

Whatever happened that night, she knew it couldn't have been Jonathan's fault. . . .

Nicholas came out of the bathroom with a towel wrapped around his waist and groped in the darkness of Stephanie's room.

"It's all right," she said, "I'm awake." He flicked on her bedside lamp; she blinked and turned away.

"You're awake," he said, "and I'm starved. I'm going to dress and run over to see if I can get something for us in the kitchen."

"What time is it?"

"After ten," Nicholas replied. "Too late to go to dinner. We were busy for a long time, sweetheart."

She looked up at him. His mouth was turned down on one side like Humphrey Bogart's mouth, and he said *sweetheart* the way Bogart used to say it, with a twinkle in his eye. "Don't call me that even in fun," she wanted to say. "I'm not your sweetheart."

Nicholas was looking at her and the twinkle turned hard in his eyes. "That's quite an act of innocence you've been putting on," he said. "Quite an act. You should have gone on the stage, blue eyes."

What did he mean? She didn't like the way he sounded—so sinister. She didn't know what he was talking about—

"I'll see what Gabriel can scrape up for us," Nicholas said, and turned toward his clothes that were thrown over the chair in front of her dressing table.

"You should have gone on the stage, blue eyes," she repeated to herself. Why did he sound so sinister? "You should have gone on the stage. . . ."

The stage. The theater. Two nights before Jonathan died they had gone to the theater. She had forgotten about that night. She had made a scene in the theater and Jonathan was becoming suspicious of her and Fitz, and worried about his wife's behavior, and his worry and suspicions were dangerous for him. That was why Fitz thought she had to kill him, Stephanie realized. He must have found out about the two of them—she and Fitz—together.

Nicholas had dropped the towel and was pulling on his jockey shorts, watching Stephanie while he dressed. *I'm bisexual now,* she thought. *I can't be bisexual. It's disgusting; I don't want to be. But that's not why I made a scene at the theater. It wasn't because I was turned on by the female star; it was because I envied her so much . . . and yet Fitz was loving me every night. . . .*

Nicholas was still watching her and buttoning his shirt, and suddenly it all came back to Stephanie, the Curran Theater on Geary Street, two nights before Fitz killed Jonathan. She and Jonathan had gone with Carol and Jack Simpson to see *A Little Night Music,* and the star was Jean Simmons, who was so beautiful and talented, and danced and sang so perfectly. Her name was Desirée, and Stephanie kept thinking that *she* could have been Jean Simmons. She had become angry with Jonathan on the way out, walking up the aisle. . . .

Nicholas zipped up his trousers, bent over to pull on his espadrilles, and straightened up again. "I'll be back soon," he said to Stephanie. "You might plug in the coffee maker. I'll try to get some wine." He put on his wristwatch and went out the bedroom door.

And Stephanie was walking up the aisle of the Curran Theater with Jonathan. . . .

○●

"Did you enjoy it?" Jonathan had said, smiling at her. He was wearing the silk patchwork tie she had given him for Christmas.

"I liked Jean Simmons."

"Sure," he had answered, "she was terrific."

Stephanie was belting her coat. "I'm almost as pretty as she is, in a different way."

"What?" Jonathan moved closer to her. "I didn't hear you."

"I said, 'I'm as pretty as she is.' "

One of Jonathan's eyebrows rose. "Of course you are." He smiled. "Prettier."

"I'm as pretty as she is," Stephanie had repeated, "and my figure is practically as good as hers." Suddenly she was fighting to control her voice. "I *said* I can dance as well as she can, and with a little training I could sing as well, and maybe act as well too."

"Sure, Stephie." He squeezed her arm.

"I could have been in her place."

"Of course." Jonathan was maneuvering her past an elderly couple. The crowd was noisy; everyone was talking about the sell-out performance.

"I could have been in her place, but you wouldn't want a wife in show business, would you?"

"Hey," Jonathan said, "are you angry at *me?*"

"And my parents. They would never have allowed me to go into the theater. *Nice* girls didn't go into the theater, did they? My parents wouldn't even let me model, before we were married. I had an offer to model in New York once, but my goddamned fucking bourgeois parents wouldn't let me—"

"Stephanie, what's wrong? Why are you so angry?"

"Because I've been stifled!" she burst out. "Because my whole life has been a wet blanket. Because I've never been permitted to say what I think or do what I really want to do. Because I've always been a good girl! I'd like to be a strip-teaser, Jonathan. So there. I'd like to bump and grind and take it all off in front of hundreds of men and—"

"Shhh!" Jonathan admonished. "People might hear you—"

"Oh, well. I wouldn't want to upset the people, would I? I wouldn't want to shock the neighbors; I'll be a good bourgeois girl—"

"Stephie—"

"I could have been an actress, Jonathan. Don't you understand?"

"Of course, darling. Shh now, hush." His arm was around her shoulder like a vise as they emerged into the crowded lobby. "You know," he confided, "I think lots of women here tonight wanted to be in her shoes, if it's any consolation. The way she sang—"

"No!" Stephanie hissed at him. "It's not any consolation because I'm not 'lots of women'! I'm me, and I could have been her, I could have been good enough! I could have been a singer, or a dancer, or a movie star, or many things. It's in my nature! I simply didn't realize it, and now I'm too old—"

"Hey, you two!" she heard Jack Simpson call. "Over here!" They were standing outside under the marquee. "Shall we hit the Buena Vista for a nightcap?"

"Oh yes. That would be jolly good fun," Stephanie said sarcastically. "How about Sardi's, while we're at it? We could all fly to Sardi's."

"No thanks, Jack." Jonathan squeezed her hand and looked at her hesitantly. "I think I'd better get Stephanie home to bed. She doesn't realize how tired she is. . . ."

○●

Fitz had been waiting for her in the dark studio, later that night. The night of the theater, two nights before Jonathan's death. Fitz was waiting for her in the darkness of the studio and there was no moon outside, no natural light to outline the dark beams that stretched over Fitz's head, or the black bulk of the Steinway hunched in the corner. The large room waited quietly with Fitz, waited in the still blackness for Stephanie to arrive and bring it to life.

She entered and switched on a dim lamp in the corner.

"I've been waiting," Fitz had said, "and thinking. You're late, dear heart."

"I'm sorry. We went to the theater."

"It's not working," Fitz remarked. "Jonathan's going to find out about us." She stood up and walked toward Stephanie, slinked toward her like a tall shadow. "He and I are exhausting you. You can't keep this up, this strain of being his all-purpose patsy and trying to be your own woman with me, day and night. I'm afraid you'll have to choose between us."

"No! I can't, I don't want to—"

"It's *his* fault that you've been torn apart this way," Fitz said, pouting, "like in my horrible dream. Jonathan's stubborn and stupid. I've been back for over a month now and he hasn't listened to me. He isn't trying to change anything; he's letting you die slowly. You'll be stuck with his dull routine and his shirts forever—"

"I won't give him up!" Stephanie whispered. "It's *not* his fault, and I love him! It's *you* who—"

"You won't leave him?"

"No!"

"Okay, okay." Fitz shook her head. "We can try again: we'll have to keep trying. There's something I want you to see." She smiled strangely. "I think it's time for you to help me out. Over there, in the entry closet. Dig around behind the coats and the suitcases, and you'll find what I want to show you. It's a painting I've done, a large one. A present for you."

Stephanie walked over to the closet, opened the door, and fished around behind the coats. The painting was propped up against the back wall; Fitz certainly had hidden it well. Stephanie took hold of the edges and dragged it out into the half-light.

"Don't look at it yet!" Fitz commanded. "Bring it over here."

Stephanie propped it against the leather sofa, keeping her head turned away from it. And then she stepped back. She remembered stepping back. . . .

Jonathan's brain, his eyes, his hands, and his penis leapt out at her.

"Oh God!" She clutched her throat. "It's . . . it's a horrible, unbelievable painting!"

"You like it, naturally," Fitz said, "because you have to. It's your last hope. There's still so much you don't understand, my poor Stephie, but maybe this portrait will help you. I'm going to show you a little telepathy trick now, some super concentration on Jonathan. He's got to change his life and yours; he's got to understand that you're afraid to do it on your own. . . ."

The light from the corner lamp shone on the multicolored brain, on the brown eyes, on the grasping hands and the erect penis. The glowing colors danced and swam before their eyes as they stood together in the large, quiet room, and concentrated once more on Jonathan. The glowing colors of the portrait shimmered and expanded in the stillness of the night.

○●

"Where have you been?" Jonathan had rolled over in the bed and reached for her. His clock glowed a green 4:53 A.M.

"Shh," Stephanie had whispered. "Go back to sleep."

"What have you been doing?" His voice was loud in the dark bedroom.

"I couldn't sleep. I've been in the living room drinking hot milk and reading. Now hush, darling. Let's go back to sleep." She curled up close to him.

He looped his arm over her. "Why are you having so

much trouble sleeping lately? What's bothering you, Steph?"

"Nothing, darling, just . . . just some bad dreams, some horrible nightmares. I don't want to think about them now; I want to sleep."

"All right," Jonathan sighed. "But I'm worried about you. It's not normal to prowl around the way you do, night after night. . . ."

○●

The screen door opened and closed; Nicholas was back with food and wine. She saw him standing in the doorway, looking at her with a less interested look than before, now that he'd had his way with her. She noticed that after-the-conquest attitude which was more than indifference but less than fascination. Did all women, she wondered, feel that degrading loss of self-respect, particularly after the first sexual encounter? She should have taken a shower while he was gone, she thought; her body smelled of his.

Nicholas held a white cardboard box in his hands and a bottle of wine under his arm. He placed the box on the bed, opened it to remove two glasses and a corkscrew, poured them each a glass of wine, clinked his glass against hers, and said with a sinister smile, "We're going diving together again tomorrow, to celebrate our new pact."

"What pact?"

"It's illegal, blue eyes, but that makes it all the more exciting, don't you think?" His hair was a darker blond in the diffused light from her bedside lamp.

"I don't know what you're talking about." She held the stem of the wine glass tightly in her fist. There were too many shadows on the wall.

"I'll tell you in a minute," Nicholas said. "Want some chicken? It's still hot." He sat down on the edge of the bed and reached for the white box.

218 ○●

"I'm not hungry."

"We'll go back to our reef and I'll take you down deep for a real thrill," he said. "It's obvious now that you like thrills, and pardon my immodesty."

She saw the sexy, turned-down, sinister smile again. Very sinister.

"I planned to go by myself; I had a tank filled this afternoon. It's waiting for me on the same boat, and I can easily pick up another one for you tomorrow. Everything else is arranged."

"No." She shook her head. "I won't go down again."

"I'll make love to you underwater."

"No." Why was she trembling? She didn't want to know what his illegal pact was; wouldn't ask him.

"We'll see," Nicholas said, and reached for a piece of chicken. It was covered with a dark sauce and looked messy to eat. He ate slowly, a paper napkin spread on his lap, watching her while he chewed. "Now about our pact," he finally said, wiping his hands on the paper napkin. "Let's split the two hundred and fifty grand."

Stephanie inhaled. *You do not know what that money is,* she told herself. *Hold on; you are alone.* "I don't know what you're talking about," she heard herself say.

Nicholas wiped his mouth. "The insurance money, blue eyes. It's a great set-up. We make a hot pair in bed: we can spend it together and no one will ever know. You'll be safe. I haven't told anyone yet."

He hadn't told anyone yet, *what* hadn't he told anyone yet? He couldn't know that she might have killed Fitz in desperation, because Fitz had killed Jonathan. There was no way he could know.

"You haven't told anyone what?" she asked.

Nicholas's eyes were serious now. The shadows in them probed like a thousand uncertain inquiries.

"I think," he said, "that you honestly may not realize you killed your husband. There *is* no Fitz."

●○ 219

Stephanie exhaled, relieved. They hadn't found Fitz's body after all. She must have killed Fitz and hidden her body, but she couldn't remember where. Thank God they hadn't found her. But Nicholas was trying to blackmail her; she'd have to show him there was a Fitz. She must have time to think. She could never have killed Jonathan; Nicholas was wrong. She had to remember *why* Fitz had killed Jonathan and tell Nicholas, so that he would understand. And then she would split the money with him. She had to remember what she had done with Fitz's body—

"There's no record of Fitz anywhere," Nicholas said. "I'm investigating Jonathan's death for the insurance company. They thought he might have killed himself. You were hiding the thought that Fitz killed him because *you* did it, and there's no person named Fitz. Not in Jonathan's diary, not in the records anywhere."

"That's a lie!" Stephanie exclaimed. "There's no record of her because she was visiting San Francisco, and she'd lived abroad for seven years!"

"Listen," Nicholas said. "I've been watching you and you're all screwed up, believe me. If I turn you in they'll put you in the loony bin and you'll never see your kids again. You probably belong there. But I need the money; I need the hundred and twenty-five thousand bucks. Sorry to pull a fast one on you, sweetheart. Take your choice."

Stephanie was silent, thinking desperately.

"I can cover it up for the insurance company." Nicholas grinned. "I pulled it off once before in New York. They know nothing about your fabricated Fitz; I only asked for her name and gave no reason. It'll be easy to explain that. And you've been cleared by the police. They'll have to pay us. What do you say, blue eyes?"

"I didn't kill Jonathan."

Nicholas smiled.

"There *is* a Fitz!"

His smile lingered like floating ice on a cold, dark pond.

"There *is* a Fitz!" Stephanie hissed at him. "I need more time to remember where she is, but when I do I'll *show* you there's a Fitz!"

33

Nicholas rolled over and opened one eye into daylight, squinted, opened both eyes, blinked. He was alone in the bed, in his own room. He smiled. She had made him leave her alone last night, had told him she had to think, to remember, the same old crap. But he had her, all right. He had her and she knew it.

Brilliant, Hanson, he told himself. Brilliant.

But he'd better hide the diary just in case. He got up, splashed cold water on his face, brushed his teeth and hair, and pulled on his red-and-white swim trunks. Then he took a roll of masking tape out of his briefcase, jumped up on the bed with the diary in his hand, and taped it to the wide blade of the fan overhead. Brilliant. He slipped his feet into espadrilles, grabbed a towel from the bathroom rack, put on sun glasses, and left his *casita* for the beach, the pier, the boat, and a glorious last morning of scuba diving before he flew Stephanie back to San Francisco.

Scuba diving down deep and alone was the capstone of his three-day Mexican adventure, the epitome of rule-breaking, because one should never dive alone; one should always dive with a buddy with whom to share air. But he liked to break rules, had loved to break rules since he was a boy and had learned the thrill of being whistled down by policemen for jaywalking in New York traffic. The memory of tingling apprehension—of standing guilty, expectant, frightened, and confident of no punishment while the blue-uniformed cops walked scowling toward him—had remained; he sought that thrill of defiance whenever possible.

He was glad that Stephanie hadn't wanted to come. Solitary victory celebrations were the best.

The day was magnificent despite a low bank of thunderclouds on the horizon, beyond a shimmery blue sea. He walked eagerly along the beach, across the thin scruffy crest of the point that separated it from the village, and down to the pier. A young female tourist was trying to get into the rental shop at the edge of the water, but there was no one around; the shop didn't open that early. The boat was rocking gently, tied up next to a decrepit cabin cruiser on one side and a small Chris-Craft on the other. A young boy was fishing off the end of the pier, his bronze back gleaming in the early-morning sunlight.

Nicholas jumped aboard the fishing boat and lifted the tarpaulin in the bow to check the gear: the aluminum tank that he had watched them fill in the shop yesterday, a regulator, a knife, fins, gloves, weight belt, mask and snorkel, depth gauge, and an orange vest that lay on top of the ice chest stocked with beer and wine. He had rented the vest, called a buoyancy compensator, or BC for short, as an added precaution, since he planned to go deep. Precaution and confidence were bedmates. He grinned, thinking that that would be a good slogan for manufacturers of the Pill, and opened the picnic cooler to check the supply of sandwiches and mangoes. Christ, he wondered, was Stephanie on the Pill? What the hell; she was a big girl. That was her problem.

Everything was in order. He started the motor, cast off the bow and stern lines, and headed the boat out to sea. . . .

He touched the cliff of coral gently with his gloved hands as he descended, head first, kicking his flippers in light, even strokes, pulling himself down the cliff, exploring, pausing to pick a white anemone blossom off the coral and watch it close up like a snowball in his hand, probing the spongy center of a starfish for a spine. He pushed off from the cliff, swam down faster, chased a big gold fish with silver fins and black spots, a school of blowfish, a silver streak in the two-foot form of a spike below him, stabbing toward the armor of a crusty chest of coral. A barracuda, fence of teeth, floated to his left, eying him; it was harmless in those water, he knew, and yet he swam down and away from it.

The coral cliff widened and darkened below him; he checked his depth gauge, his watch. Eighty feet in ten minutes. He looked up; the shadow of the boat floated above him and to the left, where he could still see it. He wanted to be where he couldn't see it, wanted to get out of the sight of safety and yet know it was there if he swam faster, faster, deeper and deeper into the unknown, alone and free in the cooler blue waters, the world of fish and cool freedom, tingling apprehension and wet slippery survival, ninety feet, one hundred feet, down and away from the boat, one hundred and ten feet. . . .

He stopped and looked up. The shadow of the boat was gone; he was alone with the bubbles of his own breath in mysterious waters, alone in a dangerous and primitive universe, alive in his celebration of himself and his power. He had power, the power of perception; he had seen through Stephanie McMillan where no one else had—not her dead husband, or Sommers, or the police. Brilliant, Hanson. Brilliant.

He had fifteen minutes left, fifteen minutes of air with a dive that deep, to be safe. He could have stayed down there for twenty extra minutes without having to decompress, if he had had a surplus tank. It would have been better to rent a surplus tank and have that extra time, but what the hell; he would start back up now and he still wouldn't have to decompress. He took a big breath, removed the regulator from his mouth, and blew air into the mouthpiece on the hose of his BC to inflate the vest, to give himself neutral buoyancy. He felt the vest inflate, replaced the regulator in his mouth, breathed normally, and started swimming upward.

There was a cave of dark coral to his left, a wall of sea rock towering behind and above him, an expanse of endless ocean before him and to the right, an eternity of blue white, green white calm water through which he swam up toward a weird fish he had spotted. He'd never seen a fish like this one, with a camouflaged look to it, a large fish with blue and green spots on sand-colored scales, and dark fins—

Strange thing, nature, he thought. Full of odd varieties. He should have brought a spear gun; it would have been fun to kill the fish and take it back to the village to see if the natives had ever seen

There was no air.

There was no air in his tank, nothing to breathe. That couldn't be, he had watched them fill it the regulator must be clogged he sucked he gulped nothing he heard his gulping sucking loud blew out into the mouthpiece shook the tube sucked again nothing left to blow out of his lungs that couldn't be he had no air he'd die down this deep he'd die. Nothing left to breathe what was happening hold on to the air there was nothing left to hang on to go up he had to go up hang on to the air swim faster he had to get up chest tightening kick harder rubber legs hang on to the air light head hang on to it swim faster he was going up too fast hang on to the air chest on fire light head hang on to it slow down he couldn't slow down it was too far hang on to the air fire black. . . .

His body lurched in a violent internal explosion as the embolism burst his blood vessels. The air in his vest, which had expanded as had the air in his lungs as he ascended—shot his lifeless body eighty feet up to the surface.

34

It *was* nice, not having to do dishes.

Stephanie sat on the hotel terrace in a pair of yellow shorts and a navy-blue halter, watching the waiters clear the lunch tables and thinking how lovely it was, not having to do the dishes. Four whole days of no dishes and not being confronted every morning, every afternoon, and every evening with those damned cereal bowls, crystalized Cream of Wheat clinging to their sides, dried egg yolk between the fork tines, rubber gloves, soggy paper towels sopping up bacon and hamburger and sloppy-joe grease. The debris of nourishment, the leftovers of loving care every day of her life. . . .

Stay away from it, she told herself. She had to stay away from that last day, from the unwanted memory that was beginning to roll over her like those clouds on the horizon that were rolling toward this sunny resort. This might be their last good day; it looked like a storm brewing out there, beyond a light gray haze that hung under the sun.

There was no truth to what Nicholas had said last night; it wasn't possible. *Was it, Jonathan? Oh God,* she said to herself, *if only Jonathan were here to help me, to prove it. I need you, Jonathan—*

Her dear and threatened Jonathan—on their last evening together, alone. Her concerned and patient Jonathan, sitting in his favorite armchair after a good dinner, reading the *Examiner* and still feeling safe, still believing in his safety, in the safety of his family. How many nights had she sat across from him like that, feeling safe and average? Contented Jonathan, hiding behind the headlines but also worried about his wife who seemed strange recently. It was a stage she was going through; who knew what goes on with women these days? Sweet Jonathan, whom she loved, reading his *Examiner* and thinking that with understanding and patience he would see her through this stage. . . .

She remembered rattling the ice in her brandy and soda. "This living room is as dull as dog plop," she had announced. "I'm going to redecorate it."

Jonathan sighed, folded the newspaper, and smoothed it neatly across his knees. "But Stephie, I thought that's what you had been doing!"

"No, no. I mean radically."

"Radically? But what do you call all this?" He arched the air with his arm. "All these orange and yellow pillows? That crazy, obscene African sculpture? The big tree over there by the doors, and this flea-bitten old rug?"

"It's not flea-bitten! It's an antique from Paris, and valuable!"

"Yes, dear. I know it is; I just paid for it yesterday." He grinned sardonically. "And by the way, Kent needs a new pair of sneakers. There's a hole in his right one."

She had tried to glower at him, but she felt her face softening with shame, and her eyes wavering. And then she heard Fitz's hectoring voice: "Hang in there, baby! Hang in there!"

"I want a beautiful leather sofa, and a chair to match, and some modern paintings. I was even considering hanging some paintings on our ceiling, between the beams. How's *that* for an original idea?"

Jonathan had stared at her without speaking. Then his eyes wavered, too, and he looked to his left, out through the glass door, beyond the balcony and out at the bay. Stephanie rattled the ice in her glass again. When Jonathan looked back at her, his eyes had changed: they were full of concern. Deep concern. She saw her own weightlessness reflected in them, and felt suddenly dizzy. . . .

She remembered, now.

"Stephie," Jonathan had said, "I think maybe you'd better see a doctor. I'm worried about you, honey. Really worried. All this lack of sleep, this prowling around at night, and now a remark like that. You must be a little drunk, or else overtired. You know perfectly well that we already have a leather sofa and chairs, that we're sitting in them now, that we've had them for years!"

○●

I'm fighting. It isn't possible; I'm fighting. . . .

Stephanie stood up abruptly. She had to get away from there, away from that terrace, away from the beer she had just spilled on the tablecloth and the stares of the two waiters. She had to get away, to be alone in her fright, her dread of recognition. . . . It didn't matter that they had had leather in their living room long before Fitz had rented her studio, long before Fitz had come back. . . . It didn't matter. . . .

She had to get back to her bungalow. She had to get

back to her bedroom and lock herself in it and away from the memory. Why had she been so frightened when Jonathan said that, about the leather? Why had she sat terrified across from him, no longer safe, no longer average? Why had she suddenly felt the full power of a black fear engulfing her—

Recognition. It was the realization of how similar their room was to Fitz's studio. Yes, yes—that was it, recognition of how twin she and Fitz had become in tastes, in styles, and in mutual desires. Realization that she wanted what Fitz wanted, and Fitz wanted her to be free of Jonathan, rid of Jonathan. Was that what Stephanie had wanted, too?

Because Jonathan was dead.

Oh God, no! That was wrong. Fitz hadn't wanted Jonathan dead, at all. But she thought she *had* to kill him because he had found out about her nights with Stephanie! Fitz never *wanted* him dead! It had all gone wrong. . . .

Stephanie was walking through the palm trees, walking not on the path of round stones but next to the path, dragging her bare toes in the sand, slowly. It was all coming back to her now, that horrible last day, the day she had finally realized what Fitz was doing to her. She had fought Fitz with all her strength, fought for Jonathan, fought for their love and their life together. She had pitted her wits against Fitz, her heart, her very essence—

It was all horrible, horrible! When had Fitz become so much stronger than she? When had she let Fitz take over? She still couldn't believe it, didn't want to remember.

But she did remember, too clearly now. . . .

○●

"I've made up my mind," she had told Fitz. "I've decided to choose between you and Jonathan, and *you* have to leave. *You* have to go away again. I'm feeling too confused, too torn. I won't let you mess up my head and ruin my life! I won't let you wreck my marriage!"

She remembered that Fitz had said nothing, just continued to gaze out over the whitecapped Pacific. There was a strong breeze high on the hill where they had sat, on the stone wall that bordered the museum of the Palace of the Legion of Honor. The mouth of the bay lay frothing at their feet.

Sitting on stone walls in front of museums. It had been an old pastime of theirs, a return to their childhood. . . .

Fitz had always loved that particular museum—its majestic setting, and especially the building itself. She had gone there often to dream, to revel in the classic simplicity of its architecture, in the beauty of its great porticoed courtyard and massive stone columns. But Stephanie always felt uneasy there. She wasn't sure why; she supposed the building made her feel guilty, because there were two of them, and she had missed the original. She had never been to Paris and seen the real *Palais de la Légion d'Honneur.* She found so much to feel guilty about. . . .

"Didn't you hear me?" she had said to Fitz. "You have to leave again, and the sooner the better."

Fitz turned to her, and Stephie was shocked to see tears in her smoky eyes. Fitz never cried; Stephie had never seen her cry. The superior actress, of course; the star at work.

"You don't understand," Fitz whispered. "My poor Stephie, you still don't understand; you've never understood—"

"I understand plenty," Stephanie snapped. "I understand that your influence on me is proving disastrous to the normal routine of my life, and to my bond with Jonathan. You have to go before it's too late, before you cor-

●○ 229

rupt me completely. I can't wriggle in your clutches and still lead a normal life."

"A normal life," Fitz sighed. "An average life. Oh, Stephie, I feel for you so much, to be so torn—" The tears spilled onto her cheeks.

"Save your damn tears!" Stephanie shouted. "To hell with your sympathy! Who needs it? I'm the last person who needs sympathy, the last person in the world! Save your sympathy for the unloved, for the poor, for the sick and homeless you care so much about! They need it; I don't. I have everything—everything any woman could ever want! I have more than you do, and you know it, because I have something permanent: the joy of being a mother, and three people who need me, who really *need* my love! The knowledge of something that will last, something that will see me into old age. I'll never be alone as you will, with only fame and fortune to hold your hand, and an occasional, wrinkled roué trying to get into your pants! It's not the real world you want for me anyway, Fitz! The real world isn't as easy as you make it sound, and not as desirable; the real world is responsibility and frustration, love and tears, getting along with those you love from day to day—"

Fitz shook her head slowly, sadly. The wind blew through her beautiful, dark hair. She looked at Stephanie mournfully; her eyes glistened. "It doesn't matter," she said. "None of that matters. You still don't understand that it's already too late for me to leave. It's impossible for me to abandon you now; I can't leave you up in the air this way. I have to finish what I started, or you—"

"I won't *let* you finish what you started!" Stephanie exclaimed. "I know what it is, now. You want to ruin me and Jonathan, all in the name of your precious freedom, your cherished independence, your talent. Well, I won't let you do it. You want to blame Jonathan for the fact that there's no common meeting ground between you and me—and that's not fair to him! It's not his fault that I'll never be what you want me to be, that you've always wanted too much for me. Far too much. . . ."

Fitz stopped shaking her head and pointed out over the ocean at the thickening wisps of fog that were being sucked in swirling clouds toward the Golden Gate Bridge. "Look at the bridge," she said. "See how it stretches like a rusty red yawn over the mouth of the bay? And very soon it will be swallowed politely by the concealing boredom of the gray fog. Just like you, dear heart. You'll be swallowed up by sacrificial boredom, by days of never-ending gray . . . caring for Jonathan, caring for your children, for your house, caring for everything except yourself. Driving children in carpools and to piano lessons. Why? So they can grow up like you? Sorting laundry, planning menus, lunching with dull ladies, doing dishes? You were meant for better things."

"I was not!" Stephanie cried. "Can't you get that through your head? I was not meant for better things! I'm mediocre! What I have is the best I could hope for, what I've always wanted, what suits me—"

"What's easiest? What's safest?" Fitz narrowed her eyes and looked out over the open sea.

"Yes, goddamn it, and so what? I'm not like you, wanting to challenge the open ocean alone, for the glory of high self-esteem. I might want a little fame and glory, sure—everyone secretly dreams of that, I guess—but I don't have what it takes! Where would I start? I'm afraid to try! I don't even want to try! I simply don't have what it takes, and my soul doesn't scream out for it the way yours does. . . ."

"Oh," Fitz said, "but you do. And it does. That's what you still don't understand." Her golden eyes were misty again; she was starting to cry.

"Look, Fitz." Her tears infuriated Stephanie, frightened her. But she spoke through her fear: "Marriage is hard work, too. Permanent love is perhaps the hardest challenge of all. I'm making it; I'm doing it, and I'm proud of myself for succeeding. I'll always have the pleasure of giving, the pride of self-sacrifice. That's something you couldn't understand."

Fitz turned away from her and buried her head between her knees, hugging herself. The cold wind whipped her thick hair. She wasn't crying anymore; she was thinking, plotting. She was thinking that it was time for the final showdown; she had to force Stephanie to understand. But she needed a weapon, an ultimate weapon to say it all, to symbolize the problem as well as the solution. Otherwise, Stephie would never believe her. Her weapon had to be something stable and secure, something solid like Stephie's present life, but also something dangerous and death-dealing when misused, as Stephie's marriage had been. Something that symbolized the future as well, and the unknown potential—

Stephanie froze. She was reading Fitz's mind! It wasn't possible; they couldn't have become that close. She felt a cold black clot of fear and shouted, "Fitz! Stop it! Just go away forever, please go away and leave me alone. . . ." She was numb with hope; Fitz would leave, Fitz could leave. She had only imagined it; she hadn't really read Fitz's mind. . . .

Fitz turned to face her again. Their two faces met, high on the hill in the biting wind. Fitz had smiled at her serenely. Her white teeth parted; the golden eyes closed slowly, then opened wide. Strands of gleaming black hair blew across her face, played on her skin.

She was so much more beautiful than Stephie, so much more exotic, more sensual, more intelligent, more talented. It was not a fair match, Stephanie thought. It had never been a fair match.

232 ◦●

"Just sit quietly," she said softly to Stephanie, "while I tell you about the Golden Gate Bridge. While I tell you about your life. Because that bridge—"

"The bridge?" Stephanie felt stupid. But she would keep on fighting as long as she could. "What the—"

"Hush," Fitz had commanded, and fixed her eyes on Stephanie's. "That bridge is the story of your life. It's one of mankind's finest creations, just as you are. It's beautiful, graceful, strong, and reliable. Its roots are in stable concrete, planted deep in the solid earth, just as yours are. But its towers stretch to the sky. That bridge is the symbol of man's imaginative powers to rule over seemingly impossible obstacles; it is proof of what man can do when he has the will. Over the years that bridge has assimilated itself to nature, has become as one with the cliffs, the ocean, the sky. It's mortal, of course, just as you are, but it blends with nature because of its beauty and usefulness—"

"I've heard this before," Stephanie tried, but Fitz was too strong; she would always be too strong. "I've heard your ideas on nature and usefulness, and I'm not—"

"Listen to me!" Fitz hissed. "That bridge is *your life!* It's safety over dangerous, forbidden waters, and a direct path to new, uncharted territory. It's a beautiful gateway to the future, if you use it properly. It will support you *and* transport you, if you let it. But if you just stand still in the middle of it, you might as well jump; that becomes its only purpose, then—to be a jumping-off place for a long fall into death. Are you going to stand flat-footed in the middle of your life?"

It was the same old speech, Stephanie thought. Thank God. Nothing had changed at all, had it? It was Fitz's same old speech, and her own same old reaction. There was a greater intensity to the speech—a rather frightening intensity—but they were on familiar ground. The black fear that had clutched Stephanie earlier was only her imagination, a fear of the unknown, an unjustifiable fear that she might not be able to make Fitz leave. . . .

She felt sorry for her, suddenly. "Oh, Fitz! I *do* understand you, you know . . . and I won't say that you're not right. In fact, I think you probably *are* right; but I can't let you interfere any longer in my life. I have no choice, you see. No choice. You'll have to leave before you do any more harm, before you make me even more dissatisfied with all the good things I have. Before you tempt me and seduce me again."

It was very quiet on top of the hill, except for the wind. A wet, misty fog had sneaked in from the ocean and surrounded them, sheathed them in a diaphanous gray. Fitz had not answered her at first, had not moved. She was till staring at the bridge in the distance. She sat cross-legged; her dark hair glistened with silver drops of mist. A small vein throbbed above her right eye. When at last she spoke, it was in a low monotone, an ominous chant.

"It's not I who seduce you, Stephanie . . . it's your life. . . . You have no choice, it's true. . . . You've never had a choice. But it's not what you think, at all. . . . You've been blind. . . . I'll prove it to you now. . . . Come, sit closer to me, and stare at the bridge. . . . Come, before it's swallowed by the fog. . . . At last you'll understand; you'll see that I can never leave you. . . . You'll see why I'll always be a part of your life. . . ."

The horrible black fear again the inescapable black fear that pushed Stephanie away from Fitz, helped her to recoil from Fitz's glazed eyes, from her low, droning voice. Stephanie was backing away slowly down the hill, backing away from Fitz's terrifying words. . . .

"You must not leave," Fitz said. "It won't do any good. The bridge is your life; you can't escape it. Come stare at it with me now, and it will seduce you completely. At last you'll be a life-lover. . . ."

"You're crazy!" Stephanie screamed, and her words gushed into the wind and hung there suspended. She was stumbling backward down the steep slope, away from Fitz . . . stumbling, running, fighting for her balance, fleeing into the thick fog.

"You *must* let the bridge love you!" Fitz shouted. "You must let your *own life* love you! You don't have any choice!"

Her shout filled the thick air, floated on layers of fog, and echoed all around Stephanie as she ran blindly, insanely down the steep hill. . . .

But Fitz was smiling, on the hill above her.

○●

Fitz was smiling, Stephanie realized, *because I could read her mind, because I knew what she was thinking again, and she was thinking that I would understand everything, now. I was running away, but I was running in exactly the right direction.*

Straight toward the bridge, the double-torsoed bridge.

Straight toward the twin towers.

Of course.

35

The tide was low in the tropical gray twilight. Low and forlorn, lapping at level after level of deposed relics on the beach: empty shells, pock-marked pebbles, a few stray pieces of flat, wet wood. The sky was also low; the clouds that had sat on the horizon earlier in the afternoon had crept quietly across the bay and spread into a flat, slate sky that leaned on the water, pressing down on the listless palm leaves that hung defeated in the lack of wind. It was humid and calm; it would rain that night.

Nicholas's body floated sixty feet off shore, just beyond the first breakers. The gray of the diving tank blended with the waves that lapped around it; only a small patch of his orange vest was visible.

The terrace of the Casa del Sol was lit up earlier than usual. The large striped umbrellas in the center of each table were opened in anticipation of rain, and the waiters were busy serving cocktails and dinner. There were low murmurs among the guests clustered around the tables and under the umbrellas. They were talking of the coming storm, speculating as to whether their vacations would be ruined. It wasn't supposed to rain there that time of the year.

Stephanie McMillan sat alone at one of the tables. She was wearing a long, light blue dress and sipping a margarita.

"What's that?" said a middle-aged man at a table near hers. "What's going on?" He turned away from his wife to look over his shoulder, smiled at Stephanie, and looked beyond her toward the main building.

There was a commotion at the back of the terrace, near the door that led into the kitchen. A native of the village, a fisherman, had come running to the hotel from the south, up the beach through the palms to the swinging door of the kitchen, where he announced loudly to a waiter carrying a tray of drinks out the door that there was a *cuerpo, il meurte,* someone dead with a tank on his back close to the shore, down the beach. He needed help, they should get the body, it was terrible, they must come help!

The wife of the man at the table next to Stephanie's understood Spanish. "It's a body," she said to her husband. "Someone's drowned." Then she turned to give the information to a young couple seated behind her.

"Where?" asked the young couple together.

"Down on the beach," the middle-aged wife said.

The maître d' walked quickly across the terrace to the kitchen door. He gave permission to Gabriel and another waiter to help the fisherman.

"A body!" said a twelve-year-old boy to his sister, at the table next to the young couple. "Dad, there's a body! Can we go see. . . ."

Within a minute the terrace was emptied of guests. They filed down to the beach, the women carrying their shoes in their hands and holding up their skirts, the men reluctant to remove their shoes, the children leaving their shoes and socks scattered behind them on the sand. They half-ran down to the water's edge, expectant, horrified. They stood in a bright semicircle, like a rainbow moon under the low darkening sky, and watched the three men wade into the water knee deep, thigh deep, jumping as the breakers buffeted them, waist deep, chest deep toward the body that bobbed gently out there, was not a body that they could see, but an aluminum canister, like a small garbage can.

Stephanie stood in the middle of the semicircle, watching. The man next to her lit a cigarette and offered one to his wife, who refused. It was growing dark very fast.

They dragged his body up onto the beach by his hands, Gabriel pulling on one arm and the fisherman on the other. The orange vest made a shallow trough in the wet sand; Stephanie recognized the red-and-white swimming trunks. His skin was a darker gray blue than the water, and wrinkled. "It's a miracle the fish didn't get him," someone remarked. A woman said, "Ugh!" "Jesus Christ!" someone else exclaimed.

They tried to roll him over but the tank interfered,

so the fisherman reached under his body to unbuckle the straps. They took the tank off and set it upright on the sand, then rolled him over. One woman screamed.

"*Dios,* it's Señor Hanson," Gabriel said, and crossed himself.

"That's the second diving accident this year," the other waiter remarked.

"God, what a shame," someone said.

"Who is he?"

"How did it happen?"

"I thought they wore wetsuits, and not those vests."

"Jim, we shouldn't have let the children see this. . . ."

"You sure as hell wouldn't catch me trying scuba diving. . . ."

"He never should have gone out alone."

"Paolo rented him the boat—"

"He said that's the second diving death this year—"

"How awful—"

"Wasn't he a friend of yours?" someone asked Stephanie. "I thought I saw you dining with him often—"

She was walking away from them slowly, her head down and shoulders slumped, carrying her shoes in her hands. "Leave her alone," someone else said. She was walking away from them, walking along the beach in the near-night. It had been stupid of Nicholas, she thought, to explain to her how the tanks worked, about where one let the air out, and all about panic and embolisms. She had made sure that he had enough air to get down deep, but not enough to get back up. It had been so easy to go down to the boat in the middle of the night, and to turn that valve and listen to the air escape. So easy. It had been stupid of him to tell her he was going down so deep. So incredibly stupid. . . .

She stopped for a moment to brush away the tears on her cheeks, and then continued along the beach into the night. She walked close to the water, where the sand was wet—like quicksand, she thought. She felt as if she was slipping downward, sinking faster and faster into the truth. . . . She realized now that she never *told* Jonathan about Fitz! Why hadn't she remembered sooner that she had never, ever told *anyone* about Fitz? She would have known, if she'd remembered that. Except Nicholas. She should not have told Nicholas. . . .

Fitz had the dream about her in the swamp when she started to get involved with Nicholas; Fitz knew it was dangerous. It was incredibly stupid of Stephanie to get involved with him, and then to tell him about Fitz. It was a horrible mistake, he didn't deserve to know, he didn't deserve what Fitz did with him—

Stephanie stopped walking and looked out over the black water. It still didn't mean that she had killed Jonathan, she couldn't have. She couldn't remember what happened that night, but she knew that neither she nor Fitz could have killed Jonathan deliberately, could have plotted it in advance. . . .

The dark night would help her remember what had happened. The low black night, the cold sand, the thin horizontal ribbons of light from the breakers that crested in white flashes and then disappeared, reappeared . . . they would help her remember. She had to find a place for herself in the night, a spot on the beach.

She looked to her left and saw a flat, wet spot on the sand, within reach of the waves. As she walked toward it she pulled up her skirt, hitching up the fabric with rapid, grasping movements of her fingers along her thighs, until the skirt was bunched around her waist. Then she lay down on the cold sand.

Spread your legs the way Fitz does, she said to herself. *I have never felt so alone. So completely alone. Open your legs and arms the way Fitz does, stare up at the black sky and think about Fitz, concentrate on Fitz, on the way she does it, and the answer has to come. Please please let it come. Oh Jonathan, I loved you so much! I mustn't cry; I cannot stare at the sky if I cry. Stare now, Stephanie, stare! Stare at the low black sky; lose yourself in the barren black sky. . . .*

She arched her back, extended her arms, and spread her legs wide; her eyes were fixed on the ebony sky. A great black cloud was breaking up, dispersing into a whole galaxy of soft smoky spheres that hovered over her body. They fell upon her, skimmed across her skin, caressed her lips, her hair, the tips of her fingers. The thick tongue of water lapped over her body, licking her belly, her breasts, and forcing its way into her open mouth. The cold, dark waters of the bay rolled rapidly over her belly, surged voluptuously between her thighs, and then rushed into her, pounding, pounding. . . .

And she remembered.

The brooding, moonless night. The candlelit dinner table and far too much wine. Jonathan had been loving and kind, at first. Jonathan had wanted to help Stephanie, wanted to know why she was unhappy, dissatisfied. Jonathan wanted to know what else he could do. Jonathan drank more and more wine, began to brood, got angry at Stephanie, got drunk, said he was going to leave. Stephanie was crying. Jonathan stumbled to the hall closet, looking for something, looking for his suitcase. . . .

But he found something else. He found the painting. Jonathan found the portrait of himself deep in the hall closet. He dragged it out into the light, stared at it appalled, horrified, his brown eyes round with terror. There was no softness in Jonathan's eyes, only horror. Fitz tried to explain. It was a *good* portrait! Jonathan was sick with rage and wouldn't listen to Fitz. Stephanie defended Fitz and attacked Jonathan, screamed at him that he had to listen to Fitz; *he must listen to Fitz! He must change their lives!* Jonathan was impossible, unreachable, retreating from Stephanie, his brown eyes recoiling in horror, in the agony of comprehension. He retreated backward from her toward the balcony, while Stephanie screamed through her tears that Fitz was right about everything; he should have listened to Fitz! Jonathan was drunk, staggering backward to the rail of the balcony. . . .

Fitz pushed him then, sprang at him like a huge cat, pushed his shoulders with one hand and picked up his feet with the other, quickly, so quickly. His eyes stared and his long white scream fell into the black night. . . .

Stephanie had been numb, drunk, thunderstruck. And little Angie had run to Stephanie, crying the tears of a frightened child awakened from a nightmare. Stephanie was incoherent, rocking the child in her arms. . . .

The police had come, then—minutes later, hours later, after the portrait had been destroyed by her in a daze, curled up and disintegrated in the colored flames of the fireplace. Jonathan had disappeared once again, in the flames. . . .

The police filled the house, swarmed through it, asked questions. The police believed Stephanie's distraught story; Jonathan was drunk and clowning on the rail, and she had shouted at him to watch out! There was .22 percent alcohol in Jonathan's blood. He had been alone with his loving wife; there were testimonies of dear friends. It was an accident. What else could it have been?

The funeral had been held on a foggy day. Her beloved Jonathan was dead, gone forever, buried with her secret under the ground. Her secret was buried forever, her Jonathan was gone forever. And then there was the will, the essence of the will:

To my beloved wife, STEPHANIE FITZGERALD BORDERS MCMILLAN, *I hereby bequeath everything of which I am possessed, including all personal and real property,* . . .

A white fang of lightning ripped open the thick dark skin of the Mexican sky. It nipped at the whitecapped heels of the Pacific and then disappeared with a low, satisfied growl of thunder into a thicket of black clouds. A moist, sticky darkness rained down on the palms in front of Stephanie's lanai, where she sat on the sofa picking at a plate of fresh crab meat with her fingers—her skillful, loving fingers.

She stared at the small crab claw held between her fingers, put it back down on the plate, and reached for her glass of white wine. She couldn't eat, but she could drink. She would drink all night long.

Fitz lives inside me in my mind's extended eye. She has always lived inside me. Her dreams are my dreams, her conscience my conscience, her imagination my imagination brought to life. She is the fruit of my unripened creations and frustrations. There was never a studio on Russian Hill or in Paris, no art show, no Mike Higby or Carlos or Piero Luigi or Anna, and she never seduced Jonathan. It was all my imagination.

Stephanie gulped her wine and refilled the glass. *Fitz was my dream, but she never meant to be evil, she never would have killed Jonathan if he hadn't found the portrait. . . .*

And she never died. I only believed her to be dead, along with Jonathan. I wanted to wipe out Fitz's guilt, wanted her to die when Jonathan died because I couldn't accept that part of myself.

But it was the other way around, wasn't it? It was Fitz who lived, and who had now taken over. It was Fitz who had torn up the children's photograph. Stephanie saw Angie's and Kent's faces, wide-eyed, open, vulnerable to shadow—her own shadow. They must never have that shadow. Their cheeks must always stay as smooth as golden peaches. . . .

Stephanie drained her second glass of wine.

"Now that everything's finally clear to you," she heard Fitz say, "—and before you go back to San Francisco, I think we should make some plans. You should probably sell that big house and move to Europe. After all, we're very close to being totally free—"

Her voice darkened.

"Except for the children."